Unbelonging

A New Adult Romance Novel

SABRINA STARK

ISBN-13:
978-0615945699 (Mellow Moon)

ISBN-10:
0615945694

CHAPTER 1

Some girls might fantasize about being handcuffed in Lawton Rastor's basement.

I wasn't one of those girls.

Sure, I thought about it a time or two. Sometimes with handcuffs, sometimes without. In my fantasies, we weren't in some cold, damp basement. Usually, we were on some yacht in the Pacific. With wine. Or maybe dirty martinis.

I've never actually had a martini, and I don't know what makes one dirty. But I do know you need a special kind of drink when globetrotting with a badass billionaire from the wrong side of town.

"You need some water?" he asked.

I stared at him. "Water? Seriously?"

He shrugged. He was leaning against the opposite wall, arms crossed, eyes flat. He wore faded jeans and a black T-shirt. Tattoos snaked up and down his forearms. He looked harder than the concrete behind him and just as cold.

"It's water or nothing," he said.

Fucker. He probably didn't even own a yacht.

Lawton made his money through prizefighting. Not the kind with padded gloves and some bowtie-wearing referee. He made it through the gritty, back alley kind where sweaty money changed hands over beer and bimbos.

The billionaire part came after an Internet video led to a reality series which led to all kinds of merchandising and event opportunities. In five years, he'd gone from being a fucked-up nobody to a financial force to be reckoned with.

And he was only twenty-six.

That's three years older than me. Except looking at him, I felt like a babe in the woods – a very pissed off babe in the woods.

"You're an asshole, you know that?"

If the insult bothered him, he didn't show it. "I let you keep your panties, didn't I?"

It's true. Compared to what I'd been wearing earlier, I was minus a whole bunch of clothes, but my undergarments weren't among them. Obscenely, stupidly, I was glad they were black and silky with lace trim. If there's one universal truth in this world, it's that no one wants to die in grubby underwear.

Lawton wasn't the one who attacked me, but he sure did a number on me afterwards, and not in the way you'd think. He hadn't beaten me, raped me, or taken a single obscene picture. At least not yet.

Mostly, he just stood there with his arms crossed, watching, like he was waiting for me to sprout horns and fangs. It was like Chinese water torture, without the water.

It still shocked me how quickly he'd gone from being my knight in shining armor to my basement jailer. It's better than what I deserve, he says.

I'd heard that sort of thing before. Sure, not from him. But did it matter? If I believed half the stuff people told me, I might as well believe in Santa Claus. And I hadn't believed in him for a long, long time. Even when I was little, it's not like he spent a lot of time at my house.

My wrists ached from the handcuffs, and my lips were so dry I swear I could hear them crack. Screaming all those obscenities probably hadn't helped. How long had I yelled at him? Minutes? Hours? Was it still dark outside? Probably.

In truth, water would be heavenly, but I wouldn't give the bastard the satisfaction of asking for it, even if he did offer. I looked around the massive basement. I saw windows, or what I guessed were windows, high up near the ceiling. But they were all covered in black plywood.

I guess that's pretty standard if you're planning to lock someone up in your basement.

Except it didn't look like any of this was planned. Other than the actual handcuffs, I saw nothing that would have alarmed me if I weren't in my particular predicament.

The basement was gray and spotless with a painted floor that matched the painted concrete walls. I saw a few cardboard boxes, a weight bench, and some skis leaning against a far wall. If the basement weren't so massive, I'd have no idea it sat beneath a multi-million dollar mansion in Rochester Hills, one of Detroit's most exclusive suburbs.

Yeah, such a place exists, as hard as that may be to believe.

I didn't want to talk to him, but there was something I had to know. "The guys who attacked me, where are they now?"

"Trust me," he said, "it's better if you don't know."

"Trust you?" I rattled the handcuffs. "You're joking, right?"

"Believe what you want." His eyes were the color of coal, the same as his hair. His heart was probably a couple shades darker. There was a time I'd thought differently. God, I'd been such an idiot.

His calm demeanor grated on me. "How long are you going to

stand there?" I asked.

"As long as you're here," he said.

My tone was brittle. "And how long will that be, exactly?"

He glanced at his wrist. "Another half hour should do it."

"Do what?"

"Again," he said, "better if you don't know."

My stomach dropped. What was he saying? I forced down the panic. Stay calm, Chloe. Eyes up, jaw set. Never let them see your fear. It worked with your stepmom. It can work with this guy. I kept my tone neutral. "So you're saying you'll let me go in a half hour?"

At this, he glanced away. "Probably."

Shit.

CHAPTER 2

Full disclosure – this wasn't the first time Lawton saw me in my undergarments. But it was definitely going to be the last.

Okay, make that probably.

I can't help it. The guy is obviously insane. To do everything he's done, he'd have to be. But when I was around him, I guess I went a little crazy myself. Excluding my stepmom, who gives crazy a whole new meaning, it had been way too long since I'd had any crazy in my life.

To understand, I guess I should go back to the beginning.

I'd seen Lawton for the first time a few weeks earlier when I was walking the Parkers' Yorkie during my get-acquainted visit.

The Parkers own a massive house just down the street from Lawton's estate. They have a little Yorkshire terrier named Chucky and a whole bunch of house plants that need custom attention. Seriously.

The Parkers also like to travel, which is why I'm staying in a neighborhood that's literally thousands of times beyond my reach or comfort zone. But no one wants a pauper in their mansion, so I've learned to fake it a lot better than you'd think.

I'm the house sitter, dog-walker, plant-waterer, and truth be told, broke college graduate. When I answered the Parkers' ad, I approached it the only way I thought they'd hire me. I acted like I didn't need the money.

It helped that I had a ton of references, a spotless college transcript, and a fairly respectable wardrobe thanks to countless afternoons in thrift shops and consignment stores. Just about the only clothes I own firsthand are my undergarments, because even a poor girl from Hamtramck isn't going to wear panties that covered the hoo-ha of the richer, luckier girl before her.

Plus, I like lacy things. What's a girl to do?

The first time I saw Lawton Rastor, it was in the Parkers' neighborhood. Instantly, I knew he didn't belong there. He wasn't a surgeon, CEO, or remotely civilized.

I was on the sidewalk, just around the corner from the Parkers' two-story Tudor when I spotted him, leaning against the gate of the biggest mansion in the neighborhood. Ever wary, I slowed my pace. Chucky didn't. He was straining at his leash, trying to catch a bug or a squirrel or something. Chucky's kind of a spaz, so it's hard to be sure.

Tattooed and shirtless, the guy wore faded jeans and not much else. He was lounging, barefoot, against the thick iron fencing that surrounded the massive estate, a brick and stone monstrosity that covered at least three acres of prime Rochester Hills real estate.

If I weren't so stubborn, I'd have crossed the street to avoid him. But I was stubborn. And I'd learned the hard way that showing fear is the quickest way to bring on more of whatever it is that's scaring you.

So Chucky bounded forward, and I followed, like I wasn't all-too-aware of him. Like I'd miss some strange, shirtless guy hanging out where he shouldn't, and in weather that was already showing more than a hint of the upcoming winter's chill.

I passed the guy within an arm's reach. As I did, he stood, motionless, letting me stride past without moving so much as a muscle. I wanted to look. Who wouldn't? Instead, I kept my eyes straight ahead, acting like he utterly invisible. I swear I heard him chuckle, but the sound was so low, I couldn't be sure. I made a note to tell Mrs. Parker about him the moment I returned.

If there was one thing I learned from house-sitting for the wealthy, it was that they didn't like seeing someone there who didn't belong. I know it's practical, and probably smart too because it wasn't their own neighbors who would assault them in broad daylight.

No, if their neighbors were prone to crime, it was the other kind, the kind that involved Ponzi schemes and multi-level marketing scams. Their crimes might be just as devastating, but a whole lot more civilized.

When I'd gone a block past the guy, I resisted the urge to look back. But that soft chuckle, if I'd heard it at all, echoed through my brain in a way I found unsettling. It might've been fear. It might've been something else. Either way, I hadn't felt that unsettled in a long, long time.

I kept on walking and never did look back.

CHAPTER 3

Mrs. Parker glanced in the general direction of where I'd seen the guy. Even though I'd only met the woman a few weeks earlier, I felt a lot more at ease with her than I normally did, especially during these get-acquainted visits.

She was a couple decades older than me, but there was a freshness about her I almost envied.

Her long brown hair was tied in a loose knot at the nape of her neck, and she was wearing dark jeans and a Detroit Redwings T-shirt. But even if she had been wearing some of the designer stuff that no doubt filled her closets, there was something about her demeanor that made me feel surprisingly at home.

When had I ever felt that comfortable in my own skin? Then again, when had I ever had the chance? If she weren't so likeable, I might've hated her.

We were sitting at the counter of her designer kitchen, where we had gone over the plant-watering schedule just an hour earlier, before I'd taken Chucky out for his get-acquainted walk.

"He's a sneaky one," Mrs. Parker had warned me, ruffling the fur around Chucky's collar. "You've got to watch him every second, or he'll be out of your sight before you know it."

"Don't worry," I assured her. "I'll be careful."

"We're counting on it." Her tone grew earnest. "That's why we picked you for this job. Looking at your references, we had every confidence you'd take this seriously." She glanced down at Chucky. "If he ever got out on his own, or if something ever happened to him – " She shook her head. "We'd never get over it."

"I'll watch him like a hawk," I told her. And I would. I liked dogs, and more to the point, I liked what they were paying for my services – and my discretion. It was a classic win-win. I agreed to keep it confidential that they were out of town, and they agreed to let me live there while I took care of things.

As far as the plant-watering instructions, I'd never seen anything like it. She had a special measuring cup, custom-created plant food, and notations on the exact amount of water each plant needed.

The whole thing was kind of odd. The dog, I got. The plants, I didn't. If Mrs. Parker didn't seem so easygoing in every other way, I'd have pegged her as a massive control freak. But the more I thought about it, the more I decided it was probably her husband, the surgeon, who was the control freak. She was probably just the messenger.

A very comfortable messenger.

I glanced around, taking in my rich surroundings. If her only job was to obsess over the houseplants, she didn't have it too bad.

"Some like to drink in the morning, and some like to drink at night," she had told me when she first pulled out the list.

Drinking in the morning, drinking at night. Yeah, it was like that in my Mom's house too. Except it was Jack Daniels, not filtered rainwater.

But Mrs. Parker and I weren't talking about plants now. Returning from the walk with Chucky, I'd just finished telling her about the guy with the tattoos.

I'd given her a brief rundown, looking for some indication on whether I should call the police or simply ignore him until he found a different neighborhood to loiter in. How she responded would tell me a lot, not just about what I should do now, but how I should handle future encounters.

I was going to be living in the Parkers' house for most of the winter. I knew from experience, it's better to let the home-owner dictate what to do in cases like this.

If I called the police and the owners didn't want a scene, they wouldn't be hiring me the next time they went out of town. If I didn't call the police and something bad happened, I'd get the blame.

If it were up to me, I'd do something. What, I don't know. But I definitely wouldn't just look away and hope for the best. If there was one thing I had learned the hard way, it was that problems don't just go away on their own. They only get bigger.

This guy was a problem. I knew that as sure as I knew that the Parkers' exotic houseplants were getting a lot more TLC than I'd ever gotten, even as a kid.

Mrs. Parker bit her lower lip and thought about it.

I waited, keeping my expression studiously neutral. This was her decision, not mine. I'm completely capable of handling my own decisions. But I needed this job, more than I was willing to admit, even to myself.

If she told me to run through the neighborhood screaming that some tattooed stranger was on the loose, well, I guess I wouldn't exactly do it. But I'd still be kicking myself later if I ended up at my Dad's house, sleeping on the couch in his basement.

The couch was orange, lumpy, and smelled vaguely of sour milk. It was the one piece of furniture in his entire place that wasn't new, designer, or some priceless antique, which is why it was the one place I was actually allowed to sleep.

I hated that couch.

I was contemplating just how much when Mrs. Parker finally smiled. With her index finger, she gave a single tap to the counter and said, "I think I know who that guy is."

"You do?" Just how long had he been hanging around there anyway? "So you've seen him before?"

"Not in person," she said, "but I think I know who you're talking about. You said you saw him in front of that big stone house? The one with the iron gate?"

"That's the one," I said.

She nodded, looking oddly pleased. "He lives there. Just moved in last week."

"Really?" I said, trying to keep the shock out of my voice. "Is he like the owner's son or something?"

She shook her head. "Guess again."

I threw out my second-best guess. "The gardener?" Sure, I'd never seen a gardener who looked like that, but hey, you never know.

This time, she laughed. "Hardly."

I gave it some thought. Trophy husband? No, too many tattoos. Gigolo? He certainly had the body for it, but that was too ridiculous for words. Gigolos didn't loiter outside the front gate after giving someone a nooner. They'd take their money and run. Drug dealer? Possible, but somehow, I didn't think so. He looked tough, but not slimy.

I didn't speak any of these guesses out loud. I couldn't – not if I wanted to keep up the sheltered rich-girl act.

"Cable guy?" I finally said.

Mrs. Parker gave me a strange look, like she was trying to decide if I was kidding or clueless.

"Just kidding," I laughed. "But honestly, I'm out of guesses."

"Hang on," Mrs. Parker said. She strode out of the room and came back a minute later. She was holding a magazine. She plopped it on the counter in front of me.

And there he was, gracing the front of Celebrity Watch. I felt my jaw drop. The image was oddly familiar. He stood, leaning against some brick wall, shirtless and tattooed, his six-pack glistening with what I guessed was sweat. He had that same half smile, that same dark hair, those same dangerous eyes.

My eyes drifted back to his abs. Absolute perfection. I swallowed, and then caught myself. Didn't the guy own a shirt?

Pulling my gaze from the image, I glanced at Mrs. Parker.

She was grinning. "So that's the guy, huh?"

Boy was it ever.

CHAPTER 4

I'd been living in the Parkers' house for just over a week.

I never did meet the husband, although I'd seen a bunch of framed photos here and there throughout the house. The Parkers in Paris. The Parkers skiing. The Parkers on some sailboat.

In some of the photos, it was just the two of them, looking for all the world like second-honeymooners. In others, it was the Parkers with their son – a cute kid who'd apparently grown up and moved to Chicago.

The husband was noticeably older than the wife, and it was pretty obvious it wasn't the guy's looks that had gotten him the house – or the wife for that matter. But they looked happy, at least from what I could tell.

And now, they were in Costa Rica for the winter.

And I was living in their house, along with Chucky, the plants, and my growing obsession with Lawton Rastor.

While walking Chucky, I saw him almost every day, sometimes outside his fence, sometimes inside. Sometimes, the gate to his estate was open. Sometimes, it was shut. I continued to act like he was invisible. He continued to act like he owned the

15

place, which, well, I guess he did.

After that first time, he always wore a shirt, normally a simple T-shirt, sometimes gray, sometimes black. They were never tight, but didn't matter. Thanks to my Internet-fueled obsession, I knew exactly what was underneath them.

Now, every time I looked at the guy, I had a hard time not filling in the blanks, seeing those perfect abs, the muscular chest, the intricate tattoos that would send any sane girl running.

Normally, I was sane and then some, but there was something about the guy that was making me a little crazy. It wasn't his wealth, and it wasn't his celebrity status. It wasn't even his body, as mouth-watering as it was.

It was the way he'd looked on that very first day – the way he stood, the look in his eyes, and the unbridled energy that fell off of him in waves. One night, I actually dreamed about him. The dream should've been a nightmare, except it wasn't. I woke in a fevered confusion, burning for him in a way that made me blush in the pale morning light.

It made no sense. He wasn't my type.

I'm not a star-fucker, literally or otherwise. I didn't own a TV and rarely went to the movies. I find celebrity worship too stupid for words, especially with celebrities like Lawton Rastor, some pretty boy with a death wish.

But with him, I couldn't help myself. I devoured that first magazine article word-by-word, and then dozens more on the Internet. What I learned horrified me. But I couldn't stop. What is it about train wrecks that you just can't look away?

Hell if I know. But Lawton Rastor was a train wreck for sure.

He was a bad boy heartbreaker with more baggage than any airline. His fights were brutal and so were his breakups. He'd once left some starlet half-naked in the bathroom of a posh Beverly Hills restaurant, then beat the crap out of the bouncers who tried to stop him from leaving.

There were also some pictures, along with a sex tape – all supposedly taken without his knowledge.

Yeah, right.

Why people put up with him, I had no idea. Well, actually I did. He was rich. He was famous. And he oozed raw power, the primitive kind that made girls go weak in the knees, until they grew up and realized that raw power didn't pay the bills. Except in Lawton's case, it did.

That didn't matter. I already knew how Lawton's story would end. He'd be broke in five years, maybe less. In ten years, he'd return to reality television, but this time he wouldn't be the hot newcomer. He'd be the washed-up has-been, trying to kick some coke or cupcake addiction while the world watched in morbid fascination.

Ten years after that, he'd be six feet under or working as a security guard at some low-rent shopping mall. And even that gig wouldn't last. He'd be canned, either for snorting coke in the bathroom or beating the ass of some clueless customer who just wanted to take his picture.

It was settled. The guy was doomed.

I was telling all this to Erika, my best friend since high school, when she stopped me in mid-sentence.

"But he doesn't have a drug problem," she said.

"Not that you know of."

"And you can't go through that much money," she said. "It's not even possible."

"Oh yeah?" I said. "Tell that to Mike Tyson."

We were walking Chucky down the tree-lined streets, catching up on girl talk while we strolled. Erika was on her last semester at Michigan State, two hours away by car. I hadn't seen her in a few weeks, but it felt like months. I didn't have a ton of friends, probably because I didn't have a ton of time for fun.

Erika was in town for the weekend and wouldn't be coming back for weeks. If I had my way, she'd be staying with me at the Parkers', but overnight houseguests were strictly prohibited.

I'd agreed to those terms and intended to honor them. I wasn't a liar, and I wasn't a deal breaker. And even if I were, there was no way I'd get myself fired just because some nosy neighbor reported an unauthorized sleepover. Still, it was nice to have Erika around, even if only for a few hours.

I lowered my voice. "It's up here on the left," I told her.

Looking at Lawton's estate, Erika gave a low whistle. "Wow, that's seriously huge." She laughed. "Like the rest of him, huh?"

I hadn't actually seen the sex tape, but I'd read enough about it to know exactly what she meant. I made no comment. Not on that. It would only encourage her, and when it came to sex, Erika didn't need a whole lot of encouragement. It was probably one of the reasons we were friends. We balanced each other.

Picky. That's what she called me. But I had my reasons.

"What I can't figure out," I said, "is why he's living in Rochester Hills of all places."

"Well, he is from Detroit," Erika said.

"Yeah, but shouldn't he be living in Hollywood or New York by now?"

Erika made a scoffing sound. "Want to know what a million bucks buys in New York? A coat closet."

Knowing the guy's reputation, I saw the problem. "No room for orgies?"

That's when a low, deep masculine voice sounded behind us. "Yeah. That's it."

In unison, Erika and I whipped around to see him, Lawton Rastor, looking a lot like he did on that very first day. He was standing just a couple feet away on the sidewalk, his hands thrust into the pockets of his jeans. He was wearing a gray T-shirt and no jacket in spite of the cool weather. His glossy black hair was slightly damp, like he just got out of the shower.

Looking at us, his gaze held more challenge than interest. "So, uh, you volunteering?"

I couldn't help it. I swallowed as I craned my neck to look up at him. Then, as if my eyes had a mind of their own, my gaze travelled slowly downward, pausing too long to be decent at the half-way point, and ending at his feet. He wore old-fashioned red tennis shoes, no laces.

I looked up to meet his gaze. His mouth was tight, and I had the distinct impression that my comment hadn't been appreciated. Something about his expression made me look down, studying the sidewalk while I tried to think of a snappy comeback.

"Yeah," he said. "I own shoes. Surprised?"

By habit, I went immediately into upscale, polite mode. "No. Of course not," I said. It wasn't exactly true, but it did seem like the sort of thing someone who actually lived in this neighborhood might say.

I glanced at Erika. She was looking from Lawton to me. Finally, she gave Lawton a tentative wave. "Hi. I'm Erika, and you are –?"

Oh. My. God. She wasn't seriously doing the whole, I-have-no-idea-who-you-are routine.

He paused a beat, glancing at Erika and then at me. "Just the neighbor guy."

Before she could respond, he stepped around us and kept on walking. That's when Chucky chose to start yapping his fool head off, straining at the leash as he lunged toward Lawton's receding back.

I bent down to ruffle his fur, whispering, "Why couldn't have

19

you done that five minutes ago?"

Chucky gave a single bark.

I gave him a stern look. "Remember," I told him, "you're supposed to bark before someone sneaks up on us. Got it?"

I glanced up at Erika. She burst out laughing.

"It's not funny," I said.

"Yes," she laughed. "Actually it is."

I felt my own lips tug up at the corners. "Fine," I said. "Maybe just a little."

CHAPTER 5

"Chucky! You come back here!"

For a little dog, he sure moved fast. He was also smart, a lot smarter than I'd given him credit for. The instant I cracked open the back door to take out the garbage, he shot past my legs like a furry land-rocket.

As I watched, he dodged a lounge chair, sideswiped a potted plant, and leapt off the raised brick patio, running full speed ahead toward the shrubbery-lined iron fence that ran along the back property line.

It was a cold, drizzly night, and the entire backyard was cast in shadows. I groaned in frustration. "Chucky!" I dropped the trash bag and plunged after him. "You come back here this instant!"

For a moment, I thought he might actually obey, because he appeared suddenly out of the shadows, skidding to a stop just a few feet from my legs. But the instant I reached for him, he gave a playful yip and swerved away, continuing full speed ahead on his original path.

"That's not funny!" I yelled, chasing after him in my unlaced tennis shoes. I hadn't planned on going for a run and certainly hadn't planned on playing tag with some furry prankster. I so wasn't prepared for this.

For one thing, I wasn't dressed for it. Aside from the tennis shoes, I was wearing my favorite ratty T-shirt and black sleeping shorts, no coat, no socks. The drizzle seeped into my thin T-shirt and made the already cold night seem absolutely freezing.

By the time I reached the fence, Chucky was nowhere in sight.

And that's when I noticed it. The smell of someone grilling. It smelled like burgers, or maybe steak. No wonder Chucky had taken off so fast. Even to me, it smelled mouth-watering, and it wasn't like red meat was my favorite.

I leaned my forehead between two fence spires and peered into the shadows. The foliage was thick on the other side, so I couldn't see much, only the barest glimmer of light somewhere up in the distance.

And then, from somewhere near the glimmer, I heard it, that same playful yip, followed by the muted sounds of deep male laughter.

In high school, I hated geometry. It wasn't that I hated math in general. I loved algebra, and actually ended up majoring in accounting. Still, geometry remained my major source of irritation. For one thing, the story problems drove me nuts. I didn't see the point to them, just a bunch of made up stuff that would never apply in the real world.

Until now. Because considering this real-life story problem in my head, it didn't take me long to grasp the implications of that yip and laugh. When it comes to destinations, a long stroll by sidewalk equals a short run by dog, at least when you ignore little things like iron fences.

Just great.

Fifteen minutes later, I was standing outside the gate where I'd seen Lawton Rastor that very first time. Moving at a frantic pace, I'd barely taken the time to throw on a gray hoodie, pulling the hood over my already damp hair as I ran along the sidewalk, sloshing in puddles with every step.

The drizzle had turned to rain, a steady downpour that left me feeling like a drowned rat. But given the circumstances, I hardly cared. Was Chucky still there? I sure hoped so, because if anything happened to that dog, I'd sorely regret it, and not just because of the Parkers. He might've been a prankster, but he was growing on me.

By the time I reached Lawton's gate, I was soaked, breathless, and beyond irritated. Growing on me or not, Chucky was a very bad dog.

But now that I was here, I didn't quite know what to do. The gate was shut. And I had no idea how to gain access to the grounds. There was a covered keypad off to the right, but I didn't see a call button on it, and I couldn't tell if it had an intercom. So I did the only thing I could. I cupped my hands around my mouth and yelled out toward the house, "Hey! Excuse me! Anyone home?"

Nothing.

With a deep breath, I ratcheted up the volume. "Hey! Anyone home?"

No answer.

"I'm looking for my dog!"

Even to my own ears, I sounded like an idiot. Patio grilling aside, it was way past the dinner hour. It was dark, I was wet, and the dog in question wasn't really even my own. Still, I wasn't about to give a long explanation while standing outside in the pouring rain.

Still no answer.

"Hey!!!" I called as loud as I could. "Chucky! Where are you? Anyone there!"

A moment later, I heard the sound of static, followed by a male voice. "Yeah?"

I looked at the keypad. Was the voice coming from there? I couldn't tell. In the end, I decided it didn't matter. I simply called out in the general direction of the house. "I'm looking for my dog! Is he here?"

"Come on up," the voice said. A moment later, the gate slid slowly open.

"I'll take that as a yes," I muttered, pulling the soaked hoodie further down over my face as I walked through the now-open gate. When it shut behind me, I turned to look. If I needed to get out of here, could I? The iron fencing was tall, with minimal space between the spires, and I still had no idea what controlled the gate.

I wasn't some naïve girly-girl. I'd probably seen way more of life than anyone else here in this neighborhood. Okay, except for Lawton Rastor.

Yeah, it might've been stupid to walk blindly into the gated estate of someone I didn't know. And sure, the guy had a terrible reputation. But hey, I told myself, he was technically a neighbor. And besides, what were my other choices? Call the police? Contact animal control? No way I'd be doing either of those things. I wasn't even two weeks into this job, and getting fired for stupidity wasn't part of my plan.

It wasn't just that I needed the money. I didn't have anywhere else to go. Not really.

By the time I dashed up the brick driveway to the massive covered front entrance, I was soaked down to my skin. I reached a dripping hand toward the doorbell, but never got the chance to actually ring it. Because before I could, the wide door swung open, revealing a massive entryway, a huge crystal chandelier, and Lawton Rastor in the flesh, literally.

CHAPTER 6

Dripping water onto his front porch, I stared up at him. He stood in the entryway, bare-chested, with faded jeans and no shoes. His left hand rested on the elaborate silver doorknob. In his right hand, dangled a metal spatula.

I swallowed. It reminded me of the first time I'd seen him. Only this was much worse, because I couldn't exactly ignore him and walk away.

For Pete's sake, didn't the guy own a shirt? Or shoes? Oh, that's right. He did. He told me so, and besides, I'd seen them the last time I'd run into him.

Still, why couldn't I stop staring? His wavy dark hair was slightly damp, and a smattering of what I guessed were raindrops still glistened on his bare shoulders and trickled down toward his flat, muscular abs.

I pulled my gaze up to his face and choked out, "I'm looking for my dog. Uh, Chucky. A little terrier?"

"Chucky?" He gave me a slow, deliberate smile. "Like the possessed doll?"

The smile, along with the sound of his voice, set my world

spinning. I stared up at him. My lips parted, and my mind suddenly went vacant. "Huh?"

"It's a movie," he said. "A bunch of them, actually."

I shook off the stupidity. "I don't watch a lot of movies."

He shrugged. "Probably not missing much."

"And besides," I said, "it's Chucky like –" I hesitated. Honestly, I had no idea. And then, I heard myself blurt out, "Like my uncle." My uncle? Where on Earth had that come from? I certainly didn't have an Uncle Chucky, and neither did the Parkers as far as I knew. "Um, so is he here?"

His mouth twitched. "Your uncle?"

I was cold, tired, and determined to skip the part of the script where I fell all over him, just because he was Lawton Rastor and, well, intoxicating. Luscious. Sexy beyond all reason. I gave myself a mental slap to the face. "No," I told him, very slowly, like speaking to an unruly toddler. "Chucky, my dog."

"Yeah. He's here." He stepped aside and flicked his head toward the interior of his house. "Come on in."

"Thank you," I muttered, following him inside.

My reaction to him was totally unlike me. But it didn't matter. Primitive attraction aside, the guy wasn't my type. Even if I were looking, which I wasn't, some gorgeous bad boy with a death wish wasn't on my life's shopping list.

I wasn't my Mom. I wasn't a one-night stand type of girl. I was a relationship kind of girl. And when I settled down – if I ever did settle down – it would be with someone safe. And stable. Someone exactly the opposite of Lawton Rastor.

I hadn't experienced a lot of safety or stability as a kid, and I intended to make up for it in spades as an adult.

Inside, I pushed back the soaked hood from my equally soaked head. And that's when I saw them, two nearly identical blondes in tight black dresses, leaning against the open staircase.

Their long hair was untouched by any rain, humidity, or, from what I could tell, any other force of man or nature.

They looked absolutely perfect. Perfect makeup, perfect clothing, perfect looks of contempt as they eyed me standing just inside the doorway, dripping water all over the marble floor.

Suddenly, I was very conscious of my wet hair and squishy tennis shoes. I looked down. My laces were still untied. Now they were muddy too.

"Your mutt ate our dinner," one of them said.

"And chewed up my purse," said the other one.

I resisted the urge to smile. Good boy.

Instead, I lifted my chin. "He's no mutt," I said with the pretended disdain of someone who might actually care about such things. "He's a purebred Yorkie. He has papers if you'd like to see them." I smiled. "Assuming you can read?"

I heard something like a chuckle. I glanced at Lawton Rastor. His mouth lifted at the corners as he eyed me with a curious look. Was he laughing with me? Or at me? Probably at me, I decided. I didn't need a mirror to see what he saw – a soggy girl with no fashion sense. He was probably wondering what rock I crawled out from under.

Maybe I should've taken more than thirty seconds to get ready, and brought an umbrella or a raincoat. I pointed vaguely toward the Parkers' house. "We share a fence."

"I know," he said.

He knew? How? I didn't even realize that fact myself until Chucky's great escape. Speaking of which, where was he? "You have my dog?" I said.

"I'm pretty sure your dog had me first," he said.

"Yeah," the first blonde broke in. "He chewed up Lawton's shirt."

I turned toward Lawton, making a conscious effort to not

stare. But in working so hard to control my eyes, I lost control of my mouth. "So, you were actually wearing a shirt?"

He rubbed the back of his neck. "Hey, it happens."

I suddenly occurred to me how rude I was being. I'd shown up uninvited, and apparently my dog, or rather the Parkers' dog, had eaten his dinner, and possibly his clothing. If I were the blushing type, I'd be blushing big-time right about now.

I shook my head. "Sorry. Rain makes me crabby." It wasn't true. I loved the rain. I just didn't like being out in it. "So," I cleared my throat. "I apologize." I blew out a breath. "For Chucky. And the shirt. And um, for my big mouth."

At this, his gaze briefly dipped to my lips. His own lips parted, like he was about to say something. But he never did. Instead, he studied me with a look that made my knees go weak and my mouth start running like it had a mind of its own.

"Of course," I continued, "it's none of my business what you wear, or don't wear around your own house. I mean, you could go naked, and it'd be no one's business, right?" Oh God. Shut up, Chloe. Shut up, shut up, shut up. I clamped my lips together and glanced away.

"Yeah?" he said with a crooked grin. "Good to know."

"So, uh, I'd better get going," I said.

"What about my purse?" the second blond said.

Lawton threw purse-girl half a glance. "Zip it, Bethany."

She frowned. "It's Brittney."

"Whatever."

This is when Chucky bounded in from somewhere near the back of the house, sliding on the marble floor as he took a corner at full speed. When he saw me, he gave a yip of greeting and then dove for my legs, nearly toppling me over when he slammed into them.

I couldn't help but laugh as I choked out, "Bad dog." From

the tone of my voice, he probably thought I was praising him. But I couldn't help it. Chucky was more soaked than I was, but I swear, I saw him smile.

No wonder he was happy. He'd had steak and a purse for dinner. Oh yeah, and some guy's shirt. It was a total doggie buffet.

A few feet away, Brittney edged toward Lawton and pouted in a way she probably thought was pretty. "But the purse," she persisted, "it was a Louis Vuitton."

I felt my smile fade. This was so not good.

"If you so say so," Lawton said.

She turned to glare at me. "You're gonna have to pay for it, you know."

I felt myself pale. I'd never owned a Louis Vuitton, not even secondhand. But I did know that even a basic one probably cost more than my car. Granted, my car was a piece of crap. It was old, ugly, and the heat didn't always work. But more to the point, I definitely didn't have nearly that kind of money lying around.

"Your ass," Lawton told her. "It was a knock-off, and you know it."

Her perfect face showed a hint of pink. "Well, it wasn't a cheap knock-off." She pursed her lips. "She's still gonna have to pay."

With something like a sigh, Lawton reached into his back pocket. He pulled out a black wallet and peeled off several hundreds. He held the money vaguely in her direction.

She hesitated just a moment before sauntering over and snatching it out of his hand. She gave me a dirty look as she stuffed it into her ample cleavage and then stood, possessively by Lawton's side.

"You're lucky he's such a gentleman," she said.

I was immensely grateful that Lawton had taken care of the

purse, but the idea of him as a gentleman was beyond ridiculous. I'd seen one of his fights on the Internet. The guy was a brute, and from what I'd seen in the tabloids, there was nothing gentlemanly about him.

But I'd never say that out loud. I'd had years of suppressing my real thoughts and feelings behind a mask of civility, and this was no time to break that pattern.

"Yes," I said, summoning up my very best upper crust persona. "He's very kind."

At this, Lawton gave me a curious look, and for the briefest moment, I felt like he saw straight through me. And then, just as quickly as it had come, the look was gone. Or maybe I'd been imagining it all along.

Besides, I had more important things to think about. How much money had he tossed at her? I couldn't tell the exact amount, but it looked like a lot, at least by my budget-conscious standards. Given that the purse was a fake, she'd probably made a tidy profit from the deal.

Thinking about it, I realized something that made my mouth go dry. Now, I owed him money instead of her. This hadn't solved anything. Not really.

Swallowing, I turned to him and made myself say, "If you'd like to send me a bill, I'll make sure you're promptly reimbursed."

Oh God, I sounded like an accountant. No wonder, since that had been my major and all. Still, what the hell was I saying? Reimbursement would be anything but prompt. Unless – maybe I could ask the Parkers to pay for it.

They checked in about once a week, and I had a cell phone number for emergencies. Was this an emergency? It was their dog, after all. But then I'd be forced to explain how I'd let Chucky get out in the first place.

No. This was my fault, and I'd need to pay for this fiasco

myself.

Damn it. Whatever amount Lawton had thrown at her, it was too much. That chick's profit was going to come out of my hide, and I didn't have anything to spare. Lamely, I continued on, "I'd just need a receipt, uh, for my records."

Records? What records? Shit, I didn't know.

"Nah, I've got it," he told me with a half-shrug. He spared Brittney a glance. "Besides, that'll show Barbie for leaving her purse on the floor."

"It's Brittney," she corrected for the second time.

Ignoring her, he gave me a slow half-smile. "How about a compromise? You replace dinner, and I'll worry about Becky's purse."

I snuck a glance at Brittney. This time, she didn't bother correcting him. But her look said it all. She was so not amused.

His offer was tempting, but I hated the idea of being in his debt. Sure, the guy could afford it, but I hated owing people. Those debts always came due at the worst time, in the worst way.

Brittney was looking daggers at both of us. By now, I was fairly certain Lawton was a lot better with names than he let on. Was he just goading her? If so, she certainly wasn't enjoying it. With an exasperated sigh, she gave the other blonde a pleading look.

The girl took the hint. "Forget dinner," she practically purred. "Let's get straight to dessert."

Lawton gave her the briefest glance, and then returned his attention to me. "Is it a deal? I'll get the purse. You get dinner."

"A foursome, Lawton?" the second blonde said. "Really? Isn't that a bit much?"

This time, I did blush. A foursome? We were still talking about dinner?

I leaned over and scooped up Chucky. "I've got to go."

"You're not walking back," he said.

"Sure I am."

"In the rain?"

"I walked here, didn't I?" Outside, a crack of thunder sounded loud enough to rattle the windows. Chucky whined. I wanted to whine too, but instead I clamped my lips shut and glanced toward the front door.

"Wait here," Lawton said. "I'll pull up the car."

Maybe I should've argued, but why bother? Walking home in a raging thunderstorm was stupid by anyone's definition. And besides, refusing the offer just made everything more awkward. Things were awkward enough as it was.

Still, it wasn't exactly comfortable when Lawton headed out some side entrance to pull up a car.

Brittney and her friend looked at me with undisguised loathing.

"You're not his type, you know," Brittney said.

I grinned. "Whatever you say, Betty."

She scowled. "Ha ha."

Meanwhile, Chucky was looking at their shoes with more than casual interest. As I knew firsthand, Chucky loved to chew up footwear.

Too bad we were leaving. I'd love to give Chucky the chance.

CHAPTER 7

The car wasn't what I expected. I'd been expecting something late-model and definitely expensive. Maybe a Lamborghini, possibly a Porsche. But what pulled up in the circular driveway was something I couldn't exactly place.

The car was at least double my age, and nothing I recognized. It was some vintage muscle car. Between the dark and the rain, I couldn't tell the exact color, but just looking at its sleek lines and listening to the roar of its engine, I could tell one thing flat-out. It was a lot like Lawton Rastor, all speed and muscle, not a lot of comfort.

As soon as the car skidded to a stop in the turnaround, I fled Lawton's house, plunging out of the open doorway and holding onto Chucky for dear life. No way the little monster was getting away this time.

By the time I reached the car, the passenger's side door was already open, with Lawton leaning across the seat, his tattooed arm stretched toward the door handle like he'd just shoved at it. Still clutching Chucky, I jumped into the vehicle and closed the door behind me, surprised by how heavy the door was. The thing had to be all metal, compared to whatever they made car doors out of nowadays.

I glanced over at Lawton. His hair was still damp, but at least he'd put on a shirt, some basic black T-shirt with a miscellaneous logo on the front.

When he hit the accelerator, the car's roar briefly drowned out the sound of the rain, and the seats vibrated with the engine's power. When we neared the gate, it slid open automatically, probably on a motion-sensor. A moment later, he pulled out onto the street with barely a glance in my direction. Easy to see why, with two beautiful girls waiting in the wings.

He said nothing, and neither did I until we were just a couple houses away from the Parkers'.

"I'm up here on the left," I said, pointing toward their house.

"I know," he said.

"Really? How?"

"We share a fence. Remember?"

"Oh. Yeah. Sorry." Of course, I knew that. Where was my brain tonight anyway?

"And I saw you before," he continued. "Walking your dog. Chucky, right?"

On my lap, Chucky gave a yap of affirmation.

Lawton chuckled, a low sound that blended nicely with the rumble of the engine.

Funny he could remember Chucky's name, but not the blonde's. Then again, I was still convinced most of that was an act. For whatever reason, he seemed to enjoy goading her. Maybe they had that kind of relationship, if you could call it that.

Soon, we were pulling into the Parkers' long, tree-lined driveway, the car rumbling to a stop. "Thanks for the ride," I said, reaching for the door.

"Hang on," he said. "You still owe me dinner."

I gave him a sideways glance. "The foursome? I think I'd better pass."

He gave me a wicked grin. "How about a twosome?"

My stomach did funny things at his smile, along with the image his words conjured up. But I paid no attention. I couldn't afford to pay attention. A guy like him was the last thing I needed. Besides, what did he think? That I'd jump in his pants just because he drove me home?

"Are we still talking dinner?" I asked. "Or something else?" Because if it was something else, I wasn't interested. Okay, maybe I was interested. He was mouth-watering, plain and simple, and I'd been thinking about him far too much for my own good.

In my fantasies, half the time we were naked. The other half, we were naked on his yacht, assuming he owned one. Sometimes we were naked on his yacht and drinking dirty martinis or drinks I couldn't pronounce.

In my fantasies, I didn't have too many responsibilities. Instead, I had more than enough time and plenty of money. Oh yeah, and I had parents who cared, not just about me, but for my kid brother too.

It was a pretty picture, even if it wasn't real. In my fantasies, I got to enjoy life for once, free and easy. That's where the yacht came in. I could just sail off into the sunset with a beautiful guy and no responsibilities except what came day-to-day.

But real life just wasn't like that, and even if it were, I'd never abandon my commitments. I was nothing like my parents, and I had too many things on my to-do list.

Besides, there was a fine line between fantasy and reality. The reality could never live up to anyone's imagination. I knew where that road ended. It didn't end up on a yacht. It ended with a whole lot of wasted energy and some social disease I couldn't pronounce.

He cut the engine. "That's up to you."

"Huh?"

"Dinner – or something else – it's your choice." He gave me a slow smile. "Or hey, I'm up for both."

Yeah, I just bet he was. I glanced at the house. "Sorry, but I can't have guests over."

He leaned back in the seat. "Worried your folks wouldn't like it?" He lowered his voice, as if sharing a secret. "Let me guess, because I'm a bad influence, right?"

If he only knew. My parents wouldn't give a crap one way or another. But the Parkers certainly would. Again, I glanced at the house. It wasn't half as impressive as Lawton's, but it was still pretty spectacular. Did he think I actually lived here?

Of course he did. I'd been calling Chucky my dog, after all. And Lawton had just moved in a couple weeks earlier. Even if he was the type of guy to get to know his neighbors, it's not like he'd been in the neighborhood long enough to figure out the Parkers lived there alone.

"Actually, they're not here," I said. Technically, this was true, even if it was somewhat misleading.

"So what's the problem?" he asked. It wasn't a challenge so much as a question. He seemed genuinely curious.

I had to work in a few hours. House-sitting wasn't my only job. But that wasn't the most important reason to decline whatever he was offering. "You have guests, remember?"

He shrugged. "They know the way out."

Seriously? What a jerk. Sure, I didn't care much for Brittney and what's-her-name, but his cavalier attitude was beyond offensive. So how did he envision this going?

I played out the scenario in my head, trying to see things the way he saw it. I'd invite him inside. Dinner or not, we'd do the nasty, and then he'd be treating me in the same dismissive way come morning. I made a scoffing sound. Who was I kidding? No way he'd stick around 'til morning. He'd run out the door the second we were done.

"Something funny?" he asked.

I shook my head. "I've gotta go."

He gave me a crooked smile. "So dinner's a 'no' then?"

"What dinner?"

"The steak, remember?"

Oh, yeah. The steak Chucky ate.

Still, I didn't get it. He had plenty of money and two gorgeous women waiting for him. But here he was, badgering me about dinner and who knows what else.

It was too ridiculous for words. Suddenly, I was very tired. I didn't have time for whatever game he was playing. My fantasies might be hollow, but they served their purpose.

"I don't have any steak," I said.

"Well, what do you have?"

I glanced at the house. "Uh, peanut butter and jelly."

"Sounds great," he said.

At this, I couldn't help but laugh. "Seriously?"

"Why not?" he said.

"Sorry," I said, "but you can't come in. I'll just have to owe you."

"Then I'll just have to collect." He grinned. "Lucky for you, patience is my middle name."

Liar. His middle name was Anthony.

Oh crap. I knew his middle name, for God's sake. What was I? Some kind of crazy stalker-chick?

The Internet – it was a dangerous thing for a girl in my condition. And what condition was that, exactly? Frustrated? Bored with my real life? Oddly aroused by the thought of his perfect pecs and glorious abs? I licked my lips. It was definitely time for me to stop reading about him.

He turned sideways in the seat to face me. "So, uh, tomorrow morning work for you? Steak and eggs?"

I probably had eggs somewhere in the fridge, but I definitely didn't have steak. I mentally slapped myself. Why was I even thinking about this? Obviously, he wasn't serious. And obviously, I wasn't going to have some stranger over for breakfast tomorrow. Especially a stranger like him in a house that wasn't my own.

The guy did funny things to my mind, and even funnier things to parts of my body that had been sadly neglected lately. Some might call it a dry spell. I called it holding out for something meaningful.

"So Chucky," he said in a conversational tone. "How's it goin'?"

Chucky gave a yap and squirmed in my lap.

Oh crap. I never answered him, did I? What was his question again? Had there been a question? At this point, I had two choices: try to prove I wasn't an idiot or make a break for it. Since the odds of the first choice were unlikely, I opted for the second.

"I've gotta go," I said. How many times had I said that?

Clutching Chucky, I shoved open the car door. The rain was still falling in torrents. If Lawton said anything afterwards, I didn't hear it, because a moment later, I was sprinting toward the Parkers' front door, with Chucky squirming the entire time.

After I closed the door behind me, I carefully set down Chucky and tiptoed to the front window. The shades were drawn, and the house was dark. Lawton couldn't see me, but I could still see the glare of his headlights through the blinds.

What was he waiting for? With a huff of annoyance, I stalked to the nearest lamp and turned it on. A moment later, I heard the rumble of his engine, and the headlights disappeared down the long driveway.

So he'd waited for me to get inside and turn on the lights? Was that good or bad? Either he was a gentleman, as Brittney had claimed, or he was the worst kind of opportunist. Probably, he was waiting for me to grill up a steak, rip off my clothes, and run outside to tell him I'd changed my mind.

It didn't matter. I was smart to run when I did, because if I were being completely honest, that whole twosome idea was sounding way too good.

CHAPTER 8

Chomping on my gum, I squeezed into the red vinyl booth that was already occupied by two couples about my own age. I grabbed the pencil from behind my ear and said, "So, what'd'ya want, make it snappy, will ya?"

Yeah, it wasn't the politest approach, but that was part of my job. The Two-Bit Diner was a retro burger and breakfast joint, complete with roller-skating delivery outside during the summer months, and inside-dining all year round.

But it wasn't your average diner, and it wasn't your average waitressing job. In a way, it was like a dinner show, with everyone playing a part. Along with a dozen or so other girls, I played a big-haired, big-mouthed waitress with attitude. I went through a bottle of hair spray a month.

The job was a lot trickier than it sounded. There's a fine line between rude and sassy, and finding that middle ground was a nonstop balancing act. Take the act too far, and people would get pissed off. Take it not far enough, and they'd complain they didn't get their money's worth.

The food might've been simple, but it wasn't cheap, so just

41

because I was allowed to be louder and sassier than your average waitress, it didn't mean I was allowed to be slow or incompetent. Plus, you had to be a damn good waitress just to keep everything straight, especially the alcohol, which flowed freely in spite of the diner theme.

It never said so in the help-wanted ads, but to work here, you had to have a certain look. My co-workers were all exceptionally good-looking. I'd never been short of male attention, but I'd never thought of myself in that way. To be honest, there were days I felt more than a little outclassed by the beautiful girls I worked with.

The uniforms were a total nightmare – bobby socks, short pink skirts, and tight white blouses that showed way too much cleavage whenever I bent down to lay a dish on the table.

But the tips were amazing. They should be amazing, given the price we charged for a burger. Those tips had paid for most of my college education, along with countless other obligations along the way.

Still, I'd expected to be long gone by now. I'd graduated from college months ago, but here I still was. In spite of respectable grades, my accounting degree was getting me nowhere.

I'd been interviewing for months and had been offered a couple of jobs. But the salaries had been laughable, less than minimum wage when you calculated it by the hour. I made triple the money waitressing. Sure, the hours stunk, and it was getting me nowhere in my so-called career. But I couldn't afford the pay cut. Not now, anyway.

Still, as I hustled through the place, taking orders, and delivering burgers, pancakes, and a whole bunch of drinks and side items, I couldn't help but wonder if I'd made a mistake by staying. Maybe I should've taken that payroll processing job. A girl had to start somewhere, right?

It was just after midnight, and I still had five hours left on my shift. I was putting together a tray of drinks when Josie rushed over and nudged me in the side.

"Oh my God," she whispered, motioning out to the dining area. "Is that who I think it is?"

I was too focused on my drinks to look up. "Who?"

"Lawton Rastor. In booth seven." She sounded breathless as she said, "I'd heard he was living around here, but I didn't expect to actually see him."

My whole body went still. "Lawton Rastor?"

"Oh c'mon," she said. "Don't tell me you don't know who he is."

"Uh –" I couldn't think. I'd just seen the guy a few hours ago. I'd been sopping wet with no makeup. And yet, for some reason, the thought of him seeing me this way, with big hair and blue eye shadow, was infinitely worse.

Josie rolled her eyes. "God, you're so pathetic." She said this with a smile. She'd been teasing me for months about my lack of pop culture savvy. "He's that guy from Hard World. You know, that reality show from a few years back?"

"I never saw it," I mumbled

Sure, I'd read about it, and that was more than enough. He'd slept with practically every girl in the household. But it wasn't the off-screen sex that had people watching. It was the fights. Not fights with him. Fights over him. The show was abruptly cancelled after one girl threw another one through a plate glass window. She'd survived, but the show hadn't.

"Well, you missed your chance," Josie said. "He's gone total mainstream. He's got a string of fitness centers or something."

From what I'd read, the fitness centers were just the tip of the iceberg. He also had a line of workout equipment and sports apparel, with nonstop publicity fueled by mixed martial arts events.

"I used to have a poster of him in my room," Josie said. "It drove my parents nuts."

My heart thumping, I peered over the half-wall that separated the waitress station from the dining area. Crap, it was him. Worse, the blondes were still with him. How long had it been since he'd dropped me off at the Parkers'? Four hours?

What had the three of them been doing this whole time? Looking at Lawton's tousled hair, it wasn't hard to guess.

I lowered my head and studied them through my lashes as while I added straws in the drinks. The blondes looked noticeably happier than when I'd seen them last. Even in the crowded restaurant, their laughter rose above the din.

Lawton, in contrast, looked pensive and almost bored. He leaned back in the booth, rewarding the girls with a half-hearted smile as they jostled for his attention. Something in his demeanor suggested a sort of weary resignation, like he was determined to finish whatever he started, if only to get it over with.

"You lucky dog," Josie said. "That's your table."

CHAPTER 9

I felt myself pale. Was it? Crap. We didn't go by sections, but rather by a weird rotation thing dreamed up by Keith, the new night manager. It was a nightmare for keeping track of things, and it meant I had to cover twice the real estate, but Keith said it made it more interesting for the customers, because they got to see all the girls in action.

The way I saw it, Keith was a dumb-ass. But I was mentally calling him something else as I considered that his stupid idea would have me waiting on Lawton and his two guests, if you could call them that.

For some reason, I just couldn't do it. I turned to Josie. "You want it? You can have it."

Her face broke into a wide smile. "Seriously?"

"Oh yeah," I said.

She grabbed her order pad. "I'm getting him now, before you change your mind." A second later, she was heading toward the table, calling over her shoulder, "The next table's yours!"

The next table turned out to be a couple of overgrown frat-boy types, obviously fresh from some nightclub or other.

45

"Hey good-lookin'," one of them said as I plopped down into the booth to take their order.

"Hey lookin'," I said, flashing him a grin.

He laughed. "What?! I'm not good-looking?"

From the look on his face, it was pretty obvious he knew the answer to that question. Yeah, he was good-looking in that all-American way, from the top of his sandy-colored hair to the tips of his expensive shoes. I'd recognized the brand before I sat down. They weren't tennis shoes, and they weren't cheap. He was dressed to kill, and he knew it.

In truth, the guys looked a few years past college age, but I'd have bet my boots, if I were wearing any, that they'd both been in a fraternity not too long ago.

I chomped my gum while I studied him, cocking my head to the side as if I were giving his question some serious thought. Finally, I winked at his equally good-looking friend, and said, "Well, someone at this table's a real looker."

Grinning, the guy sat up straighter, until I gave an exaggerated toss of my hair and chirped, "Me."

I didn't believe it for one minute, but I didn't care. It was all part of the act, and if my tips were any indicator, I played it well.

The first guy burst out laughing and turned to his friend. "Oh buuuuurn," he said. A half second later, the friend joined in the laughter while I blinked stupidly at them, as if I didn't understand what was so funny. A couple minutes later, I was giving their food order to the kitchen.

From the corner of my eye, I kept watch on Lawton's table. While he was sitting at that booth, I was determined to avoid them. In my stupid getup, they might not even recognize me, but I wasn't taking any chances.

By the time they left an hour later, I'd gotten pretty good at ducking, hiding, and turning the other way just in time to avoid catching their attention.

A few minutes after they'd gone, Josie sidled up to me. "I almost feel guilty," she said. "Look how much he left me."

I looked down. The tip was generous to a fault. Shit. Maybe I should've waited on him.

But for some strange reason, the whole idea made me ill. Even if I weren't too embarrassed to play the sassy waitress with Lawton, the thought of serving the two blondes was more than I could stomach. I knew exactly how they would've treated me.

They would've run me ragged, and nothing would've been good enough. I'd been treated that way before, plenty of times, but the thought of being treated that way by them, and in front of Lawton – well, I just couldn't. Why, I didn't know.

"Here," Josie said, holding out a few bills. "Lemme give you a cut."

I wanted to say yes. I needed the money. But it wouldn't have been right. Besides, the frat guys hadn't exactly been stingy. Along with a fairly generous tip, one of them had given me his phone number, and asked for mine in return.

I'd declined, of course. Not that he didn't seem nice and all, but there was a strict policy against picking up guys on the job. Policy or not, it wouldn't be a good idea anyway. Those kinds of things never worked out, and then I'd just have one more thing to dread when those same guys came into the restaurant later on.

Giving Josie a smile, I waved away the tip money. "Nah, you earned it, not me." I reminded myself that she did me a favor, not the other way around. Honestly, I'd have paid her to take that table.

"If you insist," Josie said, tucking the money into her apron. Still, she couldn't stop talking about it. "You know, he's even more gorgeous up close. I think I drooled on his cheeseburger."

"A cheeseburger?" I said. "He didn't order a steak?"

"No." She squinted at me. "Why do you ask?"

I shrugged. "No reason."

A few minutes later, I was lugging a fresh tub of coleslaw out of the walk-in refrigerator when I became aware that something strange was going on in the dining area.

It started slow, with the murmur of voices punctuated by random shouts. The voices didn't sound angry so much as excited, like sports fans watching a big play.

I poked my head around the corner, and I swear, I saw half the restaurant with their faces pressed against the long wall of windows that overlooked the front parking lot.

Before I had any idea what was going on, a large table of college-aged diners bolted from their seats and hurried out the front double doors, leaving behind jackets and plates of half-eaten burgers. Instantly, they were joined by about half the window-gawkers and a wave of other diners, mostly guys.

At tables throughout the restaurant, I saw random, lone women, looking either miffed or amused as their dates, husbands, or whatever abandoned them for who-knows-what.

The crowd near the door was swelling, with diners chatting excitedly as they jostled each other out the entryway.

Keith, the night manager, jumped into the mix, elbowing his way toward the wide double doors. He turned to face the crowd, which quickly parted around him and kept on moving.

"Hey!" Keith said in a loud, high-pitched voice. "You can't leave if you haven't paid."

Other than a couple of amused glances, the crowd mostly ignored him and kept on going.

"Alright, people!" Keith yelled, like a principal facing unruly students at a high school assembly. "You'd better turn around, or you're in big trouble!"

"Dude," said a beefy blond guy with a crew cut, as he jostled

Keith out of the way. "We're comin' back. Chill, will ya?"

Keith turned to holler at the guy's receding back. "When?"

"After the fight," the guy yelled over his shoulder as he exited the wide double doors. "Duh!"

"Fight?" Keith spluttered. He grabbed the arm of the next guy who jostled past him. "What fight?"

This guy didn't bother with an answer, but just shook off Keith and kept on going. A second later, Keith turned around and joined the crowd, elbowing his way out the front doors with the rest of them.

"Don't just stand there, call the police!" Keith shouted to no one in particular.

I glanced at the nearest phone, located next to the main cash register. Julia, the petite, brown-haired hostess, was already dialing.

My gaze scanned the restaurant. Most of my tables were empty, well, of people at least. I saw abandoned jackets, pushed-back chairs, and even a couple of purses. It looked like crew cut guy was right. The owners were coming back – probably – but that didn't mean they weren't incredibly stupid for leaving their belongings unattended.

I was still holding the tub of coleslaw. Unable to resist, I hoisted the tub onto a nearby counter and rushed toward the front entrance to join the others.

Outside, a crowd of at least fifty people had converged in a surprisingly tight circle, between two long rows of cars. Cheers and shouts filled the air as I wedged myself between a girl in a leather jacket and the big blond guy with a crew cut.

I stood on my tiptoes, but couldn't see a thing, except for the backs of people in front of me.

The noise was deafening. I cupped my hands around my mouth and yelled out to the crew cut guy, "What's going on?"

"Fight," he said, sparing me half a glance, followed by a much longer look when he saw my uniform in all its skimpy glory.

"You wanna see?" he asked, his eyes bright with excitement that likely had little to do with my uniform.

I nodded. A moment later, he hoisted me up into the bed of a nearby pickup truck. Grinning, he climbed up to join me. He was quickly followed by two other guys and the girl in the leather jacket.

He grinned down at me. "My truck!" he yelled over the cheers and shouts of the crowd.

I nodded. "Nice!" Then I turned my attention to what was going on inside the circle.

In the center of the circle was Lawton Rastor. Of course.

CHAPTER 10

A few feet away, on the pavement, I saw a massive guy with a shaved head. He was on his hands and knees, as if trying to push himself up, but not having a lot of luck. His face was covered in blood. It looked like his own.

"Oh my God," I said, gripping Crew Cut Guy's arm. "What happened to him?"

He grinned. "That other guy –" he pointed toward Lawton. "– kicked the shit out of him." He said it like it was a good thing.

"He's hurt," I said. "We've gotta help him."

"Nah, he'll be alright," he said. "Besides, he swung first. Serves him right, you ask me."

I looked at the guy who'd supposedly swung first. Blood dripped from the center of his face. Broken nose? I had no idea.

I looked at Lawton. He wore the same thing he'd been wearing in the restaurant – jeans and a T-shirt, no jacket. His face was a mask of calm intensity, like he knew what was coming and was fully prepared for it. As I watched, the corded muscles on his forearms flexed, making his tattoos dance in the orange glow of the tall parking lot lights as he squared off against the guy facing him.

The second guy was as big as the first one, well over six feet. He looked like he beat people up for a living, or maybe just for fun. Unlike Lawton, his face was a mask of frustration and fury, like things weren't going exactly the way he'd expected.

Around the circle, random people held cell phones out in front of them like cameras, while others ditched their phones to watch with their own eyes. I spotted Brittney and friend at the inner rim of the circle, their eyes bright with excitement as they cheered Lawton on.

If Lawton heard anything outside his own thoughts, he gave no sign. He stood, waiting and watching, like the calm within a storm.

The other guy was anything but calm. With a guttural roar, he barreled toward Lawton, only to whirl off to the side and crash into a couple of onlookers after Lawton's right fist struck the side of his jaw.

"Wow, he's fast," I said, more to myself than to the guy next to me.

The blow had seemed to come from nowhere. One instant, the guy was coming at him, and then the next, he was staggering away.

Crew Cut Guy leaned down to holler in my ear. "That's like his tenth run at him," he said. "Always ends the same way. It's fuckin' amazing, isn't it?"

I nodded.

Lawton seemed unimpressed with the whole scene – the roaring crowd, the frigid night air, and the next attack, which ended with another swift blow from Lawton, this one to the gut.

This time the guy doubled over, then fumbled a couple steps back. Lawton eyed him with a look of near boredom, like he'd be happy when the whole sordid thing was over so he could get back to what he really wanted to be doing.

For the briefest instant, I wondered what that was, exactly. I glanced at Brittney and her friend. They'd stopped yelling, probably because no encouragement was needed. Their lips parted as they devoured the scene in front of them with hungry eyes, as if the fight was the main course, and Lawton would be the dessert.

I couldn't help but wonder if you could even call this a fight. It was nothing like I'd seen on the Internet. Even to my untrained eyes, it was beyond obvious that Lawton could've destroyed the guy already, turning him into a bloody pulp without a whole lot of effort. Why didn't he? Was it because of the audience?

Nearby, the bloody guy on the ground made another half-hearted effort to rise. Lawton's gaze snapped briefly in his direction before returning to the opponent who was still standing. Sort of. He was wobbling more than anything, weaving from side-to-side like he'd be toppling over any moment.

Watching, the crowd grew almost silent, breathless, waiting for the guy to fall over, or for Lawton to finish him off. On the sidelines, I saw more than one wad of money change hands.

In the center of it all stood Lawton, his feet shoulder-width apart and arms loose at his sides. He'd barely broken a sweat. Somehow, I didn't think the cold weather was the reason for his cool demeanor.

Crew Cut Guy leaned in close to me. "You know who that is, don't you?"

I nodded, too breathless to speak.

And then I heard it, the sound of sirens somewhere off in the distance. The crowd shifted, and then as if by unspoken agreement, held its ground. It remained eerily quiet for a few seconds, then began to buzz with the low hum of excitement.

I glanced toward Lawton. He had an arm around the guy's

neck and was speaking into his ear, saying something too low for me to hear. Actually, it was too low for anyone to hear, judging from the frustration on the faces of those closest to the action.

The guy choked out something that sounded vaguely like a laugh – a forced, high-pitch sound that rang false in spite of its volume. "Oh yeah?" he said. "Well try it, and you're dead."

Lawton made a scoffing sound. "Like that scares me."

The sirens were near deafening now. The second guy glanced at his friend, then at the crowd, and then back at Lawton. Finally, with muttered curses, he wobbled off, stopping briefly to help his friend off the pavement.

Together they shuffled toward a dark sport utility vehicle with tinted windows. The bloody guy climbed into the passenger's seat, and the other guy got into the driver's side. Seconds after the door swung shut, the vehicle squealed out of the parking lot and disappeared from sight.

"Damn," Crew Cut Guy said. "Guess the show's over."

I studied Lawton across the parking lot, relishing the chance to observe him, unencumbered by the bounds of decency or politeness. I took an obscene amount of comfort in the fact I was just one of many, a face in the crowd. I felt like a Peeping Tom, but couldn't bring myself to care.

Ignoring crowds of wannabe friends and well-wishers, Lawton turned and sauntered toward his car, the blondes close on his heels. Silently, he opened the passenger door and waited as they climbed inside.

After their long legs disappeared into the vehicle, Lawton shut the car door and walked around to the driver's side door. He opened it, slid into the driver's seat, and shut the door behind him. A moment later, he roared out of the parking lot, leaving the crowd staring after him.

From somewhere off to my right, I heard a male voice say,

"Hey, Chloe!"

Standing in the tall pickup bed, I looked down and saw Keith staring up at me, his hands on his hips and a scowl on his face. "What the hell are you doing out here?"

Past Keith, in the crowd, I saw both busboys, half the cooks and at least two other waitresses. Why Keith chose to zero in on me, I had no idea. "Watching the fight," I said.

Like he didn't know.

"Yeah?" His scowl deepened. "Don't you have work to do?"

Obviously, I wasn't the only employee out here. So why was I the only one getting in trouble? Suddenly, I was so tired of Keith's crap. "Don't you?" I said.

His jaw tightened. "I'm not a customer," he said. "So don't sass me and think you're cute."

Next to me, Crew Cut Guy spoke up. "Hey, I think she's cute." He puffed out his chest. "And I'm a customer. So I'm always right." He turned to give me a wide grin. "Right?"

"Awwww...thanks," I said, genuinely touched.

But on the ground, Keith didn't look nearly as pleased. A spot of color had risen to his cheeks. "Yes, well." Keith cleared his throat and looked up at the guy. "Thank you for your patronage."

"Actually," Crew Cut said, giving me a long look, "she's more than cute. She's smokin' hot. You oughta give this girl a raise." He turned to give me another grin. "What do you think of that?"

I laughed, embarrassed but delighted, not so much with the compliment, but for the effect it had on Keith. He was looking more unhappy with every passing moment.

"Yeah, well," Keith muttered, straightening his tie and turning his gaze on me. "Get back inside, and we'll talk about it."

I gave Keith a sweet smile. "Thanks, boss. I'm looking forward to it."

I never called him boss, and I knew there wasn't going to be a raise. But the look on his face was almost reward enough.

I turned to Crew Cut Guy. "Thanks for letting me hang out in your truck." I winked at him. "And for getting me promoted."

I hopped down and headed back inside. Just as well. I did still have customers after all. I wouldn't be earning any tips if I spent all night in the parking lot.

Still, I wasn't above spending way too much time looking out the window to see what was going on. By the time the lone police car had rolled into the parking lot, there wasn't much to see.

There were only a few stragglers and Keith, who stalked over to the police car and made his complaints known, using gigantic arm gestures to emphasize whatever he was telling them.

Whatever it was, the police didn't look too impressed.

From what I learned later, the police weren't a big help. There'd been no property damage, nothing stolen, and other than Keith, no one had complained.

Keith tried to press the issue of disturbing the peace, and since at least one of the guys – Lawton Rastor – was easy to identify, the police promised to look into it. But Keith's sullen demeanor for the remainder of the night suggested he thought this unlikely.

What I couldn't figure out was what started the fight in the first place. One of my customers, a tall guy with a window seat, swore he saw the other two guys jump Lawton in the parking lot, but since I didn't see it for myself, I tried to withhold judgment and not think too much about it.

But it wasn't easy. Lawton was proving easy to think about, but hard to forget.

CHAPTER 11

The soft trilling sound made me want to throw my cell phone across the Parkers' guest room. Somehow, I'd forgotten to turn off the ringer, and no matter how soothing the sound was supposed to be, it still grated on my foggy brain.

I glanced at the digital clock on the night stand. It was just after nine in the morning. My waitressing shift had ended only four hours ago. After driving back, walking Chucky, and taking a shower, I hadn't been sleeping nearly long enough to function like a real human being.

Groaning, I fumbled for the phone and looked at the display.

Shit. It was Loretta.

For the briefest instant, I debated letting the call go to voicemail, but that wouldn't solve anything. I'd have to call her back later, and the dread of it would make it that much harder to fall back asleep. Better to get it out of the way so I could slip back into oblivion.

I took a deep breath and hit the button. "Hello."

"Don't tell me you're still asleep?" she said. "God, it's practically noon."

Obviously, noon was still a few hours off, but math had never been my stepmother's strong suit. "I worked late," I said.

"I wish I could sleep all day," Loretta said. "Must be nice."

"Nice?" I gritted my teeth. "Yeah? Well, while you were sleeping, I was working, so I guess it all evens out then, doesn't it?"

"There's no need to get snippy," she said.

I closed my eyes and counted to ten. Snippy? I could show her snippy. But telling her off wasn't an option. My short-term satisfaction would only lead to long-term misery for my younger brother, Josh, who still lived there. Sort of.

"Hey!" Her shrill voice interrupted my thoughts. "You didn't fall back asleep, did you?"

"No, I'm awake." I hated that I sounded defensive, like a teenager caught smoking in the bathroom.

"Good," she said. "Because your Dad's gotten this idea that we should all celebrate Thanksgiving together. And I'm telling you now, so you don't screw up our schedule."

"Thanksgiving?" I mumbled. "Really? Who does he mean by all?"

"Don't be dense," she said. "Him, you, me, Josh. Who else?"

I didn't bother asking about Grandma. Even if she were invited, she wouldn't go. But she wasn't the only person missing from Loretta's little list.

"What about Lauren?" I asked. Lauren was Loretta's natural daughter. She was nearly my age, but rated a lot higher than me or Josh. No way she'd be left out.

"She might come over later," Loretta said.

The whole thing was odd. Loretta loved to cook, but never for us. Honestly, I was surprised my Dad would suggest such a thing. Even for him, this was incredibly stupid.

I had a pretty good idea how the day would end, with Loretta hurling insults, and maybe a couple of dishes. Dad would pretend not to notice, I'd pretend not to care, and Josh would pretend Mom hadn't left us for some washed-up racecar driver.

Happy Thanksgiving, everyone.

Unfortunately, saying no wasn't an option. Josh wouldn't have a choice. And if Josh was going to be there, I was going to be there. If nothing else, Loretta's special brand of holiday cheer would fall on my shoulders instead of his. Still, the whole thing would be a total nightmare, unless –

"Hey, can I bring someone?" I asked on impulse.

"Like who?" she asked.

"I dunno," I said, trying to keep my tone casual. "A friend, or maybe a date, I guess it depends." No way I'd be subjecting any date to my crappy excuse for a family, excluding Josh, of course. But I needed to be vague.

My plan was to beg Erika to come, if only for part of it. My Dad liked Erika a lot more than he liked me. More importantly, Loretta was intimidated by Erika's last name, which graced a string of restaurants and shopping centers in the Rochester Hills area.

But no matter who it was, it would be better than nobody. My Dad and Loretta were always a lot nicer in front of an audience. I just needed to find an audience I could trust, someone who knew my family, loved me anyway, and wouldn't blab after the fact.

This only left Erika. If I had to beg her, I would. It wasn't just for me. It was for Josh too. She liked Josh. She'd probably do it.

"Fine," Loretta muttered. "I guess you can bring someone."

She didn't sound very happy about it. The fact she agreed at all was a total surprise. Obviously, she was just as eager for this little get-together as I was, which is, not eager at all. It was almost funny to think we agreed on anything.

I wasn't used to this.

"If you want any food, be there at noon," she said. "I'm assuming you can crawl out of bed by then?"

Before I could answer, she hung without saying goodbye.

Now this, I was used to.

I was just drifting back to sleep when the doorbell rang, causing Chucky start yapping his head off from somewhere downstairs.

With a sigh of frustration, I threw aside the covers and stumbled out of bed, making my way toward the window that overlooked the driveway. When I got there, what I saw in the driveway made me groan out loud.

There was no mistaking the vehicle. Last night, I couldn't tell the color, but in the morning light, it was beyond obvious – neon green with a black racing stripe. Lawton Rastor was here? But why?

And then, it hit me. He'd mentioned stopping by this morning, something about steak and eggs? I'd been positive he was joking. Apparently, he wasn't.

Was I supposed to be flattered? What the hell? So the guy has some threesome or whatever with those two other girls, and just a few hours after shoving them out the door, he's on my doorstep wanting breakfast?

Cripes, I wasn't even dessert, I was an afterthought. I knew one thing for sure. A guy like Lawton Rastor didn't stop by just for steak and eggs.

I could imagine how this scene was playing out in his head. I'd greet him at the door, in full makeup, with my hair done to perfection. I'd be wearing something totally inappropriate for lounging around the house, maybe some sheer nightie or a cocktail dress. Or, if I wanted to be really subtle, I'd throw on skimpy shorts and a tank top, one that showed way too much cleavage, and the barest hint of nipple if the morning were cool enough.

And then, when I opened the door, I'd still pretend to be surprised. All the while, everything about me would be screaming, "Screw my brains out!"

Fuck that.

I'd had to take a lot of crap in my life, from my stepmother, and occasionally on the job. But I didn't need to take crap from random strangers, no matter how rich, famous, or gorgeous they happened to be.

I snuck a glance in the mirror. When I'd crawled into bed after my shower, I hadn't bothered to dry my hair. And it showed. I had a wicked case of bed-head, and there were dark circles under my eyes. I was wearing an oversized gray T-shirt and pajama bottoms covered in ninja penguins.

He deserved to see this.

I felt myself smile. He deserved steak and eggs too, right? And I knew just the girl to serve it up to him.

When I flung open the front door a couple minutes later, he was still there, wearing what I'd come to recognize as his usual outfit – faded jeans and a T-shirt. This shirt was black, accenting the tattoos that snaked up his forearms. His hair still had that semi-tousled look, and his face was heart-stopping gorgeous in spite of the expression of unease that quickly settled over his features.

"Hi!" I said with an overly big smile. "I'm ever so glad you stopped by." I practically leaped out of the entryway and slammed the door behind me to keep Chucky from getting out. "Steak and eggs, right?"

He took a half step backward. "Uh, did I wake you up?"

"Of course not," I gushed, doing my best crazy stalker impression. "I've been waiting for hours and hours for you to show up. Look!" I said, thrusting the paper lunch bag in his direction. "I made you breakfast and everything, just like you wanted." I lowered my voice. "Baby."

He eyed the bag, but made no move to take it.

I shoved it closer. "Go on," I urged with another stalker smile, "Take it. I made it just for you."

Reluctantly, he took the bag. Slowly, he opened it and peered inside. I watched, breathless, as he studied the contents. For a few seconds, nothing happened. And then, his mouth twitched. He looked up. "Really, you shouldn't have," he said.

This wasn't the reaction I'd been expecting.

The bag contained a couple of whole eggs, along with a handful of steak-flavored doggie treats.

He was supposed to be offended, not amused. As I watched, he reached into the bag and pulled out a doggie treat. He held it up and gave it a quick sniff. "I think I'll save this for later," he said.

Slowly, I felt something like sanity return. And once it did, I was suddenly way too conscious that I was standing on the Parkers' front steps, looking like a crazy person. I hadn't planned for this. He was supposed to have stormed off by now, which would've given me the chance to stalk back into the house and slam the door not exactly in his face, but definitely in his back.

Now what?

He gave my outfit a long, amused look. "Penguins," he said with a slow nod of his head. "Nice."

I'm not a blushing person, but I swear, I could feel the color rise to my face. What the hell was I doing? Stupid question. I already knew the answer. I was making an ass of myself. The fight-or-flight mechanism was starting to kick in, big-time.

"I've gotta go," I said, turning to head back inside.

"Wait," he said.

I turned to face him. He wasn't laughing anymore, but I could still see the amusement in his eyes, crinkling at the corners in a way that made me want to blush for an entirely different reason. I felt myself swallow.

For a moment, he wasn't Lawton Rastor, the famous bad-ass womanizer, but merely the boy next door, which in a way he was.

His eyes were deep and dark, and I felt myself get lost in them as he stood on the doorstep, holding that paper bag of utter crap.

He reached into the front pocket of his jeans. "I found this in my car." He pulled out a small silver medallion that I recognized instantly. Chucky's ID tag. It must've fallen off his collar during the ride back last night.

"Oh," I said. "So that's why you stopped by?"

"It was one of the reasons." He held up the bag. "But hey, thanks for breakfast."

I looked at the bag. "Uh, sorry about that." I cleared my throat and took Chucky's tag from his outstretched hand. "And thanks."

"No problem."

When he hopped in his car a minute later, I shuffled back into the house, wondering what was more stupid, my misguided anger that he might show up for a pre-nooner, or my odd disappointment that he didn't. Maybe he just didn't see me in that way.

But as I caught my reflection in the hall mirror, it wasn't hard to see why. I decided that if I never saw the guy gain, it would be too soon. As bad as I looked, I should've worn that bag over my head.

It wasn't until I was halfway up the stairs that something occurred to me. He never did give his other reason for stopping by. And I'd been so distracted, I never did ask him.

Too late for that now. I stumbled back to the guest room and crawled under the covers, but no matter how hard I tried, I never could fall back asleep. □

CHAPTER 12

I stared at my cell phone, unable to believe it. The call had come. Finally. My heart racing, I felt a wide smile spread across my face. Holy crap. I had a job.

A real job.

And I'd be starting in mid-November, just a little over five weeks away. Sure, it was a long lead-time, but there was a good reason, and I wasn't about to complain.

It was the day after I'd given Lawton that stupid paper bag, and I'd been in the shower when they'd called. But the message hit all the highlights I needed – the pay, the start-date, the benefits.

They weren't anything extravagant, but they were a lot more than I was used to. I was still dripping from the shower when I returned the hiring manager's call.

It was official. A few Mondays from now, I'd be signing the paperwork.

It had been weeks since the interview, but the job was perfect. Not only would I actually be using my degree, I'd be working regular hours for the first time in my life. The company was small, and the pay wasn't spectacular, but it wasn't minimum wage either. And I'd finally get the job experience I desperately needed to move on to something bigger and better when the opportunity presented itself.

Maybe I'd even double-up and keep the waitressing job another month or two, just on weekends. Sure, it would stink. But by Christmas, I'd be rich, at least by my standards.

I'd finally have enough money to cover a security deposit and other expenses. When my stint at the Parkers' ended, I could get my own place.

No more house-sitting, no more tiptoeing around in someone else's domain. No more sleeping on my Dad's godawful couch. I'd have a place of my own, even if it was low-rent.

It was just before noon, and I wasn't scheduled to waitress that night. It made for an almost perfect day, and when I left to walk Chucky, my steps were lighter than they had been in a long time.

Sometime that night, a warm front had moved in, lending the hint of Indian summer to the fall air. Chucky and I were walking the usual route when I saw a familiar figure lounging outside the gate of Lawton's estate. The form was unmistakable: the long legs, the tousled hair, the chiseled features.

It was Lawton. He wore jeans and yet another black T-shirt, this one with long sleeves. As Chucky and I walked closer, I almost forgot to breathe. He looked like a heavenly demon, fallen from some other world just to give girls like me something to fantasize about when their ordinary lives grew unsatisfying.

Not that I was unhappy to see him, but what was he doing just standing there? Enjoying the weather? And if so, shouldn't he be lounging by a pool or something?

The sky was clear, and the air felt almost balmy, at least compared to how it had been. I was wearing jeans and a long-sleeved shirt. I'd figured out too late it was too many clothes. At least I wasn't alone. As far as I could tell, Lawton had made the same mistake.

Chucky was even more hyper than usual, and hustling to keep up with him made me wish all over again for shorts and a tank top.

When were just a couple blocks away, Chucky went nearly berserk, yapping and straining at his leash and dragging me at an unseemly pace toward Lawton, who watched the spectacle with a look of amusement in his dark eyes.

I was half out of breath by the time Chucky dragged me toward him. And that's when I noticed it, a shiny bag in Lawton's hand. The bag looked familiar. Too familiar.

I stopped a few paces away and narrowed my eyes. "Are those doggie treats?"

"This?" He held up the shiny bag. It was already open, and it made a crinkling sound as he shook it. "Yup."

Chucky went nuts, straining at the leash and yapping like crazy. The man was too devious for words. I couldn't help but laugh. "Trying to get me killed?"

"No," he said. "Trying to get you to stop."

By now, Chucky was jumping up on Lawton's jeans. He was yapping more ferociously than before.

"Care if I give him some?" he asked.

"At this point," I said, "I think you'd better – unless you want to get eviscerated." In truth, the only thing Chucky was capable of eviscerating was a pile of bacon, but it seemed undignified to admit it.

Lawton squatted down and gave Chucky a couple of the treats. He ruffled the fur on Chucky's head as the treats disappeared in record time.

When he stood back up, Lawton gave me a heart-stopping grin. "Want some company?"

The offer took me off guard. From everything I'd read and seen, he wasn't the kind of guy who'd be caught dead doing anything so normal as walking a normal, if hyper, dog, around a normal, if upscale, neighborhood. What was going on?

When I didn't answer, he pointed at his feet. "Look," he said. "Shoes."

I laughed. "And a shirt too."

He grinned. "Just for you."

"Really, you shouldn't have."

I said it as a joke, but I wasn't totally sure I was kidding. Sure, he looked great in a shirt, but he looked even better without it. Not that I really wanted him to walk around the neighborhood shirtless. True, I liked looking at him. Who wouldn't? But sometimes there's a fine line between sexy, and well, weird.

Of course, ninja penguins were weird. So was a paper bag full of breakfast snark. If I were lucky, we'd never speak of it again.

Lawton held out a hand for Chucky's leash. "Want me to take him?"

It was a tempting offer, but walking Chucky wasn't the easiest job in the world. I was a semi-professional. Lawton had probably never walked a dog in his life.

Even with little dogs, it wasn't half as easy as it looked. Between tangling the leash around street signs, trees, and anything else we came across, and lunging after squirrels, Chucky always made it a lot trickier than it should've been.

I handed Lawton the leash. "You can try," I said. This should be good for a few laughs.

We started out at the usual uneven pace, with Chucky pausing every so often to water the bushes, and bounding ahead every so often to chase after whatever caught his attention, real or imagined. But after a couple of blocks, we'd fallen into a nice rhythm. I didn't want to admit it, but Lawton handled Chucky easier than I did.

After a while, Lawton said, "About yesterday –"

"Forget it," I said. What happened on the Parkers' front steps was the last thing I wanted to talk about. I'd made a total fool of myself.

"Not gonna happen," he said.

I stopped and gave him a look. "Excuse me?"

He stopped too, turning around to face me on the sidewalk as Chucky tried unsuccessfully to drag him in the other direction. "You're not getting off that easy," he said.

"What do you mean?"

"I mean," he said, "I can't forget it."

"Why not?" I demanded.

He looked at me for what seemed like a long time. As the time passed, I felt my face grow warm, and probably not just from the sunshine. When he finally spoke, his voice was oddly quiet. "I dunno. I just can't."

"You just don't want to," I said.

"Probably."

For Chucky's sake – the dog was about to go nuts – I started walking again, and Lawton fell in beside me.

"Look," he said, "I know what you were thinking, me showing up so early, but that wasn't it."

"Oh." That was a relief. Sort of.

"I saw the tag when I got into my car, and I knew you wouldn't want Chucky running around without it."

"He's not supposed to run around, period," I said. "Well, not without me, anyway."

Lawton said nothing, and I snuck a sideways glance at him. Even in long sleeves, I saw hints and shadows of the muscular form underneath. There were things I'd like to ask him, things about the reality show and his fights, but somehow, I didn't want to be just another stalker-chick digging into his business.

Thanks to my computer, I'd done that enough already.

When he changed the subject to movies, it was a huge relief.

Walking with him was totally surreal. He acted just like a normal guy, sometimes funny, sometimes serious. We talked about nothing in particular as we made our way along the sidewalk. The thing that wasn't completely normal was how quickly time flew.

We were in front of the Parkers' before I knew it.

"Thanks for the walk," I said, reaching for Chucky's leash.

Lawton grinned, holding it just out of my easy reach. "You sure you can handle him?"

"Oh please," I said, rolling my eyes.

"Please what?" he said, his voice full of hidden meanings that I didn't dare decipher.

I reached up and snatched the leash away from him. I never did answer. Instead, I gave him a quick goodbye and headed straight down the Parkers' long driveway. When I reached the front door, I glanced over my shoulder and saw him standing on the sidewalk, waiting for me to get inside.

It was a funny habit, but I found myself smiling at the thought of it. I gave him a quick wave, unlocked the door, and went inside along with Chucky.

CHAPTER 13

Later that afternoon, I was sitting at Grandma's kitchen table, sipping hot chocolate and telling her and Josh all about my job offer. Josh had just gotten out of school, so the timing was perfect. "It's an accounting job," I was telling them. "The company sells car parts, stuff like mufflers and alternators."

Her house was rented, and it was tiny – one bedroom, one bathroom, a cozy kitchen, and small living area with windows overlooking the gardens of the much larger house that the cottage belonged to.

Technically, Grandma's place was a guest house, but it served her purposes – and mine – almost perfectly.

There was only one problem. Her landlady was a psycho. And her name was Loretta, my Dad's wife. But I wouldn't think about that now. Today, I'd only think about happy things, and that definitely didn't include Loretta.

"And I start in five weeks," I said. "Mid-November."

"Why so long?" Grandma asked.

"I'm replacing someone who's retiring," I explained. "They're leaving at Thanksgiving. This gives us like a week overlap for training." I smiled. "But then, the job's all mine. Can you believe it?"

"Hell yeah, I believe it," Grandma said, reaching out to give my hand a playful swat. "I just knew you'd get that job."

"Yeah, but you've been saying that about every job," I said. "And none of those panned out."

"Hah!" Grandma said. "Those other jobs sucked."

I raised an eyebrow. "Yeah?"

She nodded. "Yeah. Total shitholes, every one of 'em."

Laughing, I turned to Josh. "Now, remember – "

He held up a hand. "I know, I know. Just because Grandma says 'shithole,' it doesn't mean I can say 'shithole.'"

I squinted at him. "You just did. Twice."

"That?" He grinned. "Nah. That was purely for illustrative purposes."

I laughed. "Well, if nothing else, I'm glad to see your vocabulary extends beyond four-letter words." It wasn't all that surprising. Josh had always been smart. He was in the gifted program at school and already planning for college. I might worry about his home life, but I never worried about his grades.

But I did have to worry about his school in more general terms. He was in a good one. And he needed to stay in a good one, which meant he couldn't move. He needed to stay right where he was, with my Dad and Loretta. This meant Grandma had to stay right where she was, next door to my Dad.

It was a complicated, but convenient arrangement. With Grandma nearby, Josh always had a place he felt welcome, no matter what happened. In my view, that made all the difference in the world.

"Shithole has eight letters," Grandma told me. "Count 'em, Smarty Pants."

Smiling, I shook my head. "Enough. Both of you. I've given

up swearing, remember? You're not helping here."

"Yeah, right," Josh said. "You're worse than all of us."

"Not anymore," I insisted. "So, about the job, what do you think? Car supplies, pretty cool, huh?"

"Totally," Josh said. "Mom's gonna be so excited. She loves car stuff."

I felt my smile freeze. Mom wouldn't give a crap one way or another, at least not in the normal sense. "Yeah," I said, keeping my tone light, "I'll have to give her a call."

Even if I did, she probably wouldn't answer. But Josh didn't need to know that. He still thought she left by necessity, not by choice.

Josh had just turned thirteen. When I was thirteen, I'd felt ancient. But Josh, he had a sunnier disposition. Plus, I'd worked hard to spare him the worst of our parents' flaws. He might be a teenager now, but it still seemed far too early to shatter his illusions. "I'm sure she'll be excited," I said.

Yeah, she'd be excited alright. She'd probably ask me for a loan. I glanced at my phone. My waitressing shift started in a couple hours, and I still needed to give Chucky his afternoon walk. "I've gotta run," I said.

"On your way out, can you drop off some work at the mail shop?" Grandma said.

"Sure," I said, heading toward the side table where she kept the blue bin of mailing materials. The envelopes were there, all lined up and stuffed with flyers.

Grandma's job was stuffing envelopes from home. It didn't pay a lot, but it was easy work, something she could do while chatting with Josh or watching her favorite programs. It covered her rent on the cottage, and had gotten her out of the crappy, low-rent apartment she'd been living in after she'd lost her house, thanks to my deadbeat mother.

I picked up the bin, said my goodbyes, and headed out to my Ford Fiesta. It was a total beater, but had an eclectic look that might pass for fashion with my upscale clients. It ran okay, most of the time, but it wasn't exactly roomy. I set the bin on the passenger's seat and headed out of the long driveway.

On the way, I passed the house where my Dad lived with Loretta. It was an impressive place, brick, two stories, a lot like the Parkers', except for the fact it had a guest house. The garage was shut, and the shades were drawn. They both worked days, so I was spared the obligation of stopping by.

Dad and Loretta were funny like that. If I stopped by, they made me feel unwelcome. But if I didn't stop by, there'd be hell to pay later on. I could take it, but Josh couldn't, which was why I made a point to stop by Grandma's on weekdays.

Halfway to the Parkers', I swung by the recycling center and dumped the envelopes into the paper-and-cardboard bin, watching as they scattered over old cereal boxes and newspapers.

After that, I hit the office supply store to buy more envelopes and paper. Maybe this time, I'd do a flyer for cat supplies. My Grandma adored cats. She'd probably like that.

CHAPTER 14

When I walked Chucky the next day, Lawton wasn't exactly waiting for me. But he did happen to walk out his front door when I walked by his house. It might've been planned, or it might've been a spur-of-the-moment thing. I didn't ask, and he didn't say either way.

He did, however, have another bag of treats in his hand for Chucky, who had apparently decided that Lawton was the best thing since grilled steak, or maybe a designer purse. Looking at Lawton, I had to agree, but for entirely different reasons.

If Lawton were a treat, he'd be the kind that smart girls avoided. His body was too sinful, his reputation too dangerous, his face too hypnotic. It would easy to fall for him, and even easier to believe I could somehow mean more to him than some passing fling.

But he wasn't treating me like a fling. He was treating me like a friend. This was a good thing, or at least that's what I told myself. Flings came and went. Friends were harder to come by, especially for someone like me, who lived in one world and worked in another.

When he offered to take Chucky's leash, I didn't argue.

We'd gone only a couple of blocks when he said, "I always wanted a dog."

I turned my head to look at him. "Really? Then why don't you have one?"

He shrugged. "Too hard to take care of."

"Oh c'mon," I said, "they're not that hard. Besides, you're great with dogs."

"Yeah, but I'm gone a lot."

Not from what I'd seen. For someone with so many business projects – assuming everything I'd read was true – he seemed to spend an awful lot of time just hanging around the neighborhood.

"You're not gone that much," I said. "I see you around here all the time. Like almost every day."

His gave me a crooked grin. "Yeah? You been watching for me?"

"No. Of course not." I felt color rise to my cheeks. "It's just, well, I – "

He laughed. "Just kidding. Truth is, I have been around a lot more lately. But it's not always like this."

"So why is it now?" I asked. "Are you on vacation or something?"

"Something like that."

"You're not gonna tell me?"

He stopped walking. Slowly, he turned to face me. "You can't guess?"

As I met his gaze, I almost forget to breathe. The autumn breeze played with the loose ends of his tousled hair, while the rest of him was a study in stillness. His eyes met mine, and I felt my lips part. He leaned his face toward mine, and time all but stopped.

Unfortunately, Chucky didn't.

With a series of frantic yips, he tugged against his leash, breaking the spell as Lawton and I glanced in his direction. A squirrel was darting up a tall oak tree. Chucky was straining against the leash, barking as if his very life depended on it. The squirrel stopped on a high branch, chattering as it looked down on us.

I gave a nervous laugh. "I think it's taunting us."

Lawton looked up. "Probably," he said, not sounding too happy about it.

I started walking again, and Lawton followed suit. Our casual pace was a stark contrast to the tumult of my emotions. Behind us, the squirrel was still chattering, but Chucky had moved on, his attention caught by a slow-moving mail delivery truck a couple blocks ahead of us.

Probably, I should've been annoyed. The squirrel, Chucky, even my own reservations, they were wreaking havoc on the realization of what I'd almost done. I'd almost kissed him. And I was pretty sure he'd almost kissed me back.

I was glad that didn't happen.

Sort of.

Yeah, it would've been heavenly. But I wasn't about to have an impromptu make-out session with some guy I barely knew, on the sidewalk, in a neighborhood where I was house-sitting. It was insanity, at least by my standards. If any of the neighbors put two and two together, I'd probably get fired.

"So," I said, trying to pretend it hadn't happened, "why don't you get a dog of your own?"

When he didn't answer, I gave him a sideways glance. His eyes were straight ahead, and he looked a million miles away. I returned my gaze to the sidewalk and picked up the pace.

We'd gone a full block before he finally spoke. "Because then," he said, "I couldn't borrow yours."

"Oh c'mon," I said. "Be serious. Why don't you?"

"Maybe it's not fair to leave 'em alone," he said.

"You could always get a dog-walker. Or a house sitter," I said, feeling incredibly awkward even as I said it. Somehow, it felt like a lie by omission. I should've stated the obvious. I was such a person.

Lawton snorted. "Yeah, like I'm gonna trust some stranger with my dog. You hear stories." He stopped to let Chucky water the bushes. "And if anyone harmed my dog, well –" He clamped his lips together and looked away. "I wouldn't like it."

Unspoken, but completely apparent, was what he didn't say. It wasn't only that he wouldn't like it. He wouldn't put up with it. I glanced at the powerful hand that held Chucky's leash. The fist was tight, with white knuckles that had flexed convulsively as he spoke.

"You don't even have a dog," I said.

"Yeah," he admitted. "See what I mean?"

"No," I said, laughing. "You're all worked up about some stranger mistreating your dog, and you don't even have one."

"I'm not worked up," he said.

I glanced at his hands. "Really?"

He looked down, following my gaze. Slowly, he loosened the muscles in his hands and gave me a crooked grin that sent my world spinning.

"So, uh, did you have a dog growing up?" I asked.

His smile faded. "No."

I waited for him to elaborate. He didn't. From what I'd read, his home-life hadn't been spectacular, but the details had been vague, with veiled references to social services and time on his own. No wonder he didn't want to talk about it.

When he changed the subject to current headlines, I didn't fight it. It was pretty obvious he was finished with talking about himself, and I was in no position to judge. In truth, I wasn't eager to talk about myself either.

Even if I were looking to tell my life-story, where would I start? With the fact that I was merely the house sitter? That particular topic was definitely off-limits. The Parkers had a strict confidentiality clause. Most of my clients did, for obvious reasons. There was no quicker way to get robbed than to advertise that a home-owner was out of town.

Before I knew it, we had circled back to the Parkers'. Turning toward me, Lawton asked, "Got any plans for tonight?"

My heart skipped a couple of beats. Was he actually going to ask me out? No, I reminded myself. Guys like Lawton Rastor didn't ask girls out. He'd let the girl come to him, ready, willing and able. And maybe, if the two blondes were any indicator, one girl by herself might not be enough.

The fantasies aside, I didn't want to become a random notch on some famous guy's bedpost. He'd forget me the instant I left his bed. Or his countertop. Or his swimming pool. I swallowed, pushing aside the images that flooded my brain and other places.

A random encounter would mean nothing to him, but it would mean a lot of trouble for me, and not just because I was getting way too interested in him. I'd be living here most of the winter. I didn't need any trouble, and I didn't need any drama.

Besides, something strange was going on in my own head and heart. I no longer saw him as Lawton Rastor, the guy who made men bleed and girls swoon. I saw him as this incredible guy next door who made my mouth water, and my knees go week.

No way reality could live up to the fantasy. Besides, I did have plans. Maybe they weren't exciting plans, but they were plans I needed to keep, and they centered around a certain diner that I'd be vacating in a few weeks.

"Actually, I do have plans," I said, hearing the regret in my own voice. With a mental effort, I shoved that regret away. "In fact, I'd better get going if I don't want to be late."

I realized we were no longer walking. Chucky had flopped down on the sidewalk, lying across Lawton's shoes like he wanted nothing more than to bask in his mere presence. I knew the feeling.

"How about tomorrow night?" he asked.

I was working tomorrow too. This was probably a good thing. It would be easy to lose control with a guy like him. Besides, when I did have free time, it usually fell during the day. "Nights are bad for me," I said.

He looked at me a long time, as if trying to figure out exactly what I was telling him. "So, if you don't mind my asking, who do you live with, anyway?"

"What do you mean?" I asked.

"You're the only one I've seen hanging around." He flicked his head toward the Parkers'. "I'm guessing that's your parents' house? They out of town?"

At this, alarm bells started going off in my head. On the surface, the question might be harmless enough. But it bothered me that he'd noticed. Probably I should've been flattered. Hell, it was flattering that he noticed me at all.

Still, I didn't like the idea of letting anyone know I was staying in the house alone, especially since the house wasn't actually mine.

I didn't want to lie. But for too many reasons to count, I certainly wasn't going to reveal that the home-owners were out of the country. In a lame attempt to deflect his train of thought, I pointed in the general direction of his place. "Are you living in your parents' house?" I asked.

His face froze, becoming oddly devoid of emotion as he said, "No. Haven't for a while."

Oh crap. It suddenly hit me. I was such an idiot. Why'd I bring up his parents? Did he even have parents? In everything I'd read, the details had been vague about that too.

"Sorry," I said.

His voice was soft. "No." He was now staring past me, his eyes vacant. Then, as if shaking off a bad memory, he returned his gaze to mine and shrugged. "I asked, you asked. No big deal." With a tight smile, he handed me Chucky's leash.

Silently, I took it. The leather felt warm in my cool hand. "Will you be walking tomorrow?" I asked in a lame attempt to get beyond the awkwardness.

He shrugged. "Hard to say." He glanced toward his house. "I gotta run." And then he turned away. A moment later, he began walking slowly toward his house, his head down, his fists tight. Still holding the leash, the warmth of the leather faded, leaving me feeling oddly alone as I turned away, trudged into the Parkers', and got ready for work.

CHAPTER 15

I ignored the pat on my ass and summoned up something meant to be a flirty smile as I took the guy's order. He ordered, surprise of all surprises, the usual – spareribs and bourbon. After fifty-something years on this Earth, I guess he knew what he liked.

"Although," he added, licking his wet lips," I wouldn't mind a little extra, if you know what I mean."

Unless by extra he meant a kick in the pants, he wasn't getting anything extra from me. Still, I choked down the bile and gave his hand a playful slap. "Shame on you, Mister Bolger." I tossed my hair, and turned to flounce away. "I'm not that kind of girl," I said over my shoulder as I hustled away from him.

Heading toward the bar for his bourbon, I could still feel his hand on my ass. Josie was standing at the end of the long counter, adding limes to a tray of margaritas.

"He's such a creep," I said under my breath.

Josie glanced out toward my table. "Bolger?" She gave a half-shrug. "Guess the guy expects his money's worth." She flashed me a smile. "Hey, want me to take him?"

The offer was tempting, and I knew why she made it. It wasn't for my sake, or at least it wasn't all for my sake. Bolger tipped a dozen tables' worth, which was exactly why Josie, along with every other girl who worked here, jumped at the chance to wait on him.

Customers weren't allowed to touch us. But since no one was complaining, especially the ones actually being touched, he got away with the occasional – okay, more than occasional – pat and enough innuendo to fill a bad skin flick.

He made me feel cheap, not because he paid extra to take a few minor liberties here and there, but because I actually let him.

No one forced me to wait on him. And no one forced me to ignore the random pats or inappropriate commentary. I could stop him any time I wanted. So why didn't I?

I knew the answer. It was the same reason none of the girls did. And it wasn't the guy's sex appeal.

Bolger was no Lawton Rastor. He was a squat, middle-aged man with two ex-wives, wandering hands, and more money than class. If he didn't tip like some kind of mogul, there's no way they'd be fighting over him.

Unfortunately, or fortunately I guess, Bolger had been requesting my section lately. Technically, thanks to Keith's stupid rotational assignment brainstorm, I didn't have a section of my own, but it didn't matter.

What Bolger was really requesting was me. Why, I had no idea. The guy's tips had mysteriously doubled to an amount that was borderline obscene, even by his already high standards.

Was I willing to sacrifice that much income to avoid a little ass-patting and sexual innuendo? If I had an ounce of pride, I would. But pride was a luxury I couldn't afford.

I thought of my new job. Soon, I'd be signing the papers. On impulse, I made a decision. I felt myself smile. Screw the idea of holding onto this job a couple more months. I'd quit waitressing the minute I started that other job. No more double-shifts, no more degrading uniforms, no more hairspray.

And no more Mr. Bolger.

I felt my smile fade. That was still almost a month away. I was here now. And until I actually quit, I'd be stupid to let a little thing like personal dignity stop me from making the most of the time I had left.

"No, I've got it," I told Josie, feeling a sinking feeling even as I said it.

Eddie, my favorite bartender, sidled over to us. "You waitin' on Bolger?" he asked. Eddie was about my age and built like a linebacker. He doubled as a bouncer when the need arose. "He gives you any trouble, you just let me know, alright?"

I nodded and made my back toward the dining area. Just a few more weeks, I told myself.

CHAPTER 16

Over the next few days, I walked Chucky as usual, but saw no sign of Lawton. He wasn't hanging out in his yard. He wasn't leaning against his fence. And he certainly wasn't waiting on the sidewalk with shiny bags of doggie treats.

Stupidly, I missed him. So did Chucky, and somehow, I didn't think it was all because of the treats. Sure, Chucky was still a spaz. That was a given. But to me, it seemed like Chucky was just going through the motions, chasing squirrels more by obligation than for the actual joy of it.

I knew exactly how he felt.

I didn't think Lawton was out of town, because I saw signs of life at his house. Sometimes his gate was open, and sometimes it was shut. One day, I saw that same muscle car in the driveway, but no one inside. It made me think about our last conversation.

Why had he been hanging around the neighborhood so much? He made it sound like it had something to do with me. But that seemed so far beyond the realm of possibility that I refused to think about it.

And even if it were true, his interest in me had obviously

waned. I couldn't say I blamed him. I hadn't exactly been encouraging.

Still, it made me glad we hadn't actually kissed that day on the sidewalk. That kiss would've meant nothing to him, but it could've cost me plenty, starting with my house-sitting job if the wrong neighbor talked.

Besides, I knew how these things went. It wouldn't have ended with a kiss. It never did. And if all the guy wanted was an easy good time, he had the wrong girl. I might be a good time, but I definitely wasn't easy.

After going nearly a week with no sign of him, I vowed to forget him entirely. It was a good thing he lost interest, or at least that's what I told myself. He was a complication I didn't need, and a temptation hard to resist.

He had a track record, and it wasn't exactly encouraging. From everything I'd read, no girl could resist him. I could totally see why. He looked like a bad-ass, but acted like a gentleman. It would be easy to fall for a guy like that. Plenty of girls had. If nothing else, at least I was in good company.

Early Friday afternoon, as I laced up my tennis shoes and got Chucky ready for his walk, I debated taking a different route. If I changed it up by just a few blocks, I could avoid Lawton's place entirely. Out of sight, out of mind. Right?

But my feet didn't cooperate, and neither did Chucky. Before I knew it, we were coming up on Lawton's place like we always did. Chucky strained at his leash, and kept my eyes studiously ahead, repeating the same thing in my mind, "Don't look at the house, don't look at the house…"

But then, I couldn't help it.

I looked at the house.

And there he was. He stood just inside his gate, his hands in his pockets and his gaze on me. He wasn't smiling, but he wasn't frowning either. My heart rate quickened, and my mouth grew dry. Meanwhile, Chucky was going nuts, tugging me toward Lawton with a series of yips and barks that sent birds flapping from a nearby tree.

When Lawton pulled out a shiny bag of doggie treats, Chucky squirmed his way through the gate, leaving me holding the leash on the other side. Lawton crouched down beside Chucky, surrendering the treats and ruffling Chucky's fur as I stood outside his estate, locked out and feeling foolish.

And then, Lawton looked up. His dark eyes met mine. When they held, I couldn't look away.

"Hey," he said.

My heart was fluttering, but my voice was calm. "Hey yourself."

His voice was low. "Want some company?"

"Well, Chucky certainly does."

His eyebrows lifted. "Only Chucky?"

"Maybe." I gave him a smile. "Or maybe not."

"Okay." He grinned. "Stop begging. I'll come with you. Just show a little dignity, will ya?"

I laughed. "Sorry. I just couldn't help myself."

"About time you admitted it." He glanced at Chucky, and his smile faded. "Don't tell anyone, but I've missed this little guy the last few days."

"Yeah?" I said. "Only Chucky?"

"Maybe," he said, a new smile curving his lips. "Or maybe not."

Well, I certainly had that coming.

"Why don't you let go of the leash," he suggested. "I'll grab it from this side."

So I did, and a few minutes later, we were strolling along the usual route. Lawton had Chucky, and I had Lawton. Sort of. For some strange reason, everything felt right with the world. I had Lawton by my side, Chucky bounding in front of us, and fall leaves skittering at our feet.

If I were the type of girl to live in the moment, that particular moment would've been a good one, because for that brief snapshot in time, I felt safe and content. I refused to care that Lawton wasn't really mine, and that Chucky wasn't either. So I just enjoyed it for what it was. And it felt pretty heavenly.

By unspoken agreement, Lawton and I kept the conversation light. I never asked him where he'd been those few days, and he never asked me anything more about who I lived with, or what I did with my nights. It was probably a good thing, because I'm pretty sure at that point, I'd have told him almost anything he wanted to know.

When Lawton joined us the next day, and the day after that, the pattern was set. We continued to stick with general subjects, safe subjects, like movies, music, that kind of stuff. Once, we spent the entire time arguing the merits of paper versus plastic. It should've been boring, except it wasn't.

Sometimes, as we wandered the sidewalks, we got strange looks from other people we came across – dog-walkers, afternoon strollers. I could tell by the way people looked at Lawton – or rather, didn't look at him – that he made them at least a little uncomfortable.

But somehow, the presence of me and Chucky seemed to relax people a bit. Chucky was a little dog, obviously a purebred. I was a clean-cut girl in designer clothes. No one knew they were second-hand, or that Chucky wasn't mine.

It was funny in a way. Chucky and I looked like we belonged here. Lawton didn't. Little did any of these people know that Lawton was the one who truly belonged here, not the other way around.

CHAPTER 17

Thursday nights at the diner were unpredictable. Sometimes, we had a line out the door, and sometimes, we had empty tables. It was nearly impossible to predict, so we were either terribly overstaffed, or terribly understaffed. There didn't seem to be much middle ground.

On this particular Thursday, we had a line out the door as soon as night fell. I was running from table to table, trying hard to cover the massive amount of real estate made necessary by the night manager's stupid table-rotation idea. It had been so much easier even just a few weeks earlier when we each had assigned sections.

Under that system, all my tables had been nice and close together, giving me the chance to drop off extra napkins to one table while delivering drinks to another. But now, every single thing required a special trip. It was a big place, and all of us servers were run ragged as a result.

That's probably why I didn't notice the group when they first came in. No doubt, I'd been on the other side of the restaurant when they'd been seated and assigned to me. But when I glanced toward their booth, I had only one real thought.

Please don't recognize me.

It was the two blondes I'd met at Lawton's that very first time, along with two guys I guessed were their dates. The guys were two big player types with too much hair gel and enough bling to stock one of those low-rent jewelry stands in the mall.

But who was I to judge? With my ultra-big hair and bimbo-blue eye shadow, I looked a thousand times tackier than any of them. But maybe that was a good thing. I was a far cry from the soaked, makeup-free girl who'd been out searching for a wayward terrier. If I was lucky, they'd never put two and two together.

Still, I definitely didn't want to wait on them. It wasn't worth the risk. They didn't like me. I didn't like them. If they realized who I was, it would be awkward for everyone, particularly me if they chose to give me a hard time.

Suck it up, Chloe, I told myself. No one really looks at their waitresses. I glanced at a nearby table, where Josie was bending across a long booth to deliver a basket of onion rings to an athletic-looking guy sitting closest to the wall. His eyes were focused firmly on her cleavage, while a guy at a neighboring table took a good long look at her legs.

Okay, so maybe we were looked at. But from what I'd seen, the customers didn't spend a whole lot of time looking at our faces. Even with the female customers, they seemed more concerned with being seen as opposed to noticing what their waitresses looked like.

When Josie returned to the waitress station, I sidled next to her. "Want to trade tables?" I asked.

"Sorry," she said, "I'm at the end of my shift. No more tables for me tonight."

"Oh crap," I said. "You think Carmen will trade?"

"Hey," a masculine voice barked behind me. "No trading. You

know the rule."

I turned around to see Keith, the night manager, giving me a stern look.

"What rule?" I asked.

"We rotate," he said. "End of story."

"That's not a rule," I said. "It's a process. And besides, we trade all the time."

He crossed his arms. "Not under my watch, you don't." He flicked his head toward the dining area. "Now are you gonna get out there, or am I gonna have to write you up?"

Oh for Pete's sake. I glanced at Josie. Her face was sympathetic, but she only shrugged. She didn't like Keith any more than I did, but she was a lot smarter about it.

"Fine," I muttered, and headed out to the table.

When I arrived, I plastered on a big smile and whipped out my order pad. "Hiya," I said. "You here to eat, or what?"

The guy on the end snickered. "We're here to do something," he said, his voice full of innuendo. He flashed a quick grin across the booth to his friend, who was sitting next to Brittney.

"Got that right," the friend said, his eyes straying to my cleavage as he added, "You got anything special for us?"

Next to him, Brittney giggled far too loud for her amusement to be genuine. "I got something for you," she told him as her hand slipped beneath the table, doing something – I didn't want to consider what – to make her date guffaw. It was loud enough to make the people at neighboring tables glance in their direction, some with amusement, others with annoyance.

Stomaching a string of bad jokes and bad innuendos, I took their orders on autopilot, reminding myself to act normal, or at least as normal as I was supposed to act, given the nature of my job.

Thankfully, the blondes barely glanced at me while I delivered their drinks, and then their food. From the servers' area, I watched them in my peripheral vision, whenever I had a free moment.

Their table was by far the loudest in the whole restaurant, and given the rowdy nature of the establishment, that was saying something. The guys were hammering the booze, and the girls were matching them drink for drink.

It wasn't until the two girls leaned across the table to give each other a long, full kiss – with tongue – that I started to worry.

Sure, the place definitely had its trashy side, as evidenced by my own attire, and sure, we served up booze and attitude. But it was still a restaurant, and we'd all been told a thousand times that public grope-a-thons, no matter who was participating, were bad for business.

Just last week Eddie had been forced to physically evict a couple of touristy types, a man and woman around my parents' age, who'd shocked their nearby tables by playing catch the cocktail wiener under the table.

And how shall I put this delicately? If the wiener were a horse, it was most definitely out of the barn.

At least that particular couple had been quiet about it. As for Brittney's table, they were anything but. When it was time to deliver their bill, the kissing had turned to neck-licking with a side of groping, as evidenced by Britney's hand squeezing the other girl's breast while their dates hooted encouragement.

Their behavior would've been blatant enough if the girls were sitting side-by-side. But they weren't. They were sitting across from each other, which meant they were leaning across the table in a way that had everyone looking.

I glanced at the bar area. Eddie was nowhere in sight, and I didn't see Keith either. Cursing under my breath, I hustled to the back office. I found Keith with his feet propped on the desk. He was laughing into his cell phone like he had all the time in the world.

When I motioned toward the dining room, in a blatant plea for help, he held up a hand, five fingers extended.

Five minutes? Crap, at the rate those girls were going, in five minutes, they'd be naked and covered in barbecue sauce.

CHAPTER 18

Keith was still talking on his phone. I edged closer. "We've got a situation," I said in a low, urgent voice.

He waved me away with a quick, shooing motion and mouthed, "One minute."

So was it one minute? Or five?

Either way, it was too long. Muttering, I stalked out of the office and peered into the dining area. As I watched, one of the guys lifted Britney onto the table top of their booth. I stared, in stunned disgust as she started to dance, lifting her long hair off her neck and gyrating like a low-rent stripper with a nerve condition.

Alcohol was definitely not her friend.

Desperately, I glanced toward the bar. Still no Eddie. The other bartenders, Tina and Carrie, had stopped making drinks and stood, staring, along with almost every other person in the restaurant, as Britney's friend climbed up on the tabletop too. She started rubbing against Brittney in a way that elicited catcalls from the two players and a mixture of murmuring and occasional laughter from the other patrons.

Screw it. I marched across the dining room to stand, my hands on my hips, at the end of their booth. If I were lucky, I'd be able to hustle them on their way without throwing more gasoline on the fire.

"Looks like somebody's having a good time," I said, trying to make my voice lighter than it felt.

"Got that right," one of the guys said. He leaned his face over the table and peered up under Britney's dress. From the look on the guy's face, it was pretty obvious the view was panty-free.

"Alright guys," I said. "Time to take it someplace else." When they all ignored me, I rolled my eyes and added under my breath, "like the Boobie Bungalow."

Apparently, I hadn't said that last part as quietly as I intended, because one of the players immediately gave a hoot of encouragement. "Yeah!" he bellowed. "Boobies! C'mon, let's see 'em!"

He might've been talking to the blondes. Or he might've been talking to me. Or maybe, it was a general plea for boobies of any variety. Honestly, the guy didn't look too picky.

Too bad Bolger wasn't here. He had decent cleavage if you could get past the hair.

On the table, Brittney was reaching for the shoulder strap of her skin-tight dress.

"Hey!" I said, "Hoochie girls. Off the table! Now!"

One of the guys laughed. "I got a better idea," he said, giving me a look that made my skin crawl. "Why don't you join 'em?"

"Yeah," the other guy said, applauding in a way that I guessed was supposed to be encouraging. He got out his wallet and peeled off a bunch of singles. He fanned them out and shook them at me like some dog-trainer, promising a treat for a trick. "Go on," he urged, "be a good girl and show us your stuff."

I gave him a smile. "I've got a better idea," I said as I leaned in close. "Why don't you take your player ass the fuck out of here, and take that travelling skank show with you."

Around us, the dining room had grown oddly quiet. Slowly, I realized that the girls were no longer dancing. The lack of motion, both from the girls and the rest of the restaurant, made them, if possible, look even more ridiculous as they stood in their sheer cocktail dresses, their high heels surrounded by empty drink glasses and plates of half-eaten food.

"Jeez, what a bitch," Brittney said. She turned to her friend and said, "Looks like someone hasn't been laid in a while."

I flushed. She was right. I was in the midst of what some might call a dry spell, but it wasn't for lack of opportunity. The way I saw it, it was better to be too picky than screw anything that moved.

"That's okay." I gave her a sweet smile. "Because it looks like you're getting plenty for all of us."

She tossed her hair. "Don't you know it."

"And, uh, how much do you charge again?" I asked.

"Hey!" the other girl broke in. "It's not like we're hookers."

"Whatever." I slammed their bill down on the table. "Time for you to go."

With a huff, Brittney climbed down from the tabletop, and her friend followed suit. Some guy across the restaurant gave a loud cheer. Was he cheering their performance, or the fact that it was finally over? I had no idea.

The girls slumped in the booth, murdering me with their eyes while the players grinned like this was the best fun they'd had all year. From the look in their eyes, they were waiting for the inevitable three-way catfight – the one that would end with a pillow-fight and torn panties.

Dumb-asses. Had they already forgotten? The skanks weren't

wearing any.

I stood with my arms crossed as the first guy pulled out his wallet and tossed a credit card on top of the bill. "Here ya go," he said in a loud, important voice. "And add on a nice tip for yourself while you're at it."

"No way," Brittney told him, tossing her hair as she looked daggers at me. "She was a total bitch. She don't deserve anything." She sank down in her seat and added, "This place sucks donkey dick."

Donkey dick? Seriously? Like a regular dick wasn't enough?

"Well," I said, "coming from an expert such as yourself, we sure do appreciate your input."

Brittney stared up at me, as if trying to decide if I she'd just been insulted or complimented. And then, something in her expression changed. Her confusion cleared, and she smiled like she'd just gotten the best surprise since her last negative gonorrhea results.

"Heeeey," she said, "I know you." With a little laugh, she turned to her friend. "Recognize her?"

I stood, frozen in place as her friend cocked her head to the side and stared up at me. She shook her head. I forgot to breathe.

And then Brittney spoke. "It's that dog-chick from Lawton's."

At this, one of the players laughed. "Dog-chick, huh?" He gave his friend a sly grin. "I'm liking the sounds of that." He leered at me. "So, you like it doggy-style or what?"

"Or maybe," the other guy said, "she's one of them Fido fuckers, if you get what I'm sayin'." He slapped the table and guffawed at his own joke as the rest of them joined in.

For once, words escaped me. I had no snappy comeback, no smart-ass observation. All I had was the urge to flee.

Wordlessly, I snatched up the guy's credit card, along with the bill, and hustled to the cash register. I processed it with lightning speed and returned to their table, eager to get this whole thing over with.

Ignoring a running stream of jokes about doggie-style sex and bestiality, I dropped off the credit card slip for the guy's signature and started clearing away the remaining dishes. The sooner the table was empty, the sooner they'd leave – or at least that's what I hoped.

Brittney snickered. "And here, we thought you were some rich bitch." She grinned at her friend. "Didn't we, Amber?"

I tried to concentrate on the dishes, but I swear, I could hear the smile of satisfaction in Brittney's voice.

"Yeah," Amber said with a giggle. "And turns out, she's just a plain, ordinary bitch."

"The poor thing," Brittney said in a tone of mock sympathy. "Guess she won't be going to Lawton's party tonight."

"What party?" one of the guy said. "You never said nothin' about a party."

"Sorry, Max," Brittney said, blowing him a kiss. "This one's girls only."

I'd been reaching for the squeeze bottle of mustard when she made that last comment. Even now, I couldn't say for sure if my fingers flexed on purpose or by reflex.

Either way, I squeezed, mustard shot, and Brittney gave a high-pitched squeal as a stream of mustard splattered the front of her cream-colored dress, with a few stray drops grazing her face, her hair, and the guy sitting next to her.

Across from them, the guy who hadn't been hit bellowed with laughter while Amber assaulted me with a stream of profanity that would've made any drunken sailor proud. On the bright side, at least she wasn't giggling anymore.

With a screech, Brittney snatched up the bottle of ketchup, pointed in my direction, and squeezed, yelling out, "Take that, you crazy bitch!"

The ketchup hit, splattering the front of my white blouse as I backed uselessly into the table behind me, my hands full of condiments and my mouth full of curses that I let loose in Brittney's direction.

And this is when Keith, the ass-hat of a night manager, chose to finally make his appearance.

CHAPTER 19

"You can't make me pay for this," I protested. "It wasn't my fault."

We were in the manager's office, and Keith was glaring at me. "Yeah? Then whose fault was it?"

"Brittney's," I said. "She totally started it."

"That's not what I heard."

"From Brittney?" I said. "She's such a liar. And besides, you didn't see the way they were acting. I did. Just ask the other waitresses. Or better still, ask the people sitting around them. They'll tell you. They were totally out of control."

"You're the one out of control." He crossed his arms. "What I should do is fire you."

I felt myself still. He couldn't fire me. I'd been here for years. He'd only just started a couple months ago.

Across from me, he smiled. "I see I finally got your attention."

My mind was whirling. Technically, I had another job, a real job. I started in a few weeks. I should tell Keith to fuck off right now and walk out my dignity, or what was left of it.

I closed my eyes. But I hadn't started that other job yet. And even once I did, it would be over a month before I got an actual paycheck. At least as a waitress, I got paid in cash every time I showed up, thanks to the tips, which were substantial.

Sure, there were other restaurants in town, but not many like this. Girls literally stood in line for a chance to work here.

And besides, I didn't have time to start waitressing someplace else. Even if I did manage to find another serving job, I'd never make this kind of money, at least not for the first few weeks while I was in training. And by then, I'd be starting that other job anyway, so the time would be wasted.

Across from me, Keith was tallying up the total on his notepad. When he was done, he turned the notepad around to face me. I felt myself pale at the amount written in big red letters at the bottom.

"That can't be right," I said.

"Oh, it's right," he said. "Go ahead, add it up."

My pulse racing, I studied the list. In Keith's tidy handwriting, I saw the amount for the group's dinner, including drinks. Given the fact they'd been drinking like fish, this alone was enough to make my stomach clench.

Then there was the amount Brittney had claimed for her ruined outfit. Finally, there was the cost of free dinner vouchers, given at Keith's insistence, to encourage Brittney to come back and give the place another chance.

Okay, I guess I could see paying for the dress. But I couldn't see paying the amount Brittney had demanded. I leaned over and pointed at the amount in question. "That's ten times what that stupid dress was worth."

Keith looked unimpressed. "It was a high-price label."

"Bull," I said. "It was a generic knock-off."

"Say what you want, that's the amount we paid her." His eyes narrowed to slits as he leaned forward. "And that's the amount you owe."

"And why the meal-vouchers?" I said. "We don't want those skanks coming back. Their dates either. They were total animals."

"Wrong, they were customers," he said, pressing his palms flat on the table. "Now pay up, or get out. Your choice."

I stood, rigid, my fingernails digging into my palms.

He glanced at his watch. "I'm waiting."

"Fine," I muttered.

At his desk, Keith leaned back. "Great." He pointed to the bottom of his list. "Sign here."

"Uh, no. I don't think so." I tore off my apron and tossed it onto his desk. "I meant, fine, I'll get out." My heart racing, I whirled around and marched toward the office door. When I reached it, I turned around and said, "Oh, and Keith?"

"Uh, yeah?" he stammered.

I smiled. "Fuck off."

CHAPTER 20

My satisfaction lasted less than an hour. By the time I'd driven back to the Parkers', I was cursing everything from my rotten temper to my stupid foul mouth. And that doesn't even count the time I spent cursing out Brittney and her whole sordid freak show.

An hour later, I was cursing a lot more than that. I was huddled in the Parkers' backyard, with dripping hair and only the barest of clothing – just a thin white tank top and matching lace panties. I had no shoes, no socks, and no pants, no kidding.

I was so screwed.

"Chucky," I muttered under my breath, "You are a very bad dog." More to the point, I was a very stupid house sitter.

I'd just gotten out of a long, hot bath – a feeble attempt to wash away the lingering unpleasantness from work – and had been dressing for bed when Chucky bounded into the bathroom, trailing my ketchup-stained blouse behind him.

A hole was chewed in the center of the largest stain, and one of the sleeves hung by just a few loose threads. The way it looked, he'd been chewing on it the whole time I'd been in the tub. It was obviously ruined.

I closed my eyes and counted to ten. It wasn't Chucky's fault I'd left the thing lying on the kitchen floor. At the very least, I should've put it in the sink.

I didn't care about the blouse. Not anymore. I'd never be wearing it again anyway. But I definitely cared about the mess. I couldn't let Chucky drag the thing all over the house. One hop onto the sofa with it, and I'd be paying for a lot more than my own short temper.

It took me forever to wrestle the thing away from him – after a lot of chasing, cajoling, and one frantic lunge that sent me skidding in my T-shirt and panties across the oak floor in the downstairs foyer.

By the time I'd gotten the blouse back in my clutches, Chucky had been thoroughly entertained, but I was flushed, breathing hard, and my hands were damp with ketchup and dog-slobber. I did a quick rinse in the sink, and then, holding the blouse by my thumb and forefinger, I marched straight out the back door and stalked the few short steps to the trash bin near the back entrance.

It wasn't until I'd flung the ruined blouse into the bin and slammed shut the lid that I had a horrible thought. I had unlocked the back door, hadn't I?

The door had one of those annoying safety features that let you turn the knob from the inside whether it was locked or not, but wasn't nearly as accommodating the other way.

My pulse racing, I hurried to the back door and gave the knob a twist. It didn't move, well, at least not enough to count. The damn thing was locked. Of course.

I'd been outside less than a minute when the chill night air started to seep in with a vengeance. Normally, I'd have never stepped outside the house in so little clothing. But it was dark, and I'd been roasting from the hot bath and the chase with Chucky. I didn't think it would matter.

Apparently, I was wrong.

My hair was still wet, and I was dressed for bed, and then only just barely. Maybe I'd been stupid to step outside like this in the first place, but I hadn't planned to be out for more than a few seconds.

It was a clear night with a full moon, which gave me a good view of my surroundings. Frantically, I glanced around the back patio, looking for something. What, I didn't know – a blanket, a jacket, anything. It didn't take me long to realize that unless I could snuggle up with a patio chair, I was so screwed.

Shivering, I tried all the back windows within reaching distance, and then, made my way around to the side of the house, and finally to the front, the fear of someone seeing me like this fading to near insignificance compared to the fear of freezing any longer than I had to.

Returning to the backyard, I glanced in the general direction of Lawton's house. He was the only person in the neighborhood I remotely knew. He was a friend. Maybe more than a friend. I blinked hard. Maybe he wasn't anything. I'd just seen him a few hours earlier, and he hadn't mentioned anything about a party.

It was pretty obvious I wasn't on the guest list. Then again, the way Brittney talked, it wasn't exactly a normal party. If she was telling the truth, if only girls were invited, I could only imagine what the entertainment would consist of. The whole thing made me sick to my stomach.

Glancing at the back fence, I listened for the sounds of music or voices. Were Brittney and Amber there right now? Were they all laughing at me, telling Lawton all about their freaky good time? I didn't hear anything, and I didn't see any lights through the shrubbery. Then again, only an idiot would be outside in this temperature.

An idiot like me.

I couldn't go to Lawton's house. I just couldn't. Not like this.

I needed to find another solution.

It wasn't a terribly windy night, but the air was so frigid it barely mattered. Dressed as I was, even the slightest breeze cut through me. The cold burrowed deep into my bones as I hustled to the driveway and tried my car doors. They were locked. Of course.

And even if my car had been open, what then? I didn't have my car keys, so I couldn't exactly start it up. And without any heat, sleeping in my car really wasn't an option.

By now, I was cursing out loud, but even the foulest words I knew – and I knew plenty – did nothing to stop the chattering of my teeth.

It was becoming painfully clear that I had two choices – break one of the Parkers' windows or knock on a neighbor's door. And then what? If I broke a window, I'd have to pay for it. If I knocked on a neighbor's door, would they even answer at this time of night? And if they did, what then?

Even using their phone, there was nobody I could call, not now. Erika was two hours away, Grandma didn't drive, and neither of my parents were any kind of option. So my alternative was what, exactly? Asking to sleep on some neighbor's sofa until I could get a locksmith to come out tomorrow morning?

I winced. How much would a locksmith cost? And what would the neighbors tell the Parkers when they returned?

Shit. No matter how I looked at it, I was beyond screwed. I wrapped my arms as tight around my shivering body as I could, and hurried back to the back patio, where this whole asinine thing had started.

Stupid or not, I tried the back door again. And again, twisting as hard as I could. When I'd finally accepted there was no way of opening it without a crowbar, I felt the first sing of tears.

I knew what I had to do. It was the thing that had been rattling around in my brain from almost the very first moment I'd gotten locked out.

I didn't want to. Out of all my options, it was the least attractive, with the possible exception of freezing to death.

The thought of facing Lawton, along with Brittney and her friends, was almost too mortifying to contemplate. The humiliation from earlier was still fresh, and the thought of heaping on another dose made me want to throw up in the bushes.

Stop thinking about it, I told myself. Just march over there and get it over with. You can borrow some clothes, see if he knows a cheap locksmith, whatever. But you can't stand outside forever freezing your ass off.

I glanced at the back property line. Technically, only a fence separated the properties. But it wasn't your average fence. It was tall, pointy, and iron, with no place to gain a foothold.

If I were a tiny terrier, I'd simply squeeze between the posts. If I had a death wish, I'd try to climb over. If I wanted to make the evening news, I'd skip the fence and go the long way, by sidewalk.

And then I remembered the stepladder. I vaguely recalled seeing it behind the Parkers' second garage, hanging off a hook or something. Before I could give it too much thought, I rushed over and yanked the ladder off its hooks.

Shivering, I dragged the heavy thing across the back lawn and stood it next to the fence. The ladder's top platform didn't quite reach the top, but it got me a whole lot closer.

As I climbed up, the ladder's cold metal was hell on my bare feet, but I couldn't bring myself to care. On the top step, I stopped and grabbed two closest metal spires. I peered over the fence. The ground looked mulchy. Soft, right? Still, it was looked a lot longer down than I'd anticipated.

What the hell was I thinking? Maybe I should've walked after all.

Yeah. In my underpants. Down the street. On a bright moonlit night. Like that was such a good idea.

Screw it. I took a deep breath and vaulted myself over.

In my visions, I was agile as a gymnast. In reality, I was as clumsy as a flying octopus – all loose-limbed and floppy as I tumbled onto Lawton's property.

I hit the ground hard and somehow ended up on my back, staring dully up at the night sky through bare branches and my own confusion.

I closed my eyes, breathing hard to catch the wind I'd knocked out of me. The ground was cold and damp against my bare arms and legs, and not much better through the thin fabric of my tank top.

My eyes still clamped shut, I lifted my head and stifled a groan as the change in position made stars shoot underneath my eyelids. I fell back, trying to get my bearings. Just one minute, I told myself even as the cold burrowed deeper through my skin. I was shuddering now, and no matter how hard I tried, I couldn't stop.

When the stars that danced behind my eyelids changed to a steady, bright sensation, I slowly opened my eyes. I groaned again, but this time, it had nothing to do with physical discomfort. The entire backyard was flooded with light, and I heard the sound of muffled footsteps growing louder with every second.

Damn it.

CHAPTER 21

Working to reclaim my lost coordination, I pressed my palms into the mulch and struggled up to a sitting position, with my bare legs still resting on the ground.

"Don't move," an unfamiliar male voice said from somewhere behind me.

Slowly, I turned toward the sound. It hadn't been unfriendly, not exactly. But it hadn't been all warm and fuzzy either.

Twisting around, my gaze started at the ground and worked my way up. I saw black boots, dark jeans, a dark long-sleeved shirt, and finally, the guy's face. He looked a couple years older than Lawton, but with the same underlying bone structure, even if his hair was a lot shorter.

He gave me a hard look. "You hurt?"

Wordlessly, I shook my head.

He blew out a breath and turned toward the house, calling out, "Lawton! You got another one!"

"Another what?" I mumbled, pushing against the ground in a feeble attempt to get to my feet. Another girl? Were so many girls going to his party that they were literally falling over the fence?

A moment later, Lawton appeared behind the guy. He stopped only an instant before rushing to my side. He crouched next to me, his eyes frantic as he looked me over. "You okay? What happened?" He reached for my hand. "God, you're freezing." He was wearing a white long-sleeved T-shirt. "Here," he said, pulling it off and thrusting it at me. "Put this on."

For once, I didn't argue. With his help, I struggled into the shirt, still warm from his body and tinged with his scent. The shirt was thin, but at least it fell well past my hips. I pulled up my knees, tucking them under the shirt until only my bare toes peeked out.

Lawton's chest was bare, and his eyes intense as he searched my face. "You okay?" he asked again.

I nodded. I felt too exposed, not just for my lack of clothes, but for my wet, disheveled hair. As for him – with his bare chest, tousled hair, and dark, probing eyes – he looked glorious. I didn't need a mirror to know that I looked, well, definitely not glorious. I looked down at my smudged knees.

Lawton turned to the other guy. "What the hell is wrong with you? You just gonna stand there? She's hurt."

The guy flicked his gaze briefly in my direction. "That's not what she said."

"Don't listen to her," Lawton said.

"What?" I said, glaring at both of them.

The other guy shrugged. "You already gave her your shirt. What do you want me to do? Give her my pants?" He made a move to unbutton his jeans. "Well, if that's what it takes –"

"No!" I blurted out.

The guy stopped. "Alright, But hey, I offered." He turned to Lawton. "There. You happy?"

By now, I wasn't the only one glaring at him. "No," Lawton told him. "You are such a dick. You know that?"

The guy shrugged. "Pretty much."

Lawton returned his gaze to me. "Now c'mon, tell us what happened."

"Nothing," I said. "It's fine. It's just –" I lifted my hand in a vague gesture. "It's just all really stupid." I glanced toward the guy who stood nearby, looking off toward the Parkers' with a cool, calculating gaze, as if searching for something there that didn't quite belong.

I knew what didn't belong. Me.

I glanced at Lawton, and then back at the stranger, wishing he'd go away.

He didn't.

"Don't pay any attention to him," Lawton said, squeezing my hand. His voice was very calm, with a barely concealed edge I'd never heard before. "You running from someone?" He glanced toward the Parkers'. "Someone in the house?" His voice darkened. "Want us to take care of it?"

I shook my head, almost wishing there was some kind of intruder in the house. At least then I wouldn't feel like such an idiot. "No," I mumbled. "It's nothing like that."

His voice was eerily quiet as he said, "A boyfriend, then?" His trip tightened. "He hurt you?"

"God no," I said.

"Hey, Lawton," the other guy said. "Maybe instead of interrogating her, you could bring her inside, hose her off or something."

I turned to give the guy another dirty look. "Hose me off? Seriously?"

"Forget him," Lawton said, releasing my hand and reaching out with both arms. "Now c'mon, let's get you inside."

"No!" I shrunk back. Since he'd miraculously shown up outside, maybe I didn't need to go to his house. Not anymore.

Not when I knew who was probably inside. My stomach clenched. Brittney and Amber, and who knows how many other people. Maybe even all girls.

Lawton stopped in mid-reach. "No?"

"I mean, thanks. But –" I bit my lip, considering the whole mess. Just inside his property line, we were a long ways from his actual house, and the view of the mansion was mostly blocked by shrubbery, so it's not like I had any real way of knowing what was going on up there.

"But what?" he asked.

I glanced toward the house, seeing nothing but greenery, but envisioning throngs of people and a driveway packed with cars. What if Brittney were there? God, the humiliation. I couldn't stand it, now that I had another option. "I can't."

His gaze was troubled. "You sure?"

I nodded. "Maybe we could just sit in your car or something?"

He stared at me. "My car?"

"Yeah," I said. "It does have heat, right?"

"Um, yeah?" he said.

"And then," I said, "you could just give me a ride. See? Problem solved."

"A ride?" His eyebrows furrowed. "Where?"

"Um, well, I'm not sure yet."

Gently, he reached a hand to my face. His skin felt warm, and I couldn't stop myself from leaning into him, at least a little. His hand felt nice. So nice. What would the rest of him feel like?

"How's your head?" he asked. "You bump it on the way down?"

"What?" I pulled back. "No. Of course not." I glanced toward the house. "It's just that, well, you probably have people over, and – "

"So?" he said. "I'll get rid of 'em."

I shook my head. "You don't have to do that."

"No big deal," he said. "It'll take just a minute."

Again, I glanced in the general direction of the house. "How many are there?"

He shrugged. "Not that many."

From a few feet away, the other guy gave a snort of laughter.

Lawton gave him a dirty look. "Don't you have something better to do?"

"Well," the guy said, "I figure in a minute, I'll be asking fifty or so people to get the hell out of your house. So 'til then, I figure I might as well take it easy."

Lawton flicked his head toward the house. "Hey, do that, will ya?"

"Take it easy?" the guy said.

"Quit messin' around," Lawton said. "No. Go back to the house, and get rid of 'em. I dunno, use your dick powers for good, not evil, or something."

"Well, this should be fun," the guy muttered, turning to walk toward the house.

"Hey!" Lawton called after him. "On your way back, cut the lights, will ya?"

"Sure thing, Romeo," the guy said without turning around.

I stared after him. Lawton was right. The guy was a dick. Definitely.

But Lawton wasn't looking at him. He was looking at me. "Come here," he said, reaching out to gather me in his arms. He wrapped his arms tight around me, and I soaked up the solid warmth of him.

"You're freezing," he murmured into my hair. "Sure you don't want to head inside now? It's a big house. You wouldn't have to see anyone, if that's what you're worried about."

I shook my head. With my luck tonight, I'd run smack-dab

into Brittney and become the life of the party, and not in the fun way. Besides, I didn't want to move. Not yet. A part of my brain whispered not ever, but that part was obviously insane. It was best ignored.

"You sure?" he asked.

I nodded, burrowing closer to him. Suddenly, I felt like crying, but I didn't know why. It wasn't sadness. Not anymore.

CHAPTER 22

A moment later, the floodlights went off, leaving the backyard once again bathed in dark shadows. For a long time, we were quiet. His skin was warm, and his embrace was steady. I was no longer trembling, at least not from the cold.

I looked up at him. "You don't really have fifty people over, do you?"

"Eh, I didn't really count 'em," he said. "Probably not fifty though."

"So, who are they?" I asked.

He shrugged. "Friends, acquaintances, that sort of thing."

The way he talked, it wasn't a houseful of girls looking to get naked with him. I'd love to know for sure. But short of asking him, unless I were willing to ask, or march up there to see for myself, I had no way to really know.

"Wait a minute," I said, pulling away. "They've been drinking, right? You can't turn a bunch of people out on the streets all boozed up."

"Don't worry about it," he said.

I couldn't help it. I did worry. If something bad happened

because I'd stupidly let myself get locked out of the house, I'd never forgive myself. "But what if they hurt someone?" I asked.

"They won't."

His confidence annoyed me. "How can you be sure?"

"I hired drivers," he said. "Always do."

"Really?"

"Yeah. A local company. Mostly college kids. It gives me one less thing to worry about." He gave a short laugh. "Plus, it keeps people from trying to crash at my place. It's a lot easier to kick 'em out when I'm paying someone to drive them home."

"Oh."

"Although," he said with a laugh, "I don't normally kick them out quite so suddenly."

Heat rose to my face. "I'm really sorry about all this."

"Don't be." His voice was quiet in the shadows. "I'm not."

"You sure?" I gave a nervous laugh. "I literally took the shirt off your back." I swallowed, thinking how nice he looked – and felt – without one. "You're probably wishing I'd just go away already."

He leaned forward, and I swear, I felt heat emanating off him in waves. "Whatever I'm wishing for," he said, "it's not that."

My heart fluttered at that certain something I heard in his voice. It was something I hadn't heard before. Not from him, anyway. We'd been together a lot lately, but never like this, and never in the dark. "But you must be freezing," I said.

"Nope."

"Liar."

"No lie here." He wrapped his arms tighter around me to whisper in my ear. "Here a beautiful girl falls from the sky right into my lap, and you think I'm gonna let something as stupid as the temperature bother me?"

"Beautiful?" I said with a little shiver that had nothing to do with the cold.

"Don't forget half-naked," said a guy's voice from somewhere in the shadows.

With a gasp, I pulled away.

The dick was back.

Muttering a soft curse, Lawton glared in the general direction of the guy's voice. "Don't you have a bunch of people to get rid of?" he asked.

Slowly, the guy appeared out of the shadows. "Already done," he said.

I looked up. "That quick? Seriously?"

"Yup," the guy said, turning his gaze to Lawton, "but I wouldn't be expecting any thank you cards, if you know what I mean."

"I can live with that," Lawton said.

"I'm heading out," the guy said. "See ya in an hour." As we watched, he turned away and disappeared silently into the shadows.

"Well, he's interesting," I said.

"You don't know the half of it."

"Where's he going, anyway?"

Lawton shrugged. "Who knows."

"Is he like a security guy or something?"

"It's the 'or something'."

"You're not gonna tell me?" I said.

He turned his dark gaze on me, his eyes probing. "You not gonna tell me what happened tonight?"

I considered the decisions that had brought me here. Every one of them had seemed logical at the time. The bath, the chase with Chucky, the dash to the garbage-bin, the climb over the fence. But now, looking back, I felt like a world-class moron.

"Honestly?" I said. "It's pretty boring."

"Uh-huh," Lawton said, cradling me in his arms, as he got to his feet. "Boring. Got it. Now, c'mon, let's get you inside."

Soon, he was carrying me toward his house. His body felt warm and hard, and so very strong. Funny to think he was strong enough to beat someone to a bloody pulp – and strong enough to carry a stupid girl across his yard without breaking a sweat.

For the briefest moment, I almost forgot I was a dirty, damp mess. Eventually, in the light of his house, there'd be no shadows to disguise my appearance. But until then, I pressed into him, relishing the feel of his skin against mine, and his muscles moving with each step he took across the quiet yard.

For that brief moment, I didn't care that I'd just gotten fired, or quit, or whatever. And I didn't care that I had no good plan for getting back inside the Parkers' house. And I didn't care that I'd apparently just gotten fifty people kicked out of some party that I hadn't even been invited to.

I didn't care about any of it, and for once, it felt absolutely terrific.

CHAPTER 23

Crossing the back lawn, I closed my eyes and snuggled into his warmth as he carried us forward at a sure, steady pace. If the cold bothered him, he gave no sign. For one heavenly minute, I savored his steady embrace. Finally, I said the thing that needed saying. "You know, I can walk."

"So?" he said.

I opened my eyes to study him in profile. "So you don't have to carry me."

"Yes, I do." He kept right on moving. "You're not wearing shoes."

"Hey, I got this far, didn't I?" I said.

"Uh-huh."

"Seriously, you can put me down."

He gave a low laugh. "Uh. No."

By now, we'd made it to his back patio, a brick and stone annex with an outdoor fireplace, covered hot tub, massive grill, and stylish patio furniture in some sort of striped pattern. From this vantage point, his place looked more like a world-class resort than anybody's house.

With sure steps, he carried me across the brick surface, and nudged us through a back door. Soon, we were travelling down a short hallway and into a spacious great room. It had oak floors, floor-to-ceiling windows that overlooked the patio, and a large, stone fireplace that took up most of the far wall.

Looking around, I saw no sign of a party. No discarded drink glasses. No trays of hors d'oeuvres. No bowls of chips or pretzels. Definitely no Brittney. I blew out a sigh of relief.

Crossing the room, he made his way to a white sofa and started to set me down.

"Wait," I said, clinging to him.

"What?"

"I don't want to get your couch dirty."

He laughed. "Forget the couch."

"I can't." Even to my untrained eye, it looked terribly expensive. "What if I ruin it?"

With a wry laugh, he turned us around so his backside faced the sofa in question. "Hold on," he said.

"For what?"

"This." He fell backward onto the sofa, taking me in a tumbled mess with him.

My dirt-covered legs and feet landed on the white upholstery, leaving dark smudges and scattered bits of fine mulch. If the sofa wasn't ruined, it would definitely need a professional cleaning.

I frowned.

"Stop thinking about it," he said. "You didn't get it dirty. I did."

"Only by a technicality."

"Forget it," he said. "Now c'mon, tell me what happened."

Where to start? Inside the brightly lit room, I suddenly felt incredibly awkward. There were no shadows to hide in, and no added clothes to cover my grubby legs and smudged skin. I lowered my face, peeking up at him through my lashes. "I just got locked out. Okay?"

He gave me a dubious look. "There's more to the story than that."

"Yeah, there is," I said. "And it's called stupidity. Can't we just leave it at that?"

He raised an eyebrow. "Stupidity?"

"Well, that and Chucky."

At this, a slow grin spread across his face. "Now, that makes sense. What? Did he outsmart you?"

"Hey," I said. "I'm smarter than a dog." Against all logic, I wanted to smile too. "Just not as devious."

He reached out to tuck a stray strand of hair behind my ear. "You sure you're okay?"

I couldn't help it. I gave in and smiled back. "Other than my wounded pride, I'm fine."

It was true. I was more than fine, actually. For that moment, nestled on his lap, I didn't care that I'd been locked out of the house. I didn't care that I was minus one job. And I didn't care that my legs were dirty or that my hair was wet and tangled.

The way he was looking at me, I felt not just beautiful, but warm and gooey all over. I was exactly where I wanted to be, and in a surreal way, it just felt right somehow.

Glancing down, I spotted new smudges marring the tattoos on Lawton's arms and chest. My smile faded. "I'm getting you all dirty."

"Chloe," he said, "you don't know the half of it."

From the look in his eyes, it was pretty obvious he wasn't talking about his skin.

The cold had long since evaporated, and I felt a searing heat burn my face and other places, places covered by my clothes, as skimpy as they were. Slowly, I realized I was trembling again. And again, it had nothing to do with the temperature.

"Still cold?" he asked, making a move to pull away. "Need a blanket?"

I didn't release him. "No. I'm fine. Really."

His glanced down. "I'm being an ass, aren't I?"

"Huh?"

"Here, you are. You're sitting there shivering, locked out of the house, and for all I know, banged up." He pulled slightly away from me. His gaze travelled slowly over my body as if looking for bumps or bruises. When his gaze reached my breasts, he swallowed.

I could guess why. With every shift of my body, I could feel the hardness of my nipples brushing against the thin white fabric. It probably wasn't leaving much to the imagination.

His lips parted, and with a visible effort, his gaze kept on going. "Do you need a shower or bath or something?" he asked, reaching up to rub the back of his neck.

I could only imagine how I looked. I reached up to smooth my tangled hair. My hand came away with bits of dried leaves.

For some reason, it made me laugh. I'd been fantasizing about the guy for days now. But nowhere in any of my fantasies did I have crumbled leaves in my hair.

He leaned over and pressed his forehead to mine. "What's so funny?"

I pulled back, meeting his gaze with a smile of my own. "I am so incredibly – "

"Irresistible?"

"Um, no…"

"Adorable? Breathtaking? Impossible to forget?"

He couldn't be serious. Laughing, I shook my head. "Actually, I was going to say 'gross'." I looked down. "Yeah, I guess I probably do need a shower."

He grinned. "Probably. But I've gotta be honest. You look fine to me, just the way you are."

The way he said it, my insides did a funny little flip. "Yeah?"

He nodded. "And you should probably run as fast as you can for the shower now, before I get tempted to prove it."

CHAPTER 24

I felt myself swallow. My breaths were coming too shallow and too fast. I licked my lips and glanced down. Whatever he meant, I did want him to prove it. My voice was breathy as I said, "A little proof wouldn't be so awful."

He leaned his face close to mine, our lips almost touching, but not quite. The moment seemed to go on forever, and then, at last, our lips met.

The kiss started slow and soft, like the kiss of a butterfly, and built steadily to a crushing crescendo of hunger and need. I felt one hand on my upper back, and another wrapped in the tangles of my damp hair.

Following his head, I reached up and ran my trembling fingers through his tousled hair, feeling the strands thread through my fingers as our lips and tongues met, danced, and slide against each other, making my head swim and my insides smolder.

I leaned forward, pressing into him until he tumbled to his back on the sofa, with me on top of him. Our bodies pressed tightly against each other, chest to chest, pelvis to pelvis, lips to lips. My bare feet rubbed against the denim fabric of his jeans. I was probably getting his jeans dirty too, but I was beyond caring.

Pulling away, he moved his mouth to my earlobe and then that tender spot behind it, running a string of light kisses as he went. Soon, I heard his voice in my ear. "You're addicting. You know that?"

My stomach fluttered, but my mind rebelled. The guy had been linked with too many women to count. Starlets, pop stars, and even some swimsuit model. I was just the neighbor girl. Correction – I wasn't even the neighbor girl. I was someone pretending to be the neighbor girl.

I didn't even belong here.

But right now, none of that mattered. I was breaking all the rules tonight. I barely knew him, but couldn't bring myself to stop wherever this was going. Everything about him was impossible to resist – his face, his body, and a certain something I couldn't exactly place.

He was good at this sort of thing. His words, the look in his eyes, the way he touched me – I'd never experienced anything like it. If he wanted to share pretty nothings and hint that I was somehow special, I'd be an idiot to complain.

I pushed any reservations from my brain and let myself get carried away by the feel of his incredible lips on my sensitive skin. If I got lost in the fantasy, was that so bad?

His hands moved to my waist, and then lower still. Slowly, they drifted down to my backside, brushing lightly over the thin fabric of my panties. My heart beat wildly in my chest, and I had an uncontrollable urge to press our bodies closer, to feel his heartbeat against mine, to feel his skin on my skin, separated by nothing, not even the thinnest of cotton.

Soon, his lips were on mine again, and I savored the taste and feel of him. When I deepened the kiss, exploring his mouth with my tongue, he shuddered and pulled me closer, gripping my backside as I ground into him, relishing the feel of his arousal pressing against my pelvis.

When his hands slipped underneath my panties, and I felt his rough hands on the smooth skin of my ass, I pressed harder against him, wanting to savor every masculine line of him, every muscle, every ridge.

I pushed back, and ran my hands along his bare chest, doing what I'd wanted to do almost since the very first moment I saw him. I let my hands explore his spectacular physique, marveling that he felt as good as he looked.

I ran my hands over his shoulders, traced the outlines of his pecs, and let my hands slide lower, down to his abs, watching his muscles rise and fall in time with his uneven breathing.

His breath hitched, and he said in a low voice, "Chloe?"

Pausing, I let myself get lost in the moment and captured by the intensity of his gaze.

He looked at me a long moment, his tousled hair falling in his dark eyes. "I want you to know something," he said.

I ran a hand up to his neck and caressed the back of it. "Hmmm?"

"This means something to me. Whatever we do – or don't do – I want you to know that. You're not like any other girl I've ever –" His voice trailed off. "It's just, you're different. The way I feel for you, it's different. It's been different from the first time I saw you."

His words were intoxicating, but I wasn't naïve enough to believe them. If this truly meant so much to him – if I truly meant so much to him – he'd have treated me as more than some walking buddy. And he'd have definitely invited me to his party. The undeniable logic was a cold splash on my steamy thoughts. My hands froze in mid-caress.

He sat up, concern darkening his gaze. "What is it? You

okay?"

I took a deep breath. Whatever this was, I refused to ruin it by overthinking. I nodded and shook off the logic to embrace the fantasy with renewed fervor.

I had this beautiful guy right here, right now. We were in a beautiful house, and he was saying beautiful things that any girl would love to hear. Only an idiot would ruin it by letting logic get in the way.

I lowered my head to nuzzle his neck. "Actually, I'm better than okay," I murmured against his skin. And it was true. He was doing all the right things, saying all the right things, making me feel all the right things.

I couldn't help but smile. "So I'm different, huh?" I teased. "Different bad?" I ran a hand over his chest, and then trailed my fingers lower to his flat, muscular stomach. "Or different good?"

When my hand brushed lower still, he made a muffled sound of pleasure. "Different good," he ground out. "Really good." He closed his eyes. "You showing up, me finding you tonight, I swear, it's like a gift." A soft moan escaped his lips. "I wished for it. I'm not kidding. They had this stupid cake, and when I blew out the candles, swear to God, I saw your face."

Wow. That was really, really good. No wonder women fought over him.

Lots of women. I bit my lip. I wanted him. I wanted him so bad I could taste it. I could feel it too. I could feel it in my racing heart. I could feel it in my hungry core. I could feel it in my ever-dampening panties, where my body cried out to know him better.

"Cake?" My voice sounded breathy as I asked, "Is today your birthday?"

"Technically, a couple days ago," he said.

My own birthday was just a couple weeks away. It probably meant we were the same sun sign or something, not that I paid attention to any of that stuff. "But I didn't get you anything," I said, feeling all the more awkward at the realization that I'd not just ruined his party. I'd ruined his birthday party.

"Wrong." His voice was soft. "You fell right into my lap. Seems to me I got exactly what I wanted."

Still, fantasy or not, I couldn't help but speak at least a little bit of the truth. My tone was light, but the words still tumbled out before I could stop them. "Now that, I'm finding that a little hard to believe."

He ran a hand along my back. "Yeah?"

I nodded.

"Well," he said, pulling me close, "now that you're actually here, maybe it's my job to convince you."

"Funny," said a voice from the doorway, "I always thought your job was to beat the shit out of people."

CHAPTER 25

Gasping, I bolted upright and practically jumped out of my skin. Pulling away from Lawton, I scooted toward the end of the couch and looked wildly toward the sound of the voice.

There, in the doorway, stood his friend. The dick.

Lawton jumped to his feet and gave the guy a murderous look. "I sort of feel like beating the shit out of someone now."

The guy leaned against the door jamb. "Yeah?"

"Yeah," Lawton said. "You interested?"

The guy grinned. "Bring it on."

"I wasn't joking," Lawton said.

"Neither was I."

I was still catching my breath, and I was all too aware that we'd been caught nearly in the act. A few minutes later, and the stranger would've seen more than just a sweaty make-out session. I squared my shoulders and glared at the guy, refusing to be cowed by embarrassment.

"You need to stop doing that," I told him.

He looked unimpressed. "Doing what?"

"Sneaking up like that. Make a sound or something next time, will ya? Seriously. It's freaking me out. And besides, it's rude."

I looked to Lawton, waiting for him to either dispute it or back me up.

Turning toward me, his lips curved into a small, but incredibly sexy smile. "You're awesome, you know that?"

"Huh?" I squinted at him. "What?"

"I've been wanting to tell him that for years," Lawton said.

The guy gave Lawton a look. "You have been telling me that for years. Now, c'mon, I've gotta show you something."

"Not a chance," Lawton said with a vague shooing motion. "Now get the hell out. And this time, don't come back."

But the guy didn't get the hell out. Instead, he turned his gaze on me. "Still need to get back in your house?" he asked.

"No. She's staying here," Lawton said. "Too late for a locksmith."

The guy lifted his eyebrows a fraction of an inch. "A locksmith? You stickin' with that story?"

"Oh fuck off," Lawton said without any real heat behind the words. He glanced at me. "Sorry."

He didn't need to be sorry. At this point, I was kind of wishing the guy would fuck off too.

"Sure." The guy flicked his head toward the back patio. "But first you've got to check this out. Sorry, but it can't wait."

"You don't sound very sorry," I said.

"True," he said. "But it seemed the thing to say."

"Son-of-a-bitch," Lawton muttered. He gave his friend a hard look. "Fine. Gimme five minutes." Lawton turned back to give me an apologetic smile. "Sorry about this."

"That's alright," I said, giving his friend a long, annoyed look. "It's not your fault."

"Hey, still want that shower?" Lawton asked.

I nodded.

"How about this? I'll set you up, and maybe we can meet back here in, I dunno, a half hour?"

I glanced at the doorway. The guy was already gone, melted away like he'd never been there in the first place.

I felt my eyebrows furrow. "You related to that guy or something?" I asked.

Lawton hesitated. "What makes you say that?"

"Oh please," I said, "I have eyes. You could be brothers. Are you?"

"Well, since you're so curious about him," Lawton said in a teasing tone, "his name is Bishop."

"First or last?" I said.

"Last. But that's the one he goes by."

"Oh." The implication was obvious. Their last names were different. That ruled out brothers. "Cousins, then?"

Lawton gave a laugh. "No. We're definitely not cousins." He grinned. "Don't tell me you have a thing for him?" From the tone of his voice, it was pretty obvious Lawton knew exactly how I felt about that guy.

"God no," I said.

"Good. Now, forget him." He reached over to trace the side of my face with his warm fingers. "Let's talk about you. If I let you out of my sight, you're not gonna sneak off on me, are you?"

I grinned. "Not a chance."

"Good. Because I'm not kidding. You look amazing just the way you are."

I rolled my eyes.

After a quick glance at the door, he pulled me close and nuzzled my neck. "Seriously," he said. "I don't want to leave you for one minute. But if I don't, he'll just come back, and then –" He shrugged.

"Then what?" I asked.

137

"Then, well, I'd have to kill him."

CHAPTER 26

In the shower, located off the main hallway upstairs, I couldn't help but smile up into the cascade of hot water. The walk upstairs had been interesting, and that was putting it mildly.

To reach the main stairway, Lawton and I waded through an obstacle course of half-empty wine glasses, plates of half-eaten appetizers, discarded napkins, highball glasses, and bottles of beer in varied stages of emptiness.

When I'd asked why the previous room had been untouched, he told me it was off-limits to party guests.

"Really?" I'd said. "Then why'd we go in there? Is it because the rest of the place was trashed?"

"This?" He kicked aside an empty beer bottle as he led me by the hand. "You haven't seen trashed. Should've seen my place last New Year's Eve." He glanced around. "Different house. Same mess though. Times a hundred."

"So why was that first room off-limits?" I said.

"I guess, it's because," he said as if thinking it over, "no matter how many people are here, I like to keep some space private. Just in case."

"Oh." My stomach sank. "So, it's uh, for interludes?"

"Interludes?" He laughed. "Was that what I said?"

"Wasn't it?"

"No." He shook his head. "Definitely not. No interludes there."

"Well," I said in a teasing tone, "it's probably a good thing your friend came in when he did, huh?"

"What do you mean?"

"I mean," I explained, "you might've broken your own rule."

We'd been walking up the stairway, but at this, he stopped and faced me. "Except you're not an interlude." As he spoke, he rubbed his thumb lightly against the side of my palm. "You're something else."

His words, along with the feel of his skin on mine, even in this smallest way, sent a shiver of pleasure straight through me. I longed to ask him what, specifically, I was, if not an interlude.

"Mostly," he continued, "the room's an escape hatch."

"From what?" I asked.

"More like from who."

"Then who?" I said.

"Whoever."

At this, he started walking again, and I fell in step beside him.

I slid him a sideways glance. "Are we talking guys or girls?"

He blew out a breath. "With the guys, well, they're not usually a problem. If they get out of hand, I just, uh –"

I grinned. "Kick their asses?"

"No," he said, sounding almost offended. Then he gave a small laugh. "Okay, well, sometimes. But normally, I just tell 'em to leave."

"Do they?"

"Almost always."

"And when they don't?"

"Well, uh, that's when the ass-kicking comes in."

I laughed. "And the girls?"

"Girls?" He looked away, and cleared his throat. "Yeah, well, they're a little harder sometimes."

"Why?" I asked.

"For one thing," he said in a teasing tone, "I can't exactly kick their asses."

We'd made it upstairs, where he'd led me to a large bathroom off the hall, stocked with a small wicker-basket of toiletries – little soaps, shampoo, conditioner, lotion, the works. Before he left, he'd also gone to retrieve some casual clothes he said were from his own closet.

"They're not gonna fit," he said. "But at least they're clean." He leaned close to me and said, "Is it bad if I like what you're wearing now better?"

The feel of him, along with his words, had me wishing I didn't have to shower alone. But that's exactly what I needed to do, assuming I didn't want that Bishop guy barging in to join us.

After Lawton left, I locked the door and dove straight for the shower.

While in there, I couldn't help but think about him. I imagined him showering with me. In my mind, I could practically see the soapy lather running down the powerful lines of his body and the curvier lines of my own. In my imagination, our bodies slid against each other, slippery with soap and hot with desire.

The images kept coming, and I found my hands lingering in certain places – places I envisioned him touching, and hoped he'd be touching later. In my thoughts, my small hands were replaced with his rough, powerful ones. What would it feel like to have his hands on me? Really on me?

I couldn't deny it. I was aching to find out. In fact, I was planning to find out. I'd been trying to resist him, but I knew defeat when I saw it. He was like that pint of ice cream in the freezer, supposedly for emergencies. I was going to have that ice cream sooner or later, and the damage would be the same regardless.

With Lawton, my willpower had officially run out.

And the longer I lingered in the shower alone, the longer I'd have to wait before all those cravings were satisfied. I rinsed off, turned off the water, and stepped out onto the luxurious bath mat.

The bathroom was thick with steam. Wrapped in a plush towel, I stood in front of the ornate, but distinctly foggy, mirror. Using the corner of the oversized towel, I rubbed at the glass, clearing a spot large enough to inspect my face.

From my hazy reflection, it wasn't as bad as I'd feared. I'd already bathed at the Parkers', but I hadn't done much else. My face was free of makeup. This was a blessing and a curse – a blessing, because there was nothing left for the water to smudge, and a curse, because I felt naked in more ways than one without it.

I wiped at the mirror to get a better look, only to have the mirror instantly fog up again. If no one were in the house, I'd simply crack open the hallway door and release some of the steam into the corridor. But with not just Lawton, but also Bishop lingering who knows where, that simply wasn't an option.

On the bathroom's far wall, I spotted a second door. Where it led, I didn't exactly know. Walking over, I took a chance and cracked it open, poking my head barely out of the steamy bathroom to check it out.

Instantly, cool air flooded my face as I peered into the darkened space, illuminated only by moonlight, streaming in through a large double-window. I blinked a couple of times, and when my eyes adjusted, I was able to make out enough details to get my bearings.

It was a modestly sized bedroom – obviously a guest room – with a full-size bed on the far wall, a night stand on each side, and a matching dresser opposite it.

The room was ice cold, and it was easy to see why. One of the two windows was open, just a couple of inches, but more than enough to fill the room with frigid night air.

Instead of retreating, I welcomed the cold, moving toward it. The shower had been scalding, just the way I liked it, but the lingering warmth was becoming oppressive, not so much physically – I loved the heat – but intellectually, I knew that cooling down would be smart.

I had no deodorant, and hadn't seen any in the basket. I was mortified at the idea of asking Lawton for some. And, given my plans for the evening, the last thing I wanted to do was to clean myself up only to go to Lawton smelling like a locker-room. Sure, he'd probably smelled more than his share of locker-rooms over the years, but I was fairly certain he didn't consider it a particularly erotic experience.

I'd taken a couple steps toward the open window when I stopped short at the sound of male voices. They sounded like they were coming from somewhere outside the house.

Clutching my towel, I edged closer to the window. The voices grew more distinct, and I peered outside to see if I could identify the source.

By the light of the moon, I made out the vague shapes of patio furniture, along with the big outdoor fireplace I'd noticed on the way in. But I didn't see any people.

And yet, I could hear the voices clearly now. I recognized them, too. It was Lawton and Bishop. Since I couldn't see them, I figured they were standing next to the house – too close for me to see without sticking my head out the window. I had no plans of doing that any time soon.

I'd just turned away to return to the bathroom when something stopped me dead in my tracks. And that something was my name.

CHAPTER 27

Clutching the towel just a little bit tighter, I stood, listening. Apparently, they were talking about me. A better person would've kept moving. I should've kept moving. But I didn't. I couldn't. Instead, I turned back to the window, edging closer until I stood right beside it.

Bishop's tone was mocking. "So she just falls over your fence, and you're not suspicious?"

"Shut up," Lawton said with half a laugh. "She's no Brandy Blue. She's my neighbor, for God's sake."

"Yeah? Like Brandy was just a cocktail waitress."

Brandy Blue. That name rang a bell. Brandy Blue, Brandy Blue. And then it hit me. That was the name of the girl who starred with Lawton in that sex tape.

I tried to remember what else I'd read. She'd gone on to do a couple of horror flicks and a short-lived stint on a doctor drama. And there was something else. Wasn't she the so-called starlet that Lawton had left stranded in a Beverly Hills bathroom?

I didn't know her, but I already hated her.

"Listen," Lawton said, the laughter gone. "You compare

145

Chloe to Brandy one more time –" He paused. "Just don't, alright?"

"Listen to yourself," Bishop said. "What are you gonna do? Kick my ass?"

"Do I need to?" Lawton said.

"I'd like to see you try," Bishop said. "I know you don't want to hear this. But she's trouble."

I felt my jaw clench. What was up with that guy? Why did he hate me so much? I'd only just met him. Of course, I hated him too, but he started it.

"You're so full of it," Lawton said.

"I'm telling you," Bishop said, "she's hiding something."

"Yeah? Or maybe," Lawton said, "she's just a nice girl from a nice family, and the concept is so fuckin' foreign to you that you can't stop yourself from being a dick about it."

I nodded. Way to tell him, Lawton.

"A nice girl from a nice family?" Bishop said, his voice laden with scorn. "What are you gonna do? Put up a picket fence?"

"Fuck off. Just because you're still pissed about your little fortune-teller – "

"That's not it."

"Whatever," Lawton said. "Just don't take your shit out on me. Or more to the point, don't take it out on Chloe. Got it?"

"No."

"For fuck's sake," Lawton said, "what's gotten into you?

Bishop was quiet for a couple of beats. Then he answered, his voice oddly quiet. "Nothing."

Lawton's voice was also quiet. "She's different. I like her. Really like her. Don't fuck this up for me."

I felt myself smile. I liked him too. Lawton was nothing like I'd expected, but everything I'd fantasized about. And he was sticking up for me. It made me feel warm all over.

"Why?" the other guy said. "Because she's got a pulse?"

My smile faded.

"No," Lawton said. "And I told you, stop being a dick about it."

"I'll stop being a dick when you stop being stupid."

"So," Lawton said, a new edge to his voice, "I can fuck Brittney and Amber and whoever else shows up from one side of the house to the other, and you don't say jack. But when there's someone I really like, you're an asshole about it. Is that how it is?"

My stomach clenched as my emotions flip-flipped from disgust to elation and back again. Brittney and Amber. Lawton wasn't talking about tonight. Was he?

"Don't forget," Bishop said, his voice harder too, "that I'm the one who got rid of them for you. So maybe you should be thanking me instead of giving me shit."

The sick feeling grew and churned. Sure, I'd known Brittney and Amber might've been here tonight, and I realized that Lawton might've slept with one or both of them at some time or another. Somehow I hadn't envisioned them getting together right before I showed up.

Maybe it shouldn't have mattered. It's not like Lawton knew I'd be coming over tonight. And it's not like he and I were an item or anything. But still, the whole idea made me feel just a little bit sick.

"Listen," Lawton said, "if you say one word to Chloe about Brittney – or any other girl – you can get in your car and leave right now."

"Yeah? Well, what about our little side venture?" Bishop asked. "Planning to handle it alone?"

"That has nothing to do with this."

"You know she wouldn't like it," Bishop said. "Girls like that never do."

"That has nothing to do with her."

"You know what?" Bishop said. "Maybe you should just go ahead and fuck her."

Lawton's voice was tight. "What?"

"Yeah," Bishop said. "Go ahead, I'll wait."

"What the hell's that supposed to mean?"

"It means," Bishop said, "the sooner you have her, the sooner you'll move on."

"Not with her," Lawton said. "She's different."

"'Cause she's supposedly the neighbor?" Bishop said. "Yeah, that's real smart."

Listening, I felt a shiver creep up my bare legs and dance across my spine. Supposedly? What did he mean by that?

Lawton's voice was hard. "We done here?"

"Almost. Listen, I didn't want to say anything, but while you two were doing whatever –" he said "whatever" like we'd been kicking puppies, " – I checked out her house."

My mouth fell open. He what?

"You what?" Lawton said.

Yeah, that's what I wanted to know.

"Get pissed all you want," Bishop said. "But hear me out. She's not just some neighbor girl. I don't know what her story is. But she doesn't live there, never has."

Lawton's voice was eerily quiet. "And you know this, how?"

"I saw her driver's license."

Standing by the window, I froze. And it had nothing to do with the cold pouring through the slim opening. My license was in my purse. My purse was on the Parkers' kitchen counter, inside the locked house.

That fucker had broken into where I lived and rummaged through my stuff. My breathing grew harsh as I fought the urge to fly down there and choke the living shit out of him.

Lawton voice was oddly quiet. "Just how did you see her license?"

"You know how," Bishop said.

"I don't fuckin' believe you," Lawton muttered.

"Hey, I was in and out," the guy said. "Five minutes. No big deal."

"It's a big deal to me," Lawton said. "And it sure as shit would be a big deal to her."

No shit. The asshole had broken into my house. Okay, so it wasn't really my house. But it was close enough. And he'd gone through my purse. The violation struck me like a hammer to the head. Had he been in my bedroom? Pawed through my undergarments. I felt like killing him.

"Yeah, 'cause you're a regular angel," Bishop said. His tone quieted. "Listen, you're so blinded by this chick that you're not thinking straight. The way you talk, the way you look at her, you'd better be careful. If her address doesn't match, there's more to her story. There always is."

"So what if it doesn't match?" Lawton said. "My address doesn't match my license, either."

"Yeah, because you just moved. And your last place wasn't that much different from this. Hers? It matches some low-rent shithole in Hamtramck."

I stiffened. My mom's address, assuming she still lived there.

"And the owner of the house here?" Bishop continued. "It's some surgeon. Guy's not married, either."

What a liar. He was married. I'd met the wife personally. And if Bishop wasn't lying, his information, wherever he'd gotten it, wasn't nearly as great as he seemed to think.

"So?" Lawton said. "It's probably her Dad."

"Except the guy doesn't have any kids."

I felt myself frown. He did so. I'd seen pictures.

"Not that you know of," Lawton said.

"Will you listen to yourself?" Bishop said. "A single guy with money? A girl half his age acting like she owns the place? You know exactly what that means."

"I'm only gonna say this once." Lawton's voice was cold. "Lay off her. I don't care that her address doesn't match, and I don't care that you're a paranoid motherfucker, and I sure as hell don't care that for whatever fucked-up reason, you don't like her."

"I didn't say I don't like her," Bishop said. "I'm just saying she's hiding something."

"Yeah, and we're not? Stop being an asshole. If you can't, then get the fuck out."

"You know who you sound like?" Bishop said.

"Don't say it," Lawton said.

"Dad."

My jaw dropped. Dad? As in their Dad? So they were brothers? When I'd asked, Lawton had lied to me. Hadn't he? I tried to recall his exact words. I couldn't quite remember, but the implication had been obvious.

Did I even know Lawton at all?

It was too much to take in. What did I really know for sure? Lawton said he liked me. In a funny way, I believed him. My own feelings were too complicated to consider. But did any of that matter? For all I knew, the dick was right. Maybe Lawton liked any girl with a pulse.

And what was their secret side venture, anyway? Knowing Lawton, I wanted to believe it wasn't anything illegal, but it sure didn't sound good. Without specifics, what did I really know?

At the mental image of what his friend – no, his brother – had done, I felt like screaming. And then – oh my God. Chucky. How had I forgotten about him? Was he okay? Had he gotten out?

I should've thought of him first. Here, I'd been so caught up in the drama below that I'd almost forgotten my real responsibilities. I should be ashamed of myself. I was ashamed of myself.

Dropping the towel, I hustled to the bathroom and grabbed for the clothes that Lawton had loaned me.

It was definitely time for me to leave.

CHAPTER 28

With quick, jerky movements I pulled on the T-shirt and then the silky sweatpants. The clothes, far too big, swam around me as I ran a quick brush through my wet hair and plunged out of the bathroom and into the hallway.

I practically flew down the stairs. Bare feet, wet hair, no makeup – I didn't care.

On the main level, I looked around. I needed shoes. Or socks. Or something. I couldn't stay here. Not anymore. If I had to walk back to the Parkers', that's exactly what I'd do. At least I was dressed in a lot more clothing than when I'd arrived.

But I was still locked out.

Or maybe not.

Bishop had been in the house. How had he gotten in? Had he broken a window? A door? However he'd gotten in, I'd get in too. And then, later, when the repairs came due, I knew exactly who'd be paying for them, and it sure as hell wouldn't be me.

Maybe the whole thing wasn't Lawton's fault. But I couldn't help it. I blamed him. It was his guest, his house, his decision to let the whole thing go. He should've known better.

I scanned my surroundings. Near Lawton's front door was a much smaller door. A closet? Silently, I crept toward it, listening intently for footsteps or voices. I heard none.

When I cracked open the mystery door, I breathed a sigh of relief. On a row of hangers, I saw at least a dozen coats, some lightweight, some obviously meant for winter. I reached for a dark hoodie and shrugged into it, not caring that it fell nearly to my knees.

On the closet's floor, I spotted a jumbled pile of casual shoes, including the red pair of old-fashioned sneakers that I'd seen on Lawton's feet, at least once, maybe more. I dug them out and slipped them onto my feet. Like the hoodie, they were way too big for someone my size, but they were still better than nothing.

I'd already done the whole run-around-the-neighborhood barefoot and half-dressed thing, and I wasn't about to repeat it.

I took a deep breath and slowly pulled open the massive front door. It made no sound as I cracked it open barely enough to slip outside and shut it softly behind me.

The air was frigid, and my heart was racing. Still, I forced myself to move slowly, not only to keep from attracting attention, but also because Lawton's shoes felt a dozen sizes too big. The last thing I needed now was to end up face-down on his brick walkway.

Ahead of me, I saw the front gate. Shut. Of course. But there must be an easy way to open it. A keypad? Or maybe a motion detector? After all, the gate was meant to keep people out, not trap them in. Right?

But when I approached the gate, nothing happened. My heart, already racing, hammered that much harder as I rushed toward it, forgetting the shoes, forgetting to be subtle. When I was close enough to touch it, I scanned along either side, looking for whatever might control the thing.

"Looking for something?" a male voice said.

I whirled around and came face-to-face with Lawton, his face devoid of expression as he stood watching me.

"I'm leaving," I blurted out.

He crossed his arms. "Obviously."

I glared at him. "You can't keep me here."

His mouth fell open, and I saw the hurt in his eyes. "Is that what you think?" he said. "That I want to force you to stay?"

I pushed aside a rush of guilt. If anyone should feel guilty, it was him. "I don't want to fight about it," I said. "I just need to go, that's all."

"That's all," he repeated, his voice flat.

"It's just that –" I struggled to find some excuse to avoid a confrontation. "I don't want to leave Chucky alone."

"And you just realized this?"

I nodded.

"You know," he said, "you didn't have to lie to me. I would've helped you either way."

"I wasn't lying."

"Right."

He was a fine one to talk about lying. "Are you gonna let me go or not?" I asked.

"You wanna go? Fine. But you're not walking. Not alone." His gaze dropped briefly to my clothes. "And not like that."

"I'll be fine," I insisted.

"Yeah? And how are you gonna get inside your house?"

"I'll figure something out."

He looked at me a long time. "Alright." Something in his voice made my heart hitch just a little. "You win."

Funny, I didn't feel like a winner.

"But I'm still driving you. And that's not negotiable." He glanced toward his house. "I'm gonna get the car. I'm guessing you wanna wait here."

I nodded.

"Yeah. I figured." He turned away, walked a couple of steps, then turned back around to say, "And just so you know, you can run off if you want, maybe scale the fence, whatever. But so can I. And I guarantee you, I can do it a lot faster than you can."

I stood near the gate, the cold stinging my face, as I waited for him to come back. I didn't know what to think or how I felt. But whatever it was, it wasn't good.

Soon, the familiar hot-rod pulled up next to me, and the passenger side door flew open. Silently, I climbed into the car. The gate had slid magically open as Lawton's car approached, so it was a simple matter of driving through it. Except it didn't feel simple. None of this did.

Other than the rumble of the engine, the short drive to the Parkers' was utterly silent. Lawton didn't say anything, and neither did I. My stomach churned as I reviewed the highs and lows of the evening. The highs had been spectacular, the lows mortifying.

And what would I find when I arrived back at the Parkers'? The back door open? Chucky gone? The place trashed?

From the passenger seat, I snuck a sideways glance at Lawton. His hands were tight on the steering wheel, and he stared straight ahead, his face devoid of expression. My heart ached just a little when I considered the change compared to just a short time ago, when he'd looked at me with enough tenderness to make my insides melt.

I bit my lip. This wasn't all his fault. Maybe none of it was his fault. But it wasn't mine, either. Not really.

When we pulled into the Parkers' long, tree-lined driveway, I turned to him and mumbled a perfunctory thanks for his help.

Other than a silent sideways glance, he gave no indication that he'd heard me at all. Instead, he cut the engine and opened the driver's side door.

"What are you doing?" I asked.

He gave me a hard look. "I'm gonna help you get inside."

"How?"

"I don't know yet."

"Yeah, I bet," I muttered.

I didn't know either, but I had a pretty good guess. Probably through a broken window or shattered door, courtesy of his stupid brother.

Together, we walked toward the front door. As we approached, I gave it a good, long look. Surprisingly, it looked fine. When I got there, I tried the doorknob. It didn't budge. My hand still on the doorknob, I scanned the front windows. They looked exactly the same as before.

From somewhere inside the house, I heard Chucky yapping like he always did. I breathed a sigh of relief. At least he was there, and apparently okay. I crossed one worry off my list. Only a million more remained.

Together, Lawton and I walked around the side of the house, and then toward the back. I saw nothing out of order. No splintered wood, no broken glass. When we reached the back patio, Lawton stood beside me as I tried the doorknob. Still locked. How had Bishop gotten in, anyway?

Next, I watched as Lawton tried all the windows within reach. All locked.

With a sigh, I had to admit the truth. "I'm not sure what to do."

"You stay here," he said. "Maybe try the back door again. I'll try the front."

"But I already tried the front," I said. It was a total waste of time. The front door had a dead-bolt the size of an oak tree, and I distinctly recalled locking it before I'd gotten into that stupid bath forever ago.

"Yeah, but I haven't," Lawton said. "Maybe the knob's stuck."

"Fine," I muttered and went to give the back door another try. I tried a couple times, with the same result as before. With a sigh, I turned to walk around the house to the front. At the midway point, I ran straight into Lawton.

"Got it," he said.

"What?"

"The front door."

I stared at him. "How?"

He shrugged. "Probably stuck, just like I said."

Somehow, I was having a hard time believing that.

He glanced toward his car. "Well, I guess that's it."

"I guess."

He gave me a long look as if waiting for something more.

When I said nothing else, he said, "Alright. See ya around," and slowly turned away.

As I watched him walk to his car and get inside, my insides churned. When the engine roared to life, my heart ached. I didn't want him to go. But I didn't want him to stay. I had no idea what I wanted, but this definitely wasn't it.

Still, I needed some serious time to think. Until then, I knew what I had to do.

Nothing.

So I made my way to the Parkers' front door and twisted the knob. It opened on the first try. With a final glance over my shoulder, I opened the door, walked inside, and locked it behind me.

Then, and only then, did I hear Lawton pull out of the long driveway.

Inside, nothing was gone, broken, or out of place, and that included Chucky. My purse was exactly where I'd left it, with nothing missing. That should've made me feel better, but somehow it didn't. And even with Chucky sleeping at the foot of the bed, that night, I felt more alone than I had in a long, long time.

CHAPTER 29

"You didn't," Grandma said.

I buried my face in my hands. "I did."

"Fuck off?" She grinned. "Exact words? No shit?"

Lifting my head, I nodded.

It was mid-morning, and it had been only a few hours since I'd argued with Lawton. But I wasn't ready to discuss that particular fiasco. Instead, I focused on the fiasco with my job, or rather my former job, given the way everything looked.

One disaster at a time, I told myself. I'd just given Grandma a run-down of what had happened, beginning with Brittney's skank-show and ending with what I said to Keith.

I still wasn't sure how much I'd slept the previous night. Maybe not at all. The situation with Lawton tore at my heart and made me feel stupid, all at the same time. In a way, I barely knew him. But I had liked him way too much for my good. What did it matter? It was over before it began.

And then there was the thing with my waitressing job. By now, all my short-term satisfaction had completely evaporated. How was I going to pay my bills? Or more to the point, how was

I going to pay Grandma's salary for her non-existent job?

I could never tell her the whole envelope-stuffing gig had been a sham. There was only one thing Grandma hated more than Loretta, and that was charity of any sort.

If she knew how serious the whole thing was, she wouldn't be laughing. Even with the new accounting job, I'd be without a paycheck for at least a month, maybe more. I bit my lip. Maybe I could pawn something. There was only one problem. I didn't have anything of value.

"That old job sucked," Grandma said.

"Yeah." I blinked, hard. "But the pay was good."

"So what?" Grandma said. "Your boss was an asshole. Can't put a price on that."

"Yeah, I suppose."

"Hey," she said, "if it makes you feel better, tonight I'll go over and tell that Keith guy to fuck off too." She hesitated. "You'd just need to give me a ride."

At the image of this, I laughed in spite of myself. She wasn't kidding. She'd do it. In a weird, twisted way, it made everything just a little better. "I just might take you up on that," I told her.

"You know what?" she said. "In a couple months, this'll be ancient history. You'll be at your new job, meeting new people." She grinned. "Wearing regular clothes."

I nodded. "No more blue eye shadow."

"I sort of liked the eye shadow. But that hair." Grandma shuddered. "Hideous. Really."

By the time I walked out her door, I wasn't feeling too bad. Sure, I'd be without a job for a while, but I'd make it somehow. If I had to, I'd ask Erika for a loan. I'd never done it before, but she'd offered countless times. It wasn't like I didn't have options. I just hated the thought of using them.

I was halfway down the driveway when I caught movement in

my rearview mirror. It was an all-too-familiar woman with short, brown hair.

I stifled a groan. It was Loretta. She wore tailored slacks, a black turtleneck, and a deep scowl as she barreled down the driveway, waving her arms to get my attention.

It was the middle of the day. A weekday. Why wasn't she at work?

With a heavy sigh, I shifted my car into reverse. Slowly, I backed up until my driver's side window was a couple feet from where she'd stopped.

When I rolled down the window, she wasted no time with pleasantries. "So, you come all the way out here, and you weren't even going to stop by?"

"What do you mean all the way out here?" It was hardly a cross-country trek. Besides, I wasn't exactly made to feel welcome whenever I did stop by.

"Don't be dense," she said. "Every time you pull this crap, I'm the one stuck holding the bag, and I'm sick to death of it."

"What bag?" I squinted at her. "What are you talking about?"

"Fine, you wanna play dumb?" she said. "It's your Dad."

"What?"

"Yeah." She frowned. "I know you're Granny's girl and all, but would it really kill you to stop by and say 'hi' to your Dad as long as you're all the way out here?"

What I wanted to do was run her over with my car. What I did do was grip the steering wheel and take a deep breath. Josh would probably be staying at my Dad's house tonight. While I could leave if I wanted, he couldn't. Or at least, he couldn't go far.

For his sake, I had to be nice. Unfortunately, that ruled out vehicular homicide, no matter how cheery the thought.

"Hey!" She leaned in closer. "You listening to me?"

"Oh, I'm listening." In a fruitless bid for serenity, I took another deep breath. Then I turned toward her. "I'm sorry. I didn't know he was home." I summoned up a stiff smile. "But sure, I'll stop in and say 'hi'."

She stared at me like I was insane. "He's not home now," she said. "For God's sake, it's a weekday." She made a sound of disgust. "Not everyone can be gallivanting around town during business hours, you know."

"Well, since I work nights, this is really the only time I can gallivant. So sorry if – And then the full meaning of her words caught up with me. "Wait a minute. He's not even home?"

"Of course not," she said. "Some people have to work for a living, or did you conveniently forget that?"

"Then what are you doing here?" I asked.

"Meeting the electrician, not that it's any of your concern."

"I didn't say that it was."

"Then why'd you ask?"

I was still gripping the steering wheel. I didn't have to look at my hands to know that my knuckles were bone-white. But I couldn't let that steering wheel go. If I did, I was in serious danger of popping her in the face.

"I give up," I said. "Just tell me what you want me to do, and I'll do it. You want me to park the car, and come up to the house, so you can tell me he's not home? Fine, I'll do it. Whatever."

"Don't be ridiculous," she said.

"Then what exactly is it that you want?" I asked.

"Do I really need to spell it out?" She rolled her eyes. "Alright, I guess I should be used to this by now." She put her hands on her hips and spoke very slowly. "Next time, it would be nice if you made at least a little effort. I mean, really, would it kill you to at least knock on the door, or maybe leave a note?"

She glanced at her watch. "You know what? I don't have time

for this."

Yeah, that made two of us.

"Next time," she continued, "try to think, will you?" And with that, she turned on her heel and marched back toward the house.

"Oh, I'm thinking alright," I muttered as I released my grip on the steering wheel and rolled up the car window.

My heart was hammering. I hated that it was hammering. I wasn't thirteen anymore. I was an adult, a college graduate. That woman had way too much power over me. I knew exactly what I wanted. I wanted to bolt out of the car and bitch-slap the crazy right out of her.

It wouldn't get rid of the craziness, but would make me feel better, at least until the police came.

There was only one problem. And that was Josh. Me, I was a big girl. If Loretta took out her crazy on me, maybe that was a good thing. Maybe there'd be a little less crazy flowing Josh's way. Fortunately, Loretta already liked him noticeably better than she'd ever liked me. But that wasn't saying much.

With a sigh, I threw the car into drive and pulled slowly out of the driveway.

When I pulled into the Parkers' driveway twenty minutes later, I saw a familiar figure sitting on the front steps.

Lawton.

CHAPTER 30

It had been less than a day since I'd last seen Lawton, but it felt like ages.

When I turned off the engine and pulled out the key, I realized my hands were trembling. Why exactly, I wasn't sure. Nervousness? Excitement? Fear? All of the above?

When I stepped out of the car and shut the door behind me, he slowly got to his feet, his hands in his pockets, and his gaze on me. Silently, he watched me approach, his eyes hollow and his face devoid of expression.

From somewhere inside the house, Chucky was alternating between frantic barks and long, drawn-out whines.

Yeah, I knew exactly how he felt.

Lawton gave me a hard look. "I need to know something."

"Hi to you too," I muttered.

"Hi?" he said. "Or bye? 'Cause I'm having a hard time figuring it out."

I looked down at my feet. "I don't know."

"I know the feeling."

"Look," I said. "I'm sorry things got so weird last night. It's just –" I shrugged. "I dunno."

"Tell me," he said, his voice raw. "What'd I do? 'Cause I keep replaying everything in my head, and I can't figure it out. Was it something I said? Something I didn't say? Something I did, didn't do? What?"

Inside the house, Chucky was now going absolutely berserk. I heard his paws at the door, scratching frantically to get out. If I didn't do something soon, who knows what kind of mess I'd find when I finally opened that door.

"I should let him out," I said, "give him a walk or something to burn off some of that energy."

"Is this your way of telling me to leave?"

I glanced at the house. "Well, we can't be hanging around here, that's for sure."

It wasn't just because Chucky was getting too worked up. Sure, the house was set far back from the street, but it was the middle of the day. We wouldn't exactly be invisible standing out in the front yard, especially if our discussion got heated. If I was going to have an argument with Lawton, this was definitely the wrong place to be doing it.

"Why not here?" he said. "You expecting someone?"

"No," I protested. "Nothing like that."

He snorted. "If you say so."

"Look," I said. "It's time for Chucky's walk. And I need to get him out here before he trashes the place."

"Go ahead," he said. "I'll wait."

I ran a nervous hand through my hair. "You can wait if you want, but we still can't talk here." I glanced around. "And it's not what you think. I just don't want to make a spectacle for the neighbors."

"I am one of the neighbors," he said.

I rolled my eyes. "Are you gonna wait or not?"

"Oh trust me," he said, "I'm not going anywhere."

A couple minutes later, Chucky and I were almost ready to go. Like the sap I was, I'd grabbed a bag of doggie treats for the road, and started Chucky out with a pre-walk snack while I laced up my shoes.

By the time we'd gone a couple of blocks, Chucky seemed happy. Lawton didn't.

By unspoken agreement, Lawton held Chucky's leash like he always did, while I held out the dubious hope this wouldn't be as awkward as I feared.

"So, why'd you leave last night?" Lawton asked. "You got someone else? Is that it?"

"No," I said. "That's definitely not it. And I don't know why you even think that."

"Maybe," he said, "it's because you get so squirrely every time we end up at your place." He frowned. "Assuming that is your place."

"Squirrely?"

"Yeah. Like you're hiding something, and I want to know what."

I made a scoffing sound. "I'm hiding something? Well, that's rich. Wanna know what I don't get?" I blurted out. "Why you didn't invite me to your birthday party."

Of all the things I could've said to him, that one surprised me. Until this moment, I didn't quite realize how much the omission had hurt. But it had. And the hurt had been burrowing deeper with every passing minute until it was rotting somewhere in my gut, along with the other stuff that I dared not mention.

His voice was soft. "You think I didn't want you there?"

"Of course you didn't want me there," I said. "If you had wanted me there, you'd have actually, oh I don't know, invited me."

169

"Let me ask you something," he said. "If I'd asked, would you have come?"

The question lingered in the open air as Chucky darted after a blue jay, barking like an idiot when it flew off its low-hanging branch. Watching, I thought about Lawton's question. Would I have come? Not if I'd known Brittney would be there, that's for sure.

"I don't know," I admitted.

"Yeah?" His voice was hard. "I thought so."

"But you invited Brittney," I said.

"And you know this, how?"

"Does it matter?" I asked. "So you did invite her?"

He shrugged. "Yeah, she was part of some general invitation. It was no big deal."

"Sure," I said. "No big deal."

"So that's what you're mad about?" He sounded almost relieved. And for some reason, that only made me more irritated.

I gave him a dirty look. "I'm not mad," I said. "Alright?"

With his free hand, he rubbed the back of his neck. "I don't get you, Chloe."

"There's nothing to get," I said. "I'm a pretty simple person."

"You?" He stopped walking to laugh in my face. "Simple?" He shook his head. "No. You're a lot of things, but simple isn't one of them."

"You want it simple?" I held up my index finger. "Okay, one simple question. Did you, or did you not, sleep with Brittney last night?"

His face froze. "What do you mean?"

I rolled my eyes. "Oh c'mon, let's not embarrass either of us by pretending you don't know exactly what I'm asking."

His lips were clamped into a thin line, and I couldn't help but notice he wasn't quite meeting my eyes. My stomach clenched.

He blew out a breath. "What do you want me to say?"

"The truth." I could handle it. Probably.

"Alright." He glanced down at his shoes. "Yes."

CHAPTER 31

In spite of my brave thoughts, the admission felt like a kick to the gut. I closed my eyes as images of Lawton with Brittney flashed through my brain. Somehow, each image was worse than the last, but somehow, I was powerless to stop them.

When I opened my eyes, Lawton was looking at me with an anguished expression. "Chloe," he began.

"What about her friend? Amber?" I said. "You sleep with her too?"

He pushed a hand through his hair.

"Well?" I said.

He looked away. "Yeah. Well, she was there. I don't really want to get into it."

Slowly, I shook my head. I guess it wasn't a surprise. Not really. But somehow, I was hoping for another explanation, a misunderstanding, whatever. God, I was such an idiot.

Lawton's voice broke into my thoughts. "There. You happy now?"

"Thrilled," I said.

"Chloe," he said, reaching for my hand.

I yanked it away. "Well, that's really special," I said. "So here, you sleep with another girl – no, make that two other girls – what, an hour ago before I show up? And then, you get all hot and heavy with me like I was the first girl you'd seen in forever?" I shook my head. "It's messed up, you know that? Nice people don't do that."

His jaw tightened. "Yeah, well, haven't you heard? I'm not a nice person."

I looked down at my feet. "I don't believe that."

"If you say so."

Chucky was tugging at the leash, straining to move forward, and trying to tug Lawton with him. I started walking again, my head down, my thoughts cloudy. We didn't speak as we walked at an unsteady pace, passing one house, and then another.

I wouldn't even call them houses. They were mansions, every one of them. They were all so impressive that I suddenly felt more out of place than normal. Sure, I looked like I belonged here, but I didn't. Not in any sense of the word. And probably, I didn't belong with Lawton either, not that he'd actually offered.

Next to me, Lawton abruptly stopped moving. He turned to face me. Again, he reached out his free hand. When I didn't move away, his fingers closed around mine as Chucky bounded around his legs.

"Listen," he said. "The Brittney thing. Yeah, I see why you're mad. It's messed up. I know that. But she and I, yeah, and Amber too, we see it for what it is."

"Which is?" I asked.

"Nothing," he said.

"No, tell me."

"No," he said. "I mean literally, it's nothing."

"Is that supposed to make me feel better?"

His voice was soft as he said, "They aren't you, Chloe." His gaze was intense as he continued. "If I'd had any idea you were coming over, any at all, I'd have made everyone leave. Shit, I did make everyone leave. The only person I wanted there was you. Don't you get that?"

My head was pounding, and so was my heart. "I don't know what to think." I gave him a hard look. "Is that how you operate? Just go from girl to girl, doing whatever with them until the next one shows up?"

His face froze, almost like he'd been slapped. But he didn't look away. "I didn't know you were showing up."

He was totally missing the point. "But even if I hadn't –" I shook my head, not sure where to begin.

"Alright, take Brittney," he said, his voice earnest. "You think I'm using her? Is that it?"

I bit my lip, considering my response. I loathed Brittney. But yeah, if I were being honest, I guess I did think he was using her. "A little," I muttered.

"Fine, I'm not gonna argue. But let me ask you something. How about Brittney? You think she's using me?"

I cleared my throat. "You mean, like for sex?"

He made a scoffing sound. "You think it's just about sex?" He opened his arms to encompass the neighborhood, the houses, all the grandeur that surrounded us. His tone grew mocking. "For this, to hang out here, to be seen with someone who's supposedly famous. To go to the hottest clubs and get inside without a wait. To get her ass kissed by people who don't know any better, and to feel good about herself for nothing more than taking off her clothes."

Well, that was an image I didn't need. "I don't want to hear this," I said.

His gaze bored into mine. "But you asked, so you're gonna," he said. "With girls like Brittney, it's never just sex, but that doesn't mean it's anything good."

From the look on his face, it was pretty obvious what he thought of the picture he'd just painted. "Yeah, well," I said, "I guess it's none of my business."

"Yes. It is," he said. "Because I want to make it your business."

Chucky whined, straining at the leash to keep moving. I felt like whining too.

"And I want to tell you something," Lawton continued. "Fame, even as minor as mine, isn't all it's cracked up to be. People meet me, and they think they've got something to prove. Half the world kisses my ass, and the other half wants to take me down a peg, prove they're tough or whatever."

He shook his head. "You know, a couple weeks ago, two guys jumped me outside this restaurant? Right here in Rochester Hills? Un-fucking-believable."

I felt myself grow still. I knew exactly what he was talking about. That fight outside the diner. I'd seen it firsthand.

"Why'd they do that?" I asked. "You mean just for the fun of it?"

He raised his hand in a dismissive gesture. "Bad example. Those guys, I actually knew. But most of the time, it's just some dumb-ass thinking to get a rep by taking mine down. I used to actually fight those idiots, beat 'em within an inch of their lives just so they'd leave me the fuck alone. But they never did. They just kept coming back for more. The whole thing got to be such a nuisance that I stopped doing it."

"What do you mean stopped doing it?"

"If someone wants to fight me," he said, "I just let 'em fight. Hit 'em when they come close, but mostly, just let them run themselves out. If it weren't so pathetic, it'd be fuckin' hilarious."

"You swear a lot," I muttered – not that I was in any position to talk. But I was working on that.

He ran a hand through his hair. "Oh shit." He looked heavenward. "Sorry. I guess I'm kind of worked up." His voice grew ragged. "I don't want to lose you."

I stared at him, utterly confused. "But you never had me."

"I know." His voice was soft. "And that's the problem."

Looking at him, my heart ached. He wasn't anything like the guy I'd envisioned. He was tough, but not cruel. If the number of party guests was any indicator, he wasn't hurting for companions. Still, he seemed alone in ways I'd probably never understand.

Was that why he put up with his dick of a friend? No, I reminded myself. Not his friend. His brother. Not that Lawton had bothered to tell me.

That was another problem. The guy had violated my privacy. He'd also broken a few laws, probably more than I knew of. He was entirely unrepentant. Was he still at Lawton's house? And if so, was he there to stay?

And what was their little side venture, anyway? The guy was trouble. But that wasn't the worst of it. For whatever reason, he absolutely hated me.

At least the feeling was mutual.

"What about Bishop?" I asked.

"What about him?"

"Is he there to stay? Or just passing through?"

Lawton stiffened. "Why do you ask?"

"Just curious."

His voice was quiet. "No."

"No, what?"

"No," Lawton said. "He's not just passing through."

"Oh."

"He doesn't live with me," Lawton said, "but when he's in town —" He shrugged, letting the sentence trail off.

"I see." And I did. The guy was there to stay. What did I expect? It was his brother, after all.

"Does it matter?" Lawton asked.

"No," I said, not entirely sure I was telling the truth. But I did know one thing. You learned a lot about someone by the company they kept. And the company Lawton kept wasn't that great, starting with Brittney and ending with some intrusive jerk who needed a serious ass-kicking.

"Look," Lawton said, "yeah, Bishop can be a dick sometimes. Come to think of it, he's been a dick for five, six years now. Long story. But you don't know him like I do. If you did, you'd like him. Hard as that is to believe."

I didn't believe it for one minute, but it was no use arguing. "We're getting off track," I said. "You never answered my question."

"Which one?"

"Why didn't you invite me to your party? And I want the truth, even if you think it's something I don't want to hear."

"Alright," he said. "I figured you'd bring someone."

"What?"

"Yeah." His voice was quiet. "And I didn't want to see it, still don't want to see it."

"Someone?" I said. "Like a date?"

"Date, boyfriend, whatever."

I stared at him. "I don't have a boyfriend. And the only person I've been dating is, well –" I shrugged. "No one. Not really." I'd almost said I was dating Lawton. Obviously, that wasn't quite the case.

"Uh-huh," Lawton said.

"Are you calling me a liar?"

"I don't know what I'm calling you." He glanced away. "You know what? Just forget it."

"Forget it?" I said. "Is that what you want?"

"Yeah," he said, "that's why I'm hanging outside your place like some kind of idiot."

"I don't get it." I shook my head. "Until last night, I thought we were just friends. I didn't realize you even thought of me that way."

He gave me a dubious look. "You're kidding, right?"

I gave it some thought. I wasn't stupid. I'd seen signs of his interest. But for all I knew, he treated every girl that way. "I don't know," I admitted.

"Do you know how many times, walking with you, I've wanted to reach out and touch you?" he said. "Wanted to see you look at me the way I feel like looking at you? So yeah, I could've invited you to the party, but then, I'd have wondered who you'd show up with. Because I knew if you brought him –" He shook his head. "It wouldn't end good."

"For the last time," I said, "there is no him."

"Then who do you live with?" he asked.

I didn't answer.

His jaw tightened. "Some guy?" He said "some guy" like it was a dirty word.

"I don't live with anyone," I said. "Not really."

"Is he out of town or something?"

I felt myself still. The answer was complicated. I didn't want to lie to him. But stubbornly, maybe stupidly, I couldn't simply dismiss my confidentiality agreement with the Parkers. Lawton's brother had already broken into their house once, and I wasn't eager for a repeat performance.

Would the guy really break in a second time? The odds were infinitely greater if he knew the owners were out of town. And what was their side venture? If it was some sort of robbery ring, I'd be incredibly negligent to advertise the fact I was just some house sitter posing as something more.

In spite of Lawton's oh-so-pretty words, I knew very little about him. And what I did know was a mixed bag at best. I was falling for him. I was falling for him hard. And the way he talked, he might feel the same way. But that's all it was. Talk. For all I knew, he'd told Brittney the same things just before he got her naked too.

I didn't want to think so. But I'd be foolish to dismiss it out of hand.

Maybe Bishop was right about one thing at least. Maybe it all came down to my pulse. I had one, so Lawton wanted me, maybe more so because he thought I was off-limits.

"I'm waiting," Lawton said.

I glared at him. "You know, I don't appreciate the interrogation."

He gave me a hard look. "Yeah, that's about what I expected."

Without my even noticing, we'd already made our way back to where we'd started, directly in front of the Parkers'. I glanced at their house. I couldn't invite him in, and I couldn't stay out here arguing all day.

"I'd better get back inside," I said.

"Yeah," he said. "You do that."

I thrust out my hand toward Chucky's leash, and Lawton gave it to me without comment. Clutching it with a death grip, I turned and stalked back to the house, taking Chucky with me, and refusing to look back.

CHAPTER 32

I'd been unemployed for only a couple days when I started seriously climbing the walls. The whole dynamic was stupid really. Even before the blowup with Keith, I'd had the past two days off anyway, so it shouldn't have been a big adjustment.

Besides, tomorrow I'd be signing the paperwork for my new job. I wouldn't be starting for a while yet, but at least I had something on the horizon.

Still, I couldn't stop obsessing over everything. Days off when you actually have a job are a lot different than days off when you're wondering how you're going to pay your bills.

And then there was the thing with Lawton.

I'd gone back to walking Chucky alone, and Chucky didn't seem much happier than I was. I kept telling myself that our falling out was for the best. Except it didn't feel like it was for the best. In the two days since our argument, I'd been replaying the whole thing over and over in my head until I was literally sick of it.

Maybe I should've been more honest with him. Maybe I should've confronted him about that awful conversation between him and Bishop. Maybe I should've demanded to know how he'd magically opened the Parkers' locked front door with no apparent key.

But those were a lot of maybes, and I had no time machine to take me back, so what did it really matter?

When not walking Chucky, I either slept, read, or worried about money. I still hadn't called Erika to ask for a loan. In fact, I hadn't called Erika, period. I desperately wanted to talk to her, and not because of anything to do with finances.

Mostly, I wanted to tell her about Lawton, and cry on her shoulder.

But I knew that once I started talking, I wouldn't stop until I'd cried her ear off, and she had enough to worry about with midterms. Plus, I still hoped that I'd miraculously solve everything before talking to her at all. It would be nice to give her good news for a change.

Sprawled in a recliner in the Parkers' living room, I thought of Lawton. The guy was giving me mental whiplash. I went from missing him to hating him, and then back full-circle.

I'd been sleeping more than normal the last couple days, but I was still exhausted. Probably, I hadn't been sleeping all that well. When my eyelids fluttered shut, and I felt myself drift, I didn't bother to fight it. It had been forever since I'd given in to a nap, as decadent as it sounded.

I drifted off thinking of Lawton and all the things I should've said to him, followed by the things I was wishing I'd done with him. Some of those things were family-friendly. Others, not so much.

When the sound of my cell phone jolted me awake, the house was dark. How long had I slept? It had to be at least a couple of hours.

I fumbled for my phone and answered without looking.

"Hello?"

"Listen, your shift started thirty minutes ago. Are you coming in or not?" It was Keith, and he sounded beyond irritated.

"What? Huh?" I stammered, trying to clear the cobwebs from my foggy brain. "I don't have any shifts."

"That's not what the schedule says."

"What are you talking about?" I said. "I don't work there anymore. Remember?"

It was true that I had been scheduled to work tonight, but that was before I'd quit. Or been fired. I still wasn't sure how to classify what had happened.

"All I know," Keith said," is that your shift started at seven, and you're not here. You think it's fair to make the other girls cover for you? Fine. Go ahead, play hooky. But they're drowning out there, so if you can find it in yourself to waltz in here any time soon, I'm sure they'd greatly appreciate it." And then, he disconnected.

I was still holding the phone, not sure what to think. Was the guy serious? Or was it some kind of ruse to drag me in there, so he could have the pleasure of firing me in person?

I shouldn't go. But I so needed the money. And what if Keith were telling the truth? What if the other girls were swamped? I'd been in that position too many times to count, with too many tables and not enough time. Before I knew it, I was pulling on my spare uniform and reaching for the eye shadow and hairspray.

When I arrived, the parking lot was packed, and there was a long line out the door. For a Sunday night, the place was hopping. I parked in the back like I always did and sat in my car a couple of minutes longer than necessary, screwing up my courage to actually go inside. And then, I opened the car door and got out.

Inside, the place was a madhouse. Weaving through the

crowd, I clocked in and ducked into the waitress station.

"Thank God you're here," Josie said. "Three girls called in sick, and we're totally slammed."

I looked around. "Where's Keith?"

She rolled her eyes. "Hiding in his office. Where else? Hey, help me with these salads, will ya?" She thrust five empty bowls in my direction. "Four ranch, one blue cheese. Next table's yours, by the way."

I started flinging lettuce into the bowls while she assembled a tray of soft drinks. I lowered my voice. "I thought I was fired."

"I thought so too. We all did." She turned and grinned at me. "Keith was so pissed. You know that vein in his forehead? It was totally ready to pop, swear to God. The guys in the back were taking bets."

"So why'd he call me back?" I asked.

Josie glanced around. "Like I mentioned, three girls called in sick, two of the chefs too. Some kind of volcanic flu, if you know what I mean. Then Carmen's in Florida, and Keisha eloped with some football player. Anyway, I don't think Keith knew what else to do."

"So I wasn't still on the schedule?"

"Hell no," she said. "He scratched your name off the second you stormed out the other night." She lowered her voice. "Did you really tell him to fuck off?"

I nodded. "Yeah, but it wasn't half as fun as it sounds."

"I seriously doubt that," she said. "My bet? As soon as the flu thing passes, he'll find some reason to let you go. I'd give it a week. Two tops. I sure hope you're looking for another job."

"Not really," I said. "Long story."

"And he says you owe him money."

"Technically, I owe the restaurant money," I said. That reminded me, I still didn't know how I'd finally settle the incident with Brittney, but knowing Keith, that had to be in the mix somewhere. "He's probably gonna dock my last paycheck."

"Yeah. That sounds like him."

"Well, I'm here now," I said, passing her the tray of assembled salads and wading out to catch the next table. "I guess I'd better make it count."

Business was absolutely crazy. Even with my unscheduled arrival, we were still two girls short. But it wasn't all bad. Sure, more tables meant more stress, but it also meant more tips.

I barely saw Keith, mostly because he spent most of the night hiding out in his office. Probably, it had nothing to do with me, and everything to do with the fact there was actual work to be done. He finally surfaced a little after midnight when Julia, the hostess on duty, threw up in the ladies room and had to be sent home.

With no one to take her place, Keith reluctantly assumed host duty, seating customers and assigning tables. Things were going as smooth as could be expected until I glanced out at my next table, only to see Brittney and Amber sitting there, dressed to kill with facial expressions to match.

CHAPTER 33

I rushed over to Keith, who'd just returned to the hostess station. "I can't wait on those girls," I said.

He crossed his arms. "And why not?"

"You can't be serious," I said. "You know why not. After the other night, you honestly think that's a good idea?"

He flicked his gaze in their direction. "They seem to think so."

I stared at him. "What?"

"Yeah. They requested you personally. Got a problem with that?"

"Hell yeah, I got a problem with that. They're just messing with me. You know it, and I know it."

Keith lowered his voice. "All I know is that unless you're planning to curse me out again, you'll get your ass out there." He gave a nasty smile. "Unless you don't think you can handle it?"

I rolled my eyes. "Oh please. Like I'd fall for that reverse psychology crap."

"Look," he said, gripping my elbow to hustle me off to the side, "here's the deal. They asked for your section. I couldn't exactly tell 'em no, especially after what happened the other night.

So I'll make you a deal. You make 'em happy, and we'll forget about you paying for their meal vouchers."

Now that got my attention. "What about the other stuff?" I asked.

"What other stuff?"

Oh for crying out loud. Did I have to spell out everything? "I'm talking about the dress," I said. "And their dinner, all that stuff from the other night."

"I already agreed to wipe off the vouchers," he said. "Isn't that enough?"

"Hardly," I said. "Of everything on that stupid list, that was the smallest."

Okay, maybe I was being a teeny bit unreasonable. But the guy had been giving me crap since day one. And he'd flat-out lied to get me in here tonight. Besides, he was going to fire me the minute the flu bug passed, if not sooner. Money aside, this was my one chance to make him squirm. No way I'd be letting this opportunity pass.

At the nearby hostess station, customers were lined up waiting. The woman at the front of the line cleared her throat far too loudly to be genuine. Keith turned to call over to her. "Be right with you, ma'am."

He turned back to me. "Fine," he muttered. "I'll cover the meal, but the dress is on you. I wasn't the one who ruined the damn thing."

"She still inflated its value," I said.

"Tell someone who cares," he said. "It's my final offer. Take it or leave it."

Biting my lip, I looked toward Brittney's table. She and Amber were leaning forward, their eyes bright, their expressions eager. Whatever they had in mind, they were obviously looking forward to it.

I wasn't.

But there was an awful lot of money on the line. Mentally, I added up the cost of the vouchers, along with the dinner from the other night. The amount was scarily big.

"I'll take it," I said. "But I want it in writing."

Keith stared at me. "What?"

"I want it in writing," I repeated. "Spell it out. Everything. That I'm not responsible for the vouchers or that stupid dinner from before."

The way I saw it, Keith would be firing me anyway, but it wouldn't be tonight. As busy and short-staffed as we were, he couldn't afford to. But tomorrow? Or next week? He'd be giving me the boot for sure. And I sure as hell didn't want to leave with a giant bill hanging over my head.

"Fine," he muttered. As I watched, he grabbed a notebook from the nearby register and scribbled out a quick note.

"Don't forget to sign it," I told him in a cheery tone that made him bare his teeth at me.

When he finished, I snatched it out of his hand and looked it over. All the points were there, just like I'd asked. And at the bottom, I saw his signature, all nice and official.

Our entire exchange had taken less than five minutes, but as hectic as tonight was, it was more time than either of us could spare. Still, I felt myself smile. In five minutes, I'd managed to wipe out a big chunk of the disputed amount. About the dress, well, I guess there wasn't a whole lot I could do about that.

As I folded up the note and tucked it into my apron, I felt my smile fade as I recalled the other half of the bargain. My half. Waiting on Brittney and Amber, and making sure they were happy.

This definitely wasn't going to be easy.

CHAPTER 34

As I made my way out to their table, I took a deep breath and steeled myself for what was sure to be an unpleasant experience.

Whether by accident or design, they'd been seated at a center table. Brittney wore a sleek black cocktail dress and matching stiletto shoes. Amber was dressed in much the same way, except her dress was a deep shimmery green and cut slightly lower in the front.

As much as I hated to admit it, they looked great, like two cover girls out on the town. It was obvious they'd put quite a lot of time and thought into their appearance.

I suddenly felt beyond ridiculous in my too-tight, low-cut blouse and stupid bobby socks. And then there was the rest of it. Where their hair fell in soft waves over their bare shoulders, my hair was an over-teased, over-sprayed mess.

Where their makeup was flawless, with just the right shade of lipstick and the barest hint of color, my own makeup was too loud, too bold, and too much. My lips were too red. My eyelids were too blue. And my face was a little too pale, if the bathroom mirror was any indicator.

Unfortunately, it was the look required of me – of all the girls actually. Most of the time, I didn't mind too much. But tonight, with Brittney and Amber, I minded.

I minded a lot.

I also minded that they'd slept with Lawton. The last thing I wanted was to look at them, talk to them, or certainly serve them. But what I wanted and what I needed to do were two different things.

They were watching me openly as I moved toward them, with my ballpoint pen in one hand and my tray in the other.

Their eager, predatory smiles, not to mention the fact they'd asked for me specifically, told me all I needed to know. This wasn't about getting good service. And it wasn't about the food or the atmosphere. No. This was about making me pay, and not just for the last time I'd waited on them.

This was about Lawton giving me a ride home and his odd refusal to remember Brittney's name. It was about knocking me down from some imagined perch to watch me squirm under their stiletto-clad feet. And if they knew anything about the other night, it was also for me getting them kicked out of Lawton's birthday party.

But I'd been bribed handsomely to do this, and I refused to regret it. I'd made my proverbial bed. Now, I just had to lie in it. Eventually, they'd leave, and I'd be done with them. And if I were really lucky, I'd never have to see either of them again.

I arrived at their table determined to make the best of it.

"About time you made it out here," Brittney said.

I gritted my teeth and reminded myself that there was some truth to what she said. Under normal circumstances, I'd have never kept a table waiting that long. But nothing about this thing was normal, and it seemed silly to pretend otherwise.

But pretending was exactly what I'd been bribed to do, so I

plastered on a stiff smile as I placed the square beverage napkins on their table. "Sorry for the delay," I said. "Can I get you a drink or an appetizer to start?"

For the longest time, neither girl answered. Then, Brittney pursed her lips and said, "Is that it?"

"What do you mean?" I asked. Were they waiting for some kind of apology?

Brittney rolled her eyes. "Aren't you supposed to be funny or something?"

I felt myself swallow. Were they really expecting the whole sassy waitress act?

"Yeah," Amber chimed in. "If we wanted a regular, boring old waitress, we'd be eating at Denny's."

"Come to think of it," Brittney said, "how come you're not working at Denny's?" Her lip curled as she gave me a long once-over, starting at my over-teased hair and ending somewhere around my bobby socks. "Wouldn't you be more comfortable there?"

I grew very still. I had worked at Denny's, in fact, for six months my senior year in high school. My fellow waitresses had been single Moms and women whose husbands or boyfriends worked as cooks, construction workers, or not at all. There'd also been kids like me saving for college, and others my age who weren't what you'd call college material.

But they'd all had one thing in common. They had to take a lot of crap, and they worked their asses off for modest tips and a meager paycheck.

I studied Brittney's unblemished hands and perfectly manicured nails. It was pretty obvious she'd never been burned by bacon grease or scalding-hot coffee. In spite of what she seemed to think, that didn't make her better than those waitresses. It only made her luckier.

"Earth to waitress," Brittney said in a loud, biting tone. "Anyone home in there?"

Oh, someone was home, alright, and she wanted to slap someone silly.

But I wasn't going to screw this up. The last time I'd waited on Brittney, their drink tab alone had been astronomical. If I didn't want to be stuck paying it, I'd need to pull my head out of my ass and quick.

I knew exactly what they wanted. They wanted to get a rise out of me. They wouldn't be satisfied until I flipped out or started crying. If I did both, they'd be positively orgasmic. I squared my shoulders. No way I'd be giving them the satisfaction.

Giggling, Brittney said loud enough for the neighboring tables to hear, "Look everyone, I think our waitress fell asleep."

"We might have to poke her or something," Amber said in a loud stage whisper.

"Good idea," Brittney said. She craned her neck and made a show of looking around. "Anyone here got a stick?"

Standing at their table, I was gripping the pen so tightly it should've snapped. But I kept my mouth shut, refusing to give them the reaction they so obviously craved.

"From the look on her face," Brittney said, "I know where a stick is." She grinned at Amber. "Go on, I'll give you three guesses."

Amber's eyebrows furrowed. "Where?"

"Oh never mind," Brittney said.

"Oh wait," Amber said. "I've got it." She giggled. "Up her ass, right?"

"Ding, ding, ding!" Brittney said. "We have a winner!"

"If you're finished," I said in a voice far more calm than I felt, "I'd be delighted to tell you the specials."

"Oh, we're not finished," Brittney said with a menacing smile, "not by a long shot."

"Tonight, we're featuring the Mushroom Burger Plate," I said. "It comes with onion rings and a side of slaw."

Brittney scowled. "I don't care about that crap."

I gave her a bright smile. "Then, might I recommend the chef's choice? A T-bone with all the fixings?

By now, Amber was scowling up at me too. "You stop that," she said.

I blinked at them. "Stop what?"

"You know what," Amber said.

I lowered my voice as if sharing a dirty secret. "Oh, I'm so sorry. Are you a vegetarian? Then might I suggest our signature California salad?"

Silently, Brittney regarded me with undisguised hatred. Then, very deliberately, she leaned over the table until her right elbow nudged the little metal rack that held the salt and pepper. She nudged a little harder, and the rack clattered to the floor, sprinkling random splotches of salt and pepper when the rack landed sideways by my feet.

Around us, the neighboring tables grew quiet.

"Actually," Brittney said, "you can start by picking that up."

My heart was racing, but my mind was made up. I would not let her get the best of me. I looked around. "Picking what up?"

"You know what," Brittney said.

I put on my most sincere expression. "I'm sorry, ma'am, but I don't know what – "

"Ma'am?!" Brittney said. "I'm not a ma'am."

"Oh." I raised my hand to my lips. "I'm so sorry." I cocked my head to the side. "Um…" I scrunched up my face as if thinking way too hard for my addled brain. "Then, it's uh –" I squinted at her. "Sir?"

Brittney rocketed to her feet. "I am not a sir." She thrust out

195

her hips to one side and threw back her shoulders. "Does this look like the body of a sir to you?"

"No. Of course not. Sorry, ma'am."

She stomped her foot. "Stop that!"

"Hey, buddy!" a male voice called to her from somewhere near the bar. "Keep it down over there, will ya?"

I had to stifle a laugh. I recognized that voice. It was Eddie. There was a reason he was my favorite bartender.

Brittney whipped around toward the sound of the voice. "I. Am. Not. A. Man," she announced in a loud, clear voice. She turned to glare at Amber, who had remained sitting, her eyes wide, her mouth open. "Aren't you gonna say something?"

"Like what?" Amber whispered, loud enough for half the restaurant to hear.

"I don't know," Brittney hissed. "But don't just sit there for God's sake. We're in this together, remember?"

Fidgeting, Amber rose to her feet. By now, the dining room was eerily quiet. Her gaze bounced from one face to another. She cleared her throat.

Brittney tapped her foot. "Well?"

Amber stood up straighter and put her hands on her hips. She cleared her throat again and licked her lips like they'd just gone dry. And then she said in a loud, clear voice, "I'm not a man either!"

Around her, people at neighboring tables burst out laughing. Someone hooted from the bar area. Brittney looked around the crowded restaurant, glaring at anyone who met her gaze.

Amber looked wide-eyed, frozen in place, until she blurted out, "I'll be right back," and bolted for the door.

Brittney stared after her. Her gaze shifted sideways until our eyes met. The silence stretched out as she glanced again toward the door. Amber was gone. And for some reason, I didn't think she was coming back.

Brittney turned her head to face me. "You'd better watch your back," she said, "because this isn't over."

She didn't scare me. Compared to Loretta, Brittney was about as menacing as a cupcake. I blinked stupidly at her. "So, uh, you're saying you want dessert?"

She gritted her teeth. "No, that's not what I'm saying, and you know it."

"Lemme tell you our specials," I said. "Our apple cobbler –"

"Shut up!" she screeched.

Someone at a nearby table laughed.

With a noticeable effort, Brittney collected herself. She tossed her hair over her shoulder and glared around the room before announcing, "I'm outta here." After a final dirty look in my direction, she said, "And I hope you know, you're not getting a tip for this."

I nodded. "Yes, ma'am."

CHAPTER 35

Five minutes later, I was in Keith's office, giving him the vouchers, redeemed in full.

"Were they happy?" he said.

"Hard to say."

Giving me the squinty eye, he opened the top drawer of his desk and pulled out a typed sheet of paper. "Here," he said, thrusting it at me.

"What's this?" I asked, taking the sheet from his outstretched hand.

"The summary of what you owe. That's your official copy."

I looked it over. "Wait a minute," I said. "This isn't right."

He leaned back in his chair. "Sure, it is."

"But this shows me paying for their dinner," I said, "the one from the other night."

"No, it doesn't."

I held out the sheet, pointing to the line-item in question. "Yes it does. Right here."

"Oh, that's not for their dinner," he said with a big smile. "That's for their drinks."

I felt myself grow very still. "What do you mean?"

"I mean," he said with a self-satisfied smile," that our agreement stated you were off the hook for dinner. It didn't say anything about their drinks."

"Drinks were part of their dinner," I said.

"Nope. Sorry."

I glared at him. "This is total bullshit."

"You really do have a potty mouth, you know that?"

With an effort, I choked down the bile and a whole bunch of profanity. "C'mon," I said, "you know exactly what I meant when I said dinner."

"Sorry," he said, "I guess you should've been more specific, huh?" He stood. "Now, if you'll excuse me, I've got some calls to make."

My fists were clenched, and my heart racing. That asshat of a weasel had tricked me. I didn't know who I was madder at – him for doing it, or me for not seeing the loophole. I wanted to slap the smug look right off his face, but that wouldn't do any good, well, except make me feel better.

I closed my eyes. No. I wouldn't feel better. Because then, I'd be fired right now for sure. The only thing that would make me feel better was money, and I wouldn't earn anything standing around arguing with this idiot. I snatched the paper out of his hand and turned to stalk out of the office.

And I'm proud to say that I didn't let any profanity fly – well, not until I was out of earshot. Then, I focused on the tables I still had, and trying to pick up additional ones whenever I had the chance.

The sun was rising by the time I walked out of the restaurant's back door with aching feet and a sore back. Sometime over the course of the night, a cold front had moved in, lending a bitter chill to the November air.

Still walking, I was fumbling for my car keys when I stopped short at the sight of my car, still a couple car-lengths away. I stared at the passenger's side window, or rather, where it used to be. I hustled toward the car for a closer look. What I saw only made me feel worse.

Sometime during my shift, the window had been busted to smithereens, leaving bits of broken glass littering the shabby gray upholstery.

What the hell? I glanced around the parking lot. I'd parked behind the restaurant, along with the rest of the staff. As far as I could tell, mine was the only car with any damage.

Immediately, my thoughts turned to Brittney. She didn't know what I drove. Did she?

Reluctantly, I trudged back into the nearly empty restaurant and gave the remaining staff a heads-up. Then I called the police, who suggested I come by the station in the morning to file a report.

Didn't they realize it was morning? I glanced at the clock in the back room. In four hours, I'd be signing paperwork for my new job. Not a moment too soon. And I had a choice to make. I could spend those four hours either at the police station, relaying suspicions I couldn't prove, or I could return to the Parkers' and get a couple hours of sleep.

It was no contest. I trudged back to my car, used the sleeve of my quilted coat to brush aside stray bits of broken glass from the driver's seat, climbed in, and pulled out of the parking lot, praying that on tonight of all nights, the car's heater would actually emit some heat.

It didn't.

By the time I reached the Parkers' house, my hands and face were numb from the icy wind, and my feet weren't much better. Even my teeth were sore, probably from all the chattering, and yeah, maybe a little cursing, but I figured I had a good reason.

Inside the big house, I took a long, hot bath, dried off, dressed in some ratty gym clothes. Then I took Chucky for the shortest walk I could manage, just around the yard, and only long enough for him to do his business and return inside.

Crouching down with him on the kitchen floor, I promised him a longer walk when I returned from my appointment. But first, I needed to sleep at least a couple hours, or I'd be no good when I got there. The last thing I needed was to lose the job before I even got it.

Lying in bed, I broke away from what had become a pattern. I didn't fantasize about Lawton Rastor, his glorious body, or the things I wanted to do to it. Instead, I fantasized about telling Keith, Brittney, and the whole lot of them to kiss my frozen ass.

By the time I fell asleep, Keith was on his knees, begging me to stay, telling me he was the best waitress the diner had. I knew it was a load of crap, but I didn't care. I drifted off smiling, and unlike the nights I'd fantasized about Lawton, that night my panties actually stayed on.

CHAPTER 36

It was a fifty-minute drive from the Parkers' house to the company I'd soon be working for. Getting dressed for the appointment, I tried not to think about the broken window. I'd already checked the weather, and it wasn't looking good.

During the couple hours I'd slept, the cold front had taken a firmer hold, making me just a little more miserable as I considered my damaged car. I'd need to repair it, and soon, before winter settled in for good. But I didn't have time, and I wasn't exactly sure I had the money.

Sure, I had my tips from last night, and maybe a little bit of breathing room on my credit card. But that was it. I tried not to dwell on the extent of the damage, or how much the repair might cost. First things first, I told myself. Sign the employment papers and then worry about all that other stuff later.

When I dashed out the front door, I stopped short at the sight of someone in the driveway. It was Lawton. He was standing next to my car, peering into it through the broken passenger's side window.

He looked up when he saw me. "What happened?" he asked.

I was moving again, walking fast, head up, acting like it was no big deal. "As if you don't know," I muttered.

Yeah, I was being unfair. In truth, I didn't even know. Not for sure, anyway. But I had a pretty good feeling about my guess.

His eyebrows furrowed. "How would I know?"

I stopped at the driver's side door, but didn't open it. Our gazes met across the low roof of the car. "Never mind," I said. "It's nothing."

He glanced at the broken window. "It doesn't look like nothing to me."

"Forget it." Had he already talked to Brittney? Had she told him about the little fun she had last night? "What are you doing here, anyway?" I asked.

His gaze met mine. "You wanna make me say it?"

"Say what?"

He crossed his arms and gave me a hard look. "First, tell me what happened."

I raised my chin. "No. You tell me what you're doing here. Wait, lemme guess. You're just in the neighborhood?"

"I live in the neighborhood."

Well, that made one of us. But that was beside the point. "I gotta go," I told him.

"Where?" he asked. "To get it repaired?"

I let out a breath. "Not today."

"You're driving it like this?" His hands dropped to his sides. "In this weather?"

He had a point. But it's not like I had a lot of choices.

"I'm not going far," I said. Just a fifty-minute drive. I shivered just thinking about it.

"You want a ride?" he asked.

I'd love a ride. But I was heading out to sign those employment papers. What would I do? Ask Lawton to wait in the parking lot? Invite him to come in with me?

I had no idea how long the whole thing would take, and asking him to tag along was a bad idea on too many levels to count, especially since we hadn't resolved anything from our earlier argument.

"No," I said. "But thanks for the offer. Seriously."

He looked at me a long time. "What's wrong?"

"Why does something have to be wrong?" I asked.

God, why was I acting like this? I hated that whole I'm-not-going-to-tell-you-what's-wrong routine. This wasn't me. At least not usually.

He stood, lips pressed together into a thin line, looking for all the world like he wasn't going to budge until he had his answer.

"You talk to Brittney today?" I asked.

He gave me a strange look. "Brittney?" He glanced down at the window. "What's she got to do with this?"

I shrugged. "I dunno."

"She knows better," Lawton said.

I made a scoffing sound. "Really? Does she?"

"Well, she wasn't around here last night, if that's what you're getting at."

I laughed, a bitter sound that sounded fake, even to my own ears. "Yeah. Tell me something I don't know." I opened the car door. "I gotta go."

"Wait."

I paused, meeting his gaze. "For what?"

"What aren't you telling me?"

"Nothing," I said. And with that, I climbed inside.

He leaned down, studying me through the broken window. "Stop by later," he said.

He hadn't phrased it as a question.

"Your place?" I said. "Why?"

He shrugged. "Because."

"That's no kind of answer," I said.

He met my gaze. "It wasn't meant to be." And with that, he straightened and stepped away from the car.

Talk about arrogant. No way was I stopping by. I wasn't into the whole command performance thing. I started the car and shifted into reverse. I gave him a tiny wave and pulled onto the street. Did he wave back? I have no idea. I kept my eyes on the road, looking forward, the only direction that mattered.

As I drove, the frigid air poured through the broken window and whipped around inside my car, making it hard to hear anything beyond my own thoughts, which alternated between the urge to beat Brittney's ass and fantasies of winning the lottery.

If I won the lottery, I decided, I'd buy a restaurant and make Brittney work at it. Then I'd come in and dance on the tables and make her feel cheap and stupid for working for a living.

Or, I'd just move to Bermuda.

The lottery distractions did little to help. By the halfway point, my hands and feet were numb from the cold, and I couldn't stop shivering.

With my first paycheck, I decided, I'd go shopping for a new car. Sure, it wouldn't be a brand new car, and I'd still have to finance it, but it was time to let the Fiesta go. I was a professional person now, I told myself. I couldn't be tooling around in an old beater with questionable heat and a long list of other problems.

But what would I do until then? My first paycheck was still a few weeks off. I couldn't exactly pay for the repairs and still have money for a down payment on something newer. Was I really willing to drive around for the next couple of weeks with no heat and a broken window?

I felt myself smile. No. Not anymore. Because I didn't have to. Screw it. Right after I signed those employment papers, I'd head to the nearest car dealership and see about trading in the Fiesta for something better.

And if that dealership wasn't willing to cut me a fair deal, I'd just hit another one. If everything went as planned, this would be my last day with unreliable transportation.

Pulling into the parking lot of my new employer, I was so caught up in my dreams of a new car that it took me a minute to realize that something was different – and very wrong.

The company was located in an industrial section, crammed with old factories and warehouses. The business itself consisted of a small one-story aluminum-sided office building next to their much larger warehouse facility.

There was only one problem. The spot where the warehouse used to be now contained a sprawling pile of charred rubble. Off to the side, I saw piles of twisted car parts, stacked here and there, as if someone had been working to salvage and sort anything that might still be of value.

Sitting in my frozen car, I looked out over the destruction, wondering what had happened, and if anyone had gotten hurt. Had anyone been inside at the time? My stomach clenched. If anyone had, and they'd been unable to make it out, they wouldn't have survived to tell about it.

Vaguely, I realized that from somewhere inside my purse, my cell phone was ringing. Distracted, I dug through, pulled it out, and answered without looking. "Hello?"

"Jeez, who peed in your oatmeal?" Loretta said.

Goes to show what she knew. I didn't even like oatmeal. "No one peed in anything," I told her, trying to control my spinning thoughts. "Why'd you call?"

"You know," she said, "you really should work on your phone manners."

"My phone manners?"

"Yes, your phone manners," she said. "Try smiling when you answer the phone. It'll make you sound like less of a sourpuss."

"Hey," I said, "I wasn't the one who mentioned oatmeal and pee in the same sentence."

I eyed the destruction in front of me. The hiring manager had described the warehouse as the heart of the company. They would rebuild it, wouldn't they? They had insurance, right?

Loretta gave a loud sigh. "Fine. Excuse me for trying to offer some constructive criticism."

I clenched my fist around the phone. "So, did you call for another reason, or just to offer the criticism?"

"Constructive criticism," she corrected. "Oh never mind. I don't know why I bother." With another loud sigh, she said, "I called to see what you're bringing."

"Bringing? What do you mean?"

"Don't be dense," she said. "For Thanksgiving. Are you bringing a side dish, a dessert, what?"

"A dessert," I answered automatically.

"Sorry. Lauren's bringing the dessert."

Oh for Pete's sake. Then why'd Loretta mention dessert in the first place? And besides, since when did it become illegal to have more than one dessert at Thanksgiving? "What kind is she bringing?" I said. "I'll bring something different. You know, for variety."

"Chloe," she said in tone of infinite patience, "I'm not going to have you trying to upstage her."

"What?"

"This is Thanksgiving," she said, "not some bake-off. Now, pick something else so I can finalize the menu. This whole thing is a lot of work, and you're not making it easier on me."

"Fine," I snapped. "Just tell me what to bring, and I'll bring it."

"In the interest of keeping family peace," she said, "I'm going to ignore your snippy tone."

In the interest of keeping family peace, I refrained from pointing out that since she'd mentioned my snippy tone, she couldn't actually take credit for ignoring it.

"I'll bring a salad," I said.

"Now, was that so hard?" she said, then hung up without saying goodbye.

And I was the one with bad phone manners? With a sigh of disgust, I tossed the phone onto the passenger's seat and returned my attention to the burned warehouse.

While talking to Loretta, another question had been creeping slowly into my brain. Did I still have a job here? Or had that gone up in flames along with the warehouse? I felt guilty for even thinking about something so small as a job when lives might've been lost. But still, the question persisted.

Even if they did rebuild, how long would that take? Could the company survive until then? And if so, did they really need a junior accountant to invoice stuff that wasn't even available for delivery, from a distribution center that was no longer functioning?

The cold forgotten, I took a deep breath and got out of my car. There was only one way to find out.

CHAPTER 37

A half hour later, I was back in the Fiesta. I took a moment to give the car a good, long look, sparing myself nothing – the broken window, the faded upholstery, the cigarette burn on the dashboard. The burn wasn't mine. I'd inherited it from a previous owner, whoever that was.

I'd gotten the car for a steal, and I'd been happy to get it at the time. Of course, that was over five years ago, during my senior year in high school. According to the fantasy life I'd scripted out for myself, I would've ditched the car a long time ago in favor of something better.

Now, it looked like I'd be driving it a while. As it turned out, the company didn't need an accounting clerk, new or otherwise, when they had almost no inventory remaining and no way to process it if they did.

"If you're still looking, come back in a couple of months," the hiring manager had told me. "Depending on how things go, we might be looking to fill the position again."

Again? The way I saw it, the position had never been filled in the first place, except by that woman about to retire. Turns out, she'd been let go that morning. Happy early retirement, huh?

As for me, I needed a new job now, not in a couple months. But I didn't tell the guy any of these things. It wasn't his fault that some freak electrical accident had burned their warehouse to the ground. Thankfully, no one had gotten hurt, but the way it looked, the business was in serious trouble.

Here, I was worried about not getting a new job, while others were losing jobs they'd had for years. That had to be worse, right?

Still, there was no denying that for me personally, it sucked. What was I going to do? Waitress the rest of my life? Or maybe, I needed to move out of state. Our local economy wasn't exactly booming. If I broadened my job search to other areas, I'd probably have better luck.

But what about Josh? And Grandma? Would they be alright? It wasn't like I lived with either one of them, but I hated the thought of moving away.

Who would take Grandma's non-existent mailers to the non-existent mailing house? Would I need to invent another fictional job to keep her in rent money?

And then there was Josh. As long as Grandma lived so close to him, I knew he was safe from the worst of what Loretta dished out. With Grandma just a short walk away, Josh had a place to go, not just for his own sake, but to keep Loretta from getting too torqued up over stupid crap like multiple desserts.

Even though she liked Josh better than she liked me, she still liked him best when he was out of sight, no matter how much she might claim otherwise in front of my Dad.

I needed comfort, big time. A call to Erika wouldn't solve my problems, but it would definitely make me feel better. And I'd been resisting long enough. I reached for my phone, and stopped short when I realized the phone wasn't on the passenger's seat where I'd tossed it after talking to Loretta.

Confused, I looked toward the car floor and then searched the other usual spots. When it didn't turn up, I got out of my car, searched it, scanned the parking lot, dug through my purse, and went through the added humiliation of returning to the hiring manager's office to see if, by chance, I'd left it inside their building.

I don't know why I bothered. I knew exactly where I'd left it, and it wasn't there. "Stupid, stupid, stupid..." I muttered when it became painfully obvious the phone was gone. Stolen, no doubt. It was several years old, ancient by today's standards. Why anyone would want the thing was beyond me.

But what did I expect? My car had a broken window, and I'd left the phone in plain sight. It had probably taken someone all of five seconds to reach in and grab it. But I couldn't live without a phone, and besides, I had a service contract, which meant I'd be paying for cell phone coverage regardless.

By the time I pulled out of the parking lot, I was thoroughly overwhelmed. I cranked up the stereo, trying to drown out the sound of the icy wind, along with my thoughts, but it didn't help.

It especially didn't help when halfway home, the stereo crackled with static, then died a slow, pathetic death over the course of five miles in stop-and-go traffic.

I spent an hour at the cell phone store, reporting the theft and replacing the phone with money I didn't have. My old phone was so old that it had been discontinued, so I had a bright shiny new model. I should've been excited, but to me, it was an expense I didn't need and confusion I didn't want to deal with.

Sure, it had a whole bunch of new features, but at the moment, I had no energy to figure them out and no patience for the time it would take for me to get used to it.

I tried to dial Erika and ended up taking a picture of my dashboard.

That did it. Cursing, I pulled into the nearest party store. Shoving the new phone deep into my purse, I went inside and bought a bag of chips and a fifth of vodka. I'd never been one to drown my troubles, but I didn't know what else to do. I didn't want to think. I wanted sweet oblivion, and if it meant I had to get it out of a bottle, so be it.

Sometimes, reality is just too damn depressing.

CHAPTER 38

Sitting at the Parkers' kitchen counter, I spent the first hour sulking. I started with sulking about the job thing and worked my way back, sulking about everything from the stupid Thanksgiving dessert that I couldn't bring to my lost cell phone.

No matter how I looked at it, I couldn't help but feel I'd done everything wrong in spite of my determination to do everything right.

How many things had I given up over the years because I was always working? How many parties? How many football games? I'd never kissed a stranger. I'd never danced until my feet blistered. I'd never had a one-night stand.

I'd taught myself to delay gratification too many times to count. Just until the end of this semester. Just until the end of the school year. Just until I graduated from college. Just until I got a good job. And for what? Did it even matter?

I'd never get those years back. Was I any further ahead than if I'd stopped to have a little more fun on the way?

Doubtful.

I stared at the bottle of vodka. Why had I even bought the

thing? I wasn't much of a drinker. I'd seen way too many of my Mom's boyfriends shitfaced to find the whole idea appealing. Besides, what was I going to do? Sit in somebody else's living room, drowning my troubles because I wanted somebody else's life?

It was a Monday, the slowest night at the diner, which explained why I hadn't been scheduled to work that night. Probably, that was probably a good thing. I wasn't in the mood to be sassy, or even competent.

But I wanted to do something, something just once that was only for now, something that said to hell with the future and plans and obligations, and all that other stuff that had been weighing on me for as long as I could remember.

But did I even know how to live in the moment? To just let loose and experience something – anything – for the fleeting joy it might bring?

I lay my head on the kitchen counter and let my mind drift. If I could do something, right here, right now, for the sheer pleasure of it, what would I do?

And that's when it hit me. I'd visit Lawton Rastor alright, but not like any nice, sensible girl would. I'd march over there and knock on his door like all the other girls who wanted a taste of his hot body and dangerous reputation. I'd beg him – no, I'd demand of him – everything he'd give and receive from a willing partner.

If he wanted it rough, I'd do it rough. If he wanted it gentle, I'd do it gentle. I didn't care. Fire, ice, fast, slow, hard, easy – for once in my life, I'd ride the waves of whatever crashed over me and have a whole lot of fun doing it.

A minute later, I was pulling on my tennis shoes. Sure, I could've put on high heels. I could've dug through the closet for my best slinky dress. I could've done a thousand other things to force the perfect look or the perfect mood. But that was just another way I'd be planning ahead.

And tonight, there was no plan, unless you counted the one thing I was determined to do before the sun came up, and that was make Lawton Rastor moan my name the same way he had in my dreams.

So what if he didn't know my last name was Malinski? And so what if he assumed I somehow belonged here? Did it matter? From what his brother said, Lawton would forget me practically the minute he had me. But as for me, I'd have the memory to last a lifetime.

Chucky was lounging in his favorite basket. "Wish me luck," I told him as I shrugged into a white hoodie. He yipped, rolled over, and closed his eyes like I'd interrupted a nap of epic proportions. "Good dog," I said.

Stopping only to grab my keys and new cell phone, I plunged out of the house and made it only a few steps before I stopped, whirled around, dashed back into the house.

I headed straight for the kitchen counter, where the bottle of vodka remained unopened. With trembling hands, I twisted off the top and took a long swig straight from the bottle.

The liquid burned on the way down, and made me sputter and curse when I came up for air. But it was exactly what I needed. A couple of swigs later, I had enough liquid courage to send me out the door all over again. Except this time, I refused to look back.

CHAPTER 39

Although we shared a back fence, it was still a fifteen-minute walk to his house by sidewalk. The night was frigid with a bitter wind that would've made me run back inside if I weren't so flush with vodka-induced heat, and the knowledge of my own intentions.

Along the tree-lined street, my hair whipped around my face in an untamed fury as the wind came in gusts and bursts. Only a total nutcase would be out walking on a night like this.

I felt myself smile. I was acting crazy, and it felt good. No. It felt more than good. Liberating. I was nearly to Lawton's place when I heard it, the sound of keys jangling somewhere behind me, either as someone moved fast or indulged a nervous twitch.

I turned to look. I saw nothing, or at least nothing out of the ordinary. I listened intently. All I heard was the wind rustling the trees and scattering dried leaves on the pavement. I wasn't worried. I'd walked this route too many times to worry, especially in a neighborhood like this. But I was curious.

With a mental shrug, I turned back around and picked up the pace. The sooner I got to Lawton's place, the better, and not because of phantom noises or the wicked weather.

Before I knew it, I was running, the wind in my hair and warmth of my skin adding to the strange unearthly feeling that destiny was pushing me on, nudging me into the abyss of the unknown, where nothing mattered except the here and now.

I wasn't me. This wasn't real. There'd be no regrets. And no worrying about tomorrow.

At Lawton's, the gate was open. A good sign. I'd just run up and knock on his door, and to hell with the consequences. What I'd say to him, I still didn't know. I'd deal with it. And if another girl was there? Well, I'd deal with that somehow too.

I stopped in my tracks. What if Brittney were there? Was I really ready to face her? And Amber? "Fuck it," I said, feeling an instant release as I spoke the words out loud.

I was tired of playing nice. If Brittney was there, who knows? There just might be a catfight after all, and I was a lot tougher than I looked.

Before I knew it, my feet were moving again, down his driveway, and toward his front door. This time, I vowed, I wouldn't be stopping. Near his front entryway, I rounded a thick patch of shrubbery, feeling lighter than I had in forever, right up the moment I crashed into a brick wall.

And the brick wall had a name. Lawton Rastor.

I'd slammed into him with enough force to send me reeling backward. My ass would've hit the pavement a second later, if not for his strong arms snagging me lightning fast and crushing me back into him to keep me from topping in the other direction.

A whoosh of air left my body. His body was warm and rock hard, and I made no move to step away. He felt amazing. Even better than I remembered. And my memories were pretty darn good.

The top of my head was well below his chin, and I rested my

bare cheek against the front of his shirt, feeling warm and safe and carefree in a way that made no sense, given the bitter wind and shitty day that had driven me to act so out of character.

"You okay?" he asked, extending his arms and taking a step backward to study my face. Somewhere in the recesses of my brain, I registered that he was dressed in all black – black running pants, a black long-sleeved T-shirt, and black running shoes.

I nodded. My breaths were coming in shallow bursts – whether from the run, from the unexpected collision, from my own torrid thoughts, I had no idea. His eyebrows furrowed. He glanced past me, over my shoulder.

"Something wrong?" he asked.

How did I put this? What would that other girl – the more adventurous girl – say? I swallowed and met his gaze, willing him to understand without making me say it. "I was coming to see you. Like you asked. Remember?"

Something in his expression changed, like a coiled knot had been loosened, and then took hold of him in a different way. The corners of his mouth lifted. "Yeah?"

Oh come on. This couldn't be that big of a surprise. No doubt, girls threw themselves at him every day. And besides, I had been invited. Hadn't I?

I nodded. "Unless –" I cleared my throat. "– you don't have company, do you?"

His words were oddly quiet as he met my gaze head-on. "No," he said. "But I'd like to."

I grinned up at him, feeling the worst kind of tension leave my body, and another kind arrive in torrents. I screwed up the last bit of courage, and said what the other girl might say. "If you invited me in, I wouldn't say no." I reached out and ran a finger lightly up his chest. "To anything."

He suddenly grew very still. So did I, other than the wind

whipping at my hair and clothes. My fingertips remained frozen in place as I waited to see what he did next. His gaze narrowed as he studied my face.

"Have you been drinking?" he asked.

"No." I withdrew my finger and stared up at him. "Well, not much anyway." Here I was, trying to seduce the guy, and he was asking about my drinking habits? I couldn't say for sure, but I'd have bet almost anything that Britney and friend were never stone-cold sober when they'd been in my shoes.

"Why?" I said. "Does it matter?"

He met my gaze. "Yes. With you, it does."

"Why?" I blurted out, briefly forgetting my role as seductress.

"I don't know," he said, "but it does."

I let out a long breath. This wasn't going the way I'd planned. A mortifying thought occurred to me. What if his drinking comment was just an excuse? What if he just didn't see me that way anymore?

I wasn't a Brittney, and I certainly wasn't anything like the other girls he'd been linked to in the news. I wasn't a siren or a starlet or a party girl in any conceivable way. What if the other night had been a fluke? Maybe I should've dressed up after all.

Oh shit.

I'd been so naïve. I thought just because I was a girl, and he was a guy who'd expressed some interest in me, that if I showed up and offered myself to him that he'd be willing. Okay, more than willing.

Screw it. I'd come this far, and my day couldn't get any more humiliating. Bracing myself, I laid my cards on the table. "So you're saying you don't want me?" I lifted my chin. Even if the situation was humiliating, I wasn't going to slink away like some whipped dog.

I'd leave, but I'd keep my dignity. Well, what dignity remained.

I guess it wasn't much.

Something in his expression changed. He chuckled. "Chloe," he said. "If you knew how much I wanted you." He shook his head. "Well, let's just say you'd be smart to run back the way you came." He took a step closer until we were almost touching. "And you'd run right now. Before I show you exactly how much." His gaze smoldered into mine, and I swear, I felt my panties ignite.

"Yeah?" I said, feeling my earlier boldness return with a vengeance. "Prove it."

He gave me a wicked grin. "Is that a dare?"

Mutely, I nodded.

Before I knew it, he'd swooped me up in his arms, literally, carrying me the final steps to the brick steps of his front entryway. I heard myself laugh, a joyful sound that had been sadly lacking lately. His steps were sure and steady, and his arms were rock-hard under my knees, as he moved easily up the steps.

With me still in his arms, he pushed open his front door and carried me inside, turning to walk through a set of large double doors.

When I'd come here the previous times, those doors had been closed.

But now, inside this strangely cozy room, I saw cream-colored walls, gleaming oak floors, a huge unlit fireplace with brown leather furniture arranged in a square pattern around a plush, gold-colored rug.

Still carrying me, he strode toward the leather sofa that sat opposite the huge fireplace. His chest was rock-hard against my cheek as I nestled into him, soaking up the clean scent and masculine feel of him.

I couldn't see his face, but I heard the smile in his voice as he said, "If I let you go, you're not gonna run off, are you?"

I shook my head, too caught up in the moment to be embarrassed at the fact I'd done exactly that on my last visit. But tonight, I was someone different. If I ran, it would be toward him, not the other way around. "Not a chance," I said.

"Good," he said, tossing me onto the couch, "because trust me, you wouldn't get far."

CHAPTER 40

I could only imagine how I looked. My hair had to be a wild mess, and I could tell by the feel of my clothes that they were twisted around me in a way that was decidedly unfashionable. But as he stood by the sofa, looking down at me with an expression of unbridled desire, none of that mattered.

All I knew was that I wanted him. And he wanted me. And for just one night, that was more than enough.

"Don't move," he said. "I'll be right back."

When he strode out of the room, I felt the loss of his presence in a way that was totally foreign to me. The room was gorgeous with gold-framed paintings and vases with flowers in all the right places. Obviously, the guy had a decorator.

He returned a minute later and strode to the fireplace. Crouching down with his back to me, he opened the glass doors, struck a match, and tossed the lit match onto a huge stack of wood and kindling, obviously staged for quick ignition.

"Wow, real wood," I said, thinking of the gas logs I'd seen in most of the homes I'd stayed in. "I haven't seen that in a while."

Slowly, he turned his head toward me and cocked a single

eyebrow. The off-color implication of my words struck me. "I meant, uh, with the fireplace." But my eyes had a mind of their own and flicked briefly to his groin area.

"Yeah?" he said, a smile tugging at the corners of his mouth.

If I were that other girl, I'd make some remark about wanting to see his wood.

On second thought – I shook my head. That would be the stupidest thing on Earth to say, unless I was starring in a bad porn movie. Next thing, I'd be asking him to deliver my pizza with sausage.

Oh crap, had he asked me a question? "Um, excuse me?"

Something like amusement danced in his eyes, and I felt a warmth in my face that had nothing to do with the fire, or the vodka for that matter.

Slowly, like a panther stalking his prey, he approached the sofa. "Has anyone told you you're beautiful when you blush?"

"I don't blush," I said.

"Is that so?"

"Well, I don't normally blush," I said.

But the truth was, being around Lawton made me do a lot of things I didn't normally do. If I had my way, that list would be a lot longer before the night was through. "What I need to do now," I said, "is make you blush."

He laughed. "You can try."

I reached for his shirt, grabbing a handful and tugging him toward me. Before I knew it, our lips were crushed together in a ragged kiss, and we fell back together on the large sofa.

Soon, we lay side-by-side with our limbs intertwined as we began to explore each other's bodies. I ran my hands over his back, marveling in the coiled mass of perfected muscle that danced underneath my fingertips every time he moved.

Slowly he ran his hands over my back. Even through my T-shirt, I felt his strength and the heat of his touch. They roamed to my waist, and then to the seat of my jeans.

With a feather-light touch, he ran his fingers over my ass, still covered in the denim. I found myself wiggling and twisting my hips in encouragement, grinding my pelvis into his while he teased me with the lightest of touches.

I heard his voice in my ear. "This isn't what I expected."

I wasn't sure what he meant by that, but everything in his touch, and in the feel of him, told me that if anything surprised him, it wasn't necessarily a bad thing. I moved my own hands lower, rubbing down his backside and upper thighs.

I couldn't stop my own soft muffled moan of anticipation, as he slipped his hands past the waist of my jeans, edging under my panties. Skin on skin. My breath was ragged with excitement, and he'd barely touched me. He gripped a cheek in each hand and squeezed lightly. "I love the way you feel," he said.

Two could play at this game. I moved my hands higher, and reached under his waistband, sliding my hands into the back of his running pants. His ass was rock-hard, with the form of an athlete. I gripped a cheek in each hand and gave a squeeze.

I marveled at his amazing physique and briefly considered that this was the same guy who'd starred in my fantasies for days, weeks even. But now, this was reality, and I gave in to the flood of sensations that overcame me.

I wanted to feel his rock-hard body press into me, feel his strong arms around me, and feel his length inside of me. As I felt his arousal press between my thighs, I felt in danger of bursting with excitement. I wanted to feel him inside of me, to feel him thrust in and out of me, and to feel his hips grind against mine as he filled me completely.

With reluctance, I scooted backward and sat up. Meeting his gaze, I gripped the hem of my T-shirt. Slowly, savoring the lust in his eyes, I lifted the T-shirt over my head and tossed it on the floor. I was still wearing my bra, but the passion in his eyes made me feel beyond naked.

"Damn, you're sexy," he said.

Whether it was true or not, the look in his eyes, and the sound of his voice, told me that he believed it. And for the moment, that was all that mattered.

"Now you," I whispered.

Grinning, he sat back and pulled his T-shirt up over his head, taking his time, just like I had, revealing more of himself to me. I drank in the sight of him, savoring the look of his flat, muscular abs, his tattooed torso, his muscular chest, and finally, his gorgeous face.

I'd never seen anything so magnificent in my whole life as Lawton Rastor half-naked in the firelight. I ran my hands lightly down the front of him, starting at his perfect pecs and working my way down to the waistband of his running pants.

I felt him fumbling with the clasp of my bra. When he had it free, he leaned back and drank me in with his eyes before leaning forward to take a nipple into his warm mouth. Under the attention of his tongue, the nipple came to life, growing harder and needier with every motion. I couldn't help it. I arched my back in pleasure, soft moans and sighs escaping my parted lips.

He placed his hand on my other breast, trailing his fingers over its roundness. He circled the flesh again and again until he zeroed in on my waiting nipple. He rolled the sensitive knob between his fingers, and it came to life in his hands.

Murmuring against my skin, he let the first nipple fall from his warm mouth and turned to taste the nipple that waited.

Moving with him, I knelt up on the couch, my legs slightly parted. His fingers trailed lower and lower until they reached the waist of my panties. He pushed them down inch by inch, as if savoring the feel of his rough hands on my smooth skin as he continued to tease my hardened nipple with his moist tongue.

Soon, my panties rested just below my hips. He reached lower, cupping my ass with his rough hands, squeezed tenderly as he ran circles around my nipple with his hot tongue.

His hands roamed to my sides, and he gripped my hips. My pelvis was gyrating in time to my own breathing, which was coming faster and faster as he zeroed in closer and closer to the hot, moist area between my thighs.

I ached for him. I ached for him so bad that when his hand reached its destination, I couldn't help it. I gave a moan of encouragement and pressed against his hand. Something – his thumb, maybe – rubbed against that hot knob of desire, and I thought I'd climax right then and there.

I pressed my lips to his neck, drinking in the scent and feel of him.

He slid a long finger inside me, twisting his finger inside me and rubbing my clitoris with his thumb. I leaned my head back and sighed, murmuring incoherent words of encouragement.

He withdrew his finger slightly, and then pressed it in again.

"I love how you sound, how you feel," he said, circling that little knob of pleasure with his thumb. "You're so responsive, so irresistible. God, I've wanted this – wanted you – so bad, you have no idea."

"Oh yes, I do," I said, gripping the waistband of his briefs. I tugged them down until he was completely free of the confining fabric. My hands found his rigid tool, stroking and caressing it until his moans matched my own.

"Oh Chloe," he said in a muffled groan.

The sound of my name on his lips did crazy things do my insides, even crazier that what his touch was doing, and that was saying something.

He took me in his arms and lowered me gently back onto the couch. As he looked down on me, our gazes met and held. He freed himself completely from his briefs and turned to my panties.

Slowly, as if savoring each moment, he pulled them lower and lower until I was completely naked.

"Hang on," he said.

"For what?" I asked, my voice sleepy with desire.

From somewhere near the couch, he pulled out a small, foil package and started to open it.

"Oh, that?" I gave him a sheepish grin. How had I ever forgotten? I might have blamed the vodka, but in truth Lawton was ten times more intoxicating. I took the package from his hand and pulled out the condom. "Here," I said. "Lemme do it."

He didn't argue, and I slid the sheer covering onto his substantial length, caressing him as I went, until his eyes were closed and his lips parted. When I finished, he opened his eyes and gave me a look of such unbridled desire that almost by instinct, I lay back again, my thighs parting as if they had a mind of their own.

"You're so beautiful," he said.

"So are you," I said.

With a soft chuckle, he ran a finger along my slick opening, teasing, caressing until I thought I'd go crazy with wanting him. And then finally, he lowered himself down toward me. I thrust my hips upward in anticipation and placed my hand on his length, guiding him closer and closer to my hot, wet opening.

When the tip reached its destination, I gave a moan of pleasure. Lawton held himself still, looking down on me with hot, hungry eyes.

"I want this to last forever," he said.

Trembling, I felt a slow smile build. "Then don't make me

wait." I leaned back and lifted my hips, urging him onward.

Thrusting his hips slowly forward, he entered me just enough to make me want to scream for more.

"You're so hot," he murmured into my hair. "I know I should go slow, but – "

"Don't stop," I urged, my voice trembling nearly as much as my body.

To my infinite pleasure, he complied with my wishes, slowly thrusting his hips forward until inch by inch, he filled me completely. As our hips pressed together, he locked his arms around me, as if savoring the moment. His lips found my neck, and he nibbled lightly on my earlobe and caressed my neck with his tongue.

Soon, our hips were moving in unison. I reached up and ran my fingers through his thick hair, enjoying how it felt around my fingers as we moved together in ways that had me feeling more complete than I ever had in my whole life.

He knew just what to do to please a girl, thrusting in time with my motions and maintaining a pace that kept me ever on the edge of climax. As he continued to thrust in and out, I gave up trying to maintain any dignity.

The sounds I made, well, I knew they'd embarrass me if I thought about it, but I couldn't think about it. My hips rose up again and again, meeting him thrust for thrust, kiss for kiss. My hands roamed over his back, caressing his skin, kneading his buttocks, and encouraging him further.

I couldn't help but marvel at the way his sinewy muscles shifted and moved in time with his motions, at the way his rock-hard buttocks contracted with each thrust, and the way his lips teased and tantalized my neck and earlobe.

As we continued our ride of passion, he wrapped his strong arms around me and somehow, even on the sofa, managed to roll us both over, placing me on top. With him still buried inside me, I sat up straight, only barely conscious of the fact that I was naked and wild, riding him like there was no tomorrow.

I couldn't help it. I threw my head back, letting my lips part and breasts thrust forward. My eyes were shut, but I felt him reach up with both hands and caress my fullness as I moved my hips in circular motions. Faster and faster, I ground my hips into his, making his length dance inside me until I couldn't hold back any longer.

With a flood of sighs and hot wetness, I reached my peak, driving Lawton to reach his own. As we moved together, relishing the final throes of passion, our moans and sighs filled the room from wall to wall.

Finally, I collapsed in a heap on top of him, relishing the feel of his strong arms around me, and his hot skin against mine.

A few minutes later, we lay naked in front of the fire. Somehow, we'd gone from the sofa to the rug, which was a lot softer than it looked.

"Nice rug." I gave him a sleepy grin. "I bet you bought it just for interludes."

"Haven't you heard?" he said, running a warm hand along the side of my face. "You're no interlude."

I laughed. "I bet you say that to all your interludes."

"You want me to be honest?" he said. "I've wanted you, and not just like this either, since the first moment I saw you." He leaned forward to press his lips to my forehead. "But that doesn't make you an interlude." His lips travelled from my forehead to that tender spot just behind my ear. "No. You're something else, Chloe."

"So are you," I said, not bothering to analyze his words or mine. It felt too good to analyze. And when he started nibbling at my neck, and worked his way down to my nipples, then my stomach, and lower still, it felt too good to think about anything.

By the time the morning sun filtered through the blinds, I'd climaxed so many times that my stomach literally ached. And I wasn't the only one. During the night, I'd given in to almost every fantasy I'd ever had. I'd tasted and caressed him in all the ways I'd been dreaming about, and it felt so right that I knew it wasn't the vodka driving me on.

It was him.

The fire had long since died down to a bed of embers, but the heat still radiated off it in waves. And even if it had gone stone cold, I didn't want to move. And the funny thing was, he didn't seem inclined to move either.

When I made a half-hearted comment about leaving, he only gripped me tighter, pulling me toward him and wrapping his arms around me so tightly that I felt safe and wanted in a way that was utterly foreign to me. Foreign, but good.

A girl could get used to this.

CHAPTER 41

Slowly, I came awake, only vaguely aware that I wasn't at the Parkers'. I was curled up on a thick, gold rug, facing a huge fireplace, with a warm, hard body spooned around me.

And we were both naked.

I let my gaze drift downward and saw a muscular, tattooed arm resting around my waist, pulling me close, even in sleep.

I recognized that arm, just like I recognized the distinct hardness pressing into my back.

In a rush, memories of the previous night came flooding back to me. At the time, it had felt like a dream. It still felt like a dream. I vaguely recalled seeing the first hint of pale morning light filtering through the high windows at one time or another. But how long ago was that, anyway? Minutes? Hours?

When I tried to sit up, the arm around me tightened. Lawton's sleepy voice whispered in my ear. "Don't go."

I felt myself smile. "I'm not," I said in a voice that was probably just as sleepy. "I just need to check the time."

"Hmmm," he said, as if still asleep, and then, slowly, he loosened his hold and rolled onto his back. "M'kay," he murmured. "But if you don't come back, I'm gonna come lookin' for you."

"Oh, I'll be back," I said, pulling away from him. Without his warm body pressed against me, I instantly felt not just colder, but more naked, and not in a good way. Sitting up, I scanned the room, but I didn't see a clock on the mantle where I'd half-expected to find one.

I looked back to Lawton, intending to ask him where one might be, but his eyes were shut and his breathing steady. Had he fallen back asleep? Or more likely, he hadn't fully woken up in the first place. Erika was like that. She could carry on entire conversations while still asleep and not recall a darn thing later.

I gave Lawton a good, long look. He was no Erika, that's for sure. As I drank in the sight of him, I felt my breath hitch as my gaze lingered on the one part of his anatomy that was decidedly wide awake.

I felt myself smile. Maybe, if it wasn't too late, I'd take a closer look, along with a much closer feel.

I bit my lip. If only I knew what time it was. If it was too late in the morning, I'd need to leave as soon as possible. Chucky needed breakfast, not to mention his morning walk. And whether I was tempted by a beautiful guy or not, I wasn't going to make a little dog pay the price for my own pleasure.

With an effort, I pulled my gaze from Lawton's naked form and got to my feet. I tiptoed across the room and found my jeans, crumpled on the floor next to the sofa. I dug in the pocket and pulled out my cell phone to check the time.

There was only one problem. I wasn't quite sure how to check the time on the thing. On my old phone, the time displayed automatically. On this one, well, I had no idea. Again, I glanced at Lawton. This was silly. I should just wake him up and ask what time it was.

Except I couldn't bring myself to actually do it. He looked so spectacular, and peaceful, just the way he was, with his eyes shut, his lips parted, and – as much as I blushed to dwell on it – a morning erection that probably had little to do with me.

Still, I'd like it to.

I was still fumbling absently with my phone when I heard a soft click. I looked down and felt my eyes widen. Oh God. I'd accidentally taken a picture of Lawton in all his naked glory.

Frantically, I searched for the delete function, but couldn't find it, and honestly, I was afraid to mess with it too much. The last thing I needed was to accidentally text the picture to all my friends and relatives.

Granted, it was a small list, but given the nature of the image, one misdirected nakedgram was one too many. Cursing, I continued to fumble with the controls, and I never did find the delete function. I did, however, finally manage to check the time and wasn't happy with what I saw.

It was almost ten o'clock in the morning, at least an hour past the time I should've fed Chucky. Torn between guilt and the urge to crawl back into Lawton's arms, I scanned the room, spotting my panties somewhere behind the sofa and the rest of my missing clothes scattered nearby. I tugged on my undergarments and crept over to where Lawton slept.

I knelt down beside him. "Lawton?" I whispered.

"Hmmmm?"

"Sorry, but I've gotta go."

"No," he murmured, without opening his eyes. "C'mon, baby. Stay. Alright?"

I felt myself smile. Even if he wasn't awake, it was nice to be wanted. "I wish I could," I whispered. "But Chucky's waiting."

"Good dog," he murmured, and rolled onto his side with his eyes still shut and lips parted in a way that made me want to kiss him all over again.

If I had my way, that's exactly what I'd be doing later.

Still smiling, I got up, pulled on the rest of my clothes, and left quietly through the front door.

CHAPTER 42

The next couple weeks were absolutely crazy – and absolutely blissful. Chucky and I spent almost every day with Lawton, watching comedies and action movies in his massive media room, playing fetch on his manicured lawn, chasing each other from one end of the house to the other.

Honestly, I was worried about wearing out my welcome, but every time I mentioned spending more time away from him, Lawton found another way to entice us to stay. There was always a new movie that needed watching, a new hot tub that needed breaking in, or a new grill that needed to be inaugurated.

Technically, none of those things were new, not exactly, but they were new to me, and from what I could tell, Lawton enjoyed my reaction to all of it.

I still hadn't quite told him I was merely the house sitter, but he stopped pressing me about who I lived with, and I stopped worrying about pretending to be someone I wasn't.

When he joked that I was probably some surgeon's love-child, I only smiled and shrugged. Then, I distracted him the best way I knew how, and it didn't involve breaching my client's confidentiality. When the Parkers returned, I figured I could tell Lawton everything, but until then, it just seemed wrong, especially with Lawton's brother prone to entering places without permission.

When I told him about my waitressing job, he didn't take it the way I expected. For some reason, he assumed I was doing it more for the fun than for the money. I guess I could see why. The job did have a sort of celebrity status, but honestly, if Lawton had ever worked as a server, he'd know just how ridiculous that assumption was.

No one, and I mean no one, would work as a waitress if they didn't need the money. Funny too, because the job attracted more than its share of rich girls – girls who didn't need the money, but were drawn in by the glamorous idea that it didn't require actual work.

They never lasted. Then again, who was I to talk? I wasn't going to last either. Not much longer anyway.

Lucky for me, the volcanic flu was still making the rounds at the diner, so Keith couldn't fire me just yet. I was racking up some serious hours, working double-shifts whenever I could.

With the extra money, I paid for the broken car window, along with the new cell phone, and still I managed to stash away some cash for the day the job finally ended. In the meantime, I was looking for something new.

A couple weeks after first sleeping with Lawton, he made a strange announcement. "I'm being a total ass."

We were sitting in his hot tub, soaking up the steamy warmth while the cold November air kept our faces cool and then some.

"How so?" I asked.

He gave me that special smile, the one that melted my heart and turned my insides to jelly. "Because I've been keeping you all to myself."

I felt myself grow very still. Was he talking multiple partners? Filling his house with groupies and hangers-on? Passing me on to his brother? I wasn't sure what, exactly, he was talking about, but whatever it was, I didn't think I was interested.

I kept my tone studiously neutral. "What do you mean?"

He studied my face. "Well, obviously, not what you think."

"What do you mean?"

"You were thinking," he said, shifting his body closer to mine, "that I'd ever consider sharing you." I felt his hand on my thigh and his hip pressed against mine. He leaned close to whisper in my ear. "Let's get one thing straight. I'm never, ever sharing you."

I felt myself smile. "Oh yeah?"

"Oh yeah. You're all mine, and I intend to keep it that way."

The way he said it sent a bolt of heat straight into my core. I didn't want to share him either. I wanted things to stay exactly as they were.

I wanted to sleep in his arms and wake up sated. I wanted to hear him laugh and watch him sweat, both in the workout room and when we were naked, which was, to be honest, embarrassingly often. I wanted to watch bad movies and enjoy all those great make-out sessions in our own private world. I wanted a string of tomorrows just like today.

Maybe I was being foolish, but at heart, I wasn't a fool. Obviously, things couldn't stay exactly like this. Eventually, the real world would interfere, or as Lawton's dick of a brother had so nicely implied, Lawton would lose interest in whatever it was that we had.

If I were smart, I'd lose interest first. But somehow, I was never able to do it. Instead, the days had passed one after another with virtually no friction, well, unless you counted the physical kind, and that was definitely no drawback.

Soaking in the hot tub, his hand drifting up and down my

thigh reminded me of how intoxicating his particular brand of friction could be.

"So what do you think?" he said.

"Hmmmm?"

He laughed. "Am I wrong to keep you all to myself?"

"Hey," I said, "I thought you didn't want to share."

"No sharing," he said, "but you know what I just realized?"

"What?"

"I've never even taken you out, like on a real date. Aren't you pissed? You should be."

I gave it some thought. He'd bought us dinner countless times from upscale places that I didn't even know delivered. He'd taken me to the movies right in his own house. He'd powered up his sound system and slow danced with me until I'd melted straight into him.

It was like Heaven on Earth, and we were the only two people in it. Well, us and Chucky. I was juggling a lot, it was true, between the waitressing, time with Lawton, and making sure to spend enough time at the Parkers' to fulfill my obligations.

I shook my head. "That other stuff isn't really important to me."

"But what about dinner, clubbing, all that, don't you want it?"

"Truthfully?" I said. "I've kind of liked things the way they are."

Aside from the luxury of having Lawton all to myself, hanging out at his house was beyond amazing. He had a long list of luxuries, and a regular cleaning service that kept us from doing hardly any housework at all. His brother was blissfully absent, and I saw no sign of Brittney, Amber, or any of the other hangers-on that I'd been expecting to see any minute.

He leaned his head close to mine, and I felt his lips brush against my damp hair. "Yeah," he said. "I've liked it this way too.

But I don't feel like I'm being fair to you."

"Why not?" I asked.

"Because you deserve all that. To go places, to be seen, all that stuff. I've carted around other girls —" He shrugged. "It's just that you deserve all that and more."

I tried not to think about other girls. So instead, I focused on the other stuff.

"Are you kidding?" I lifted a hand to encompass his back patio, which was probably nicer than most world-class resorts. "This is like a permanent vacation." As soon as that word – permanent – came out of my mouth, I felt a tinge of embarrassment creep across me.

I forced out a laugh. "Not to say I plan on hanging out here forever. I mean, I know you've got other things going on." I stood. "You know, thinking about it, I really need to get going. I've got to work in just a couple hours."

He remained seated, looking up at me with amused eyes. "That's it," he announced. "Friday night it is."

"What about Friday night?"

"I'm taking you out." He reached up to pull me back down, wrapping his arms around me as he spoke softly into my ear. "You're getting stir-crazy. I can tell."

"I am not," I said.

"Uh-huh," he said. "You still have this Friday off?"

I nodded. Usually, I got one Friday night off a month, and that was it.

"Good," he said. "Seven o'clock. I'm gonna pick you up, just like a real date."

I grinned at him. "Yeah?" Even though it wasn't what I'd been craving, the idea was oddly appealing. For some reason, I never imagined him on a traditional date. This would definitely be interesting. "Do you know," I said, almost as an afterthought,

"Saturday's my birthday?"

"It is?" he said. "No kidding?"

"No kidding."

"Then let's make it Saturday instead. We'll celebrate in style."

I sighed. "I wish I could. But I'm scheduled to work."

"So, blow it off," he said.

I gave him a sideways glance. "Easy for you to say."

"What's that supposed to mean?"

"As far as I can tell, you don't do any work at all."

At this, he actually laughed in my face. "That's what you think?"

"Isn't it the truth?"

"No," he said. "I probably work about sixty, maybe eighty hours a week."

I rolled my eyes. "You do not."

He shrugged.

"You don't, do you?" I persisted.

He shrugged again.

"Oh c'mon," I said. "Tell me."

"Alright," he said. "Yeah, it's the truth. But it's not like I put on a suit and tie and go into the office or anything."

"Do you even have an office?" I asked.

"Yeah," he said. "In downtown Detroit."

"Yikes."

"In the nice part," he clarified.

"There's a nice part?" I'd been downtown enough to know that there were some nice parts. It's just that usually, you had to go through some distinctly un-nice parts to get there. "But seriously," I continued, "We've spent practically every day together. When would you have time to work?"

"As soon as you leave."

"You can't be serious."

"Totally serious," he said. "I used to work days. Now, I work nights, mostly from home. No big deal."

I rolled my eyes. "Yeah, no big deal. What exactly do you do, anyway?"

"You're changing the subject," he said.

"There was a subject?"

He nodded. "You, me, Friday night. We'll celebrate your birthday early."

I gave him a wicked grin. "Should I wear my birthday suit?"

"Definitely," he said. "Just not in public. Unless you're ready to witness a good old-fashioned ass-kicking."

"Hey!" I said.

"Oh, it's not your ass I'm talking about." He pressed his lips to my neck. "It's the guys who'd be ogling it."

"Hmmm," I said. "Maybe I'll wear sweatpants."

"Baby," he said, "whatever you've got on, you'll look great to me."

I laughed. "I wasn't really gonna wear sweatpants."

"Good," he said, "because I wasn't really gonna pick you up at eight."

I pulled back to squint at him. "Huh?"

"I don't think I can wait that long. Let's make it six."

CHAPTER 43

"What do you mean you can't go out?" Erika said. It was Wednesday afternoon, and she'd just called to make plans for the weekend. "It's your birthday," she continued, "And it's a Saturday. You're turning twenty-three, not a hundred."

"Are you sure?" I asked. "Because I'm pretty sure I spotted a gray hair last week."

"Oh shut up," she said. "If you don't end up totally shitfaced by midnight, they'll revoke my best friend card. C'mon!"

I listened with a smile, touched that Erika would make a special trip home just to celebrate my birthday. "I wish I could," I told her, "But I've got to work that night."

"On your birthday? Seriously? Get someone to switch with you."

"I can't," I said. "The flu is going around the diner, and half the girls are out of commission. I'll probably end up working a double shift as it is."

"Maybe you should get sick too," she said, "if you know what I mean."

She sounded just like Lawton. And just like with Lawton, the offer was tempting, but I just couldn't. It would only strain my co-workers further. And I knew all too well how stressful that would be. Business didn't stop just because half the staff was home in bed. And besides, my time at the diner was quickly running out.

"I wish I could," I said, feeling a different kind of guilt. "I'm really sorry."

"Then how about Friday?" she said.

"Sorry," I said, "I can't."

"You working Friday too?"

"Not exactly," I said.

"Holy crap," she said. "You've got a date."

"Gee, you don't have to sound so surprised about it."

"Am I surprised that someone asked you out? No. But am I surprised you actually said yes? Yeah. Definitely."

I had to laugh. "I'm not that picky."

"Yes you are," she said, "and too damn busy for your own good. So, who's the guy?"

"Well," I said, "remember—"

"Wait," she said. "Don't tell me. Save it for Saturday. I want to see your face when you give me all the juicy details."

"But I'm not seeing you Saturday," I said.

She laughed. "Oh, yes you are. You're not getting off that easy. How about I'll bring the party to you? What time do you leave for work?"

I was working the graveyard shift. "A little after ten," I told her, "but – "

"Perfect," she said. "I'll swing by your house-sitting gig at seven."

"But I'm not supposed to – "

"Yeah, no parties where you're staying, I know. Don't worry," she said. "It'll just be me. Something nice and simple. A girls' night. Sound okay?"

I felt myself smile. "It sounds more than okay. It sounds awesome. Want me to make dinner?"

"Screw that," Erika said. "You're the birthday girl, remember? I'm bringing the thing that's definitely not a party to you."

CHAPTER 44

When Lawton picked me up on Friday night, I felt strangely self-conscious. I'd dug out my favorite cocktail dress, a short, black strapless number that I'd gotten for a steal at a consignment shop. The dress was obviously expensive, or at least it had been for its original owner, whoever that girl might've been.

The shoes were a different story. They matched the dress only in the sense they were black with a daring level of heel, but they were anything but expensive. I didn't care. And if the look on Lawton's face was any indicator, shoes were the last thing on his mind when I opened the Parkers' front door.

"Wow," he said, a slow grin spreading across his face. "You look –" He sucked in a breath as his gaze ran the length of me. "Wow," he said again. "You look amazing."

"Thanks," I said, my voice a little breathy, both from the look in his eyes and what he was wearing. Until now, I'd only seen him in casual clothes, or – I smiled to think of it – nothing at all.

Sure, I'd seen pictures of him on the Internet, dressed up for a night of clubbing or whatever – but in person, the vision before me was another animal entirely.

He wore black tailored slacks and a V-neck silvery shirt, set off by a sleek black blazer and designer shoes. His hair was as unruly as ever, but it only made his clothes look that much more sexy, like he was dressed for success, but ready for sin.

"You look pretty amazing yourself," I said, giving him a good, long look. "So what's the plan?"

"The plan," he said, pulling me close to whisper in my ear, "is to make it a night to remember."

The whisper turned into a kiss, which for me, turned into thoughts of rushing back to his place for an appetizer of the physical variety. "Are you sure you wanna go out?" I teased, running a hand slowly over his jawline.

I was only half-kidding. At his place, I knew what I'd find. Pure bliss. I wouldn't have to worry about my too-cheap shoes or too-small cubic zirconia earrings. I wouldn't have to worry that I was too quiet or too loud.

And honestly, I was just the teeniest bit nervous. In some ways, this felt like a first date, filled with all the unknowns, good and bad.

For a couple of weeks now, I'd been dating the boy next door – this incredibly sweet guy who had walked my dog and carried me shirtless across his lawn. He plied me with popcorn and woke me with kisses. We shared a fence, a love of comedies, and a loathing of seafood.

His public persona was very different. That guy wasn't mine. The boy next door was, or at least it felt that way.

After tonight, would I see him the same way? More to the point, how would he see me? I wasn't a Brittney. I wouldn't dance on the table or squeal like a groupie. No, if I squealed near Lawton, it was for reasons entirely unrelated to his celebrity status.

On the Parkers' front steps, my question hung in the air.

Maybe Lawton was having second thoughts about going out too.

As I stroked his jaw, he closed his eyes, and his lips parted ever so slightly. And then, as if the action took far more effort than it should have, he pulled away. "Hell yeah, I want to go out." He reached up to his face, placing his hand over mine. "It's your birthday, remember?"

"Not until tomorrow," I reminded him. "

"Then we'll celebrate at midnight," he said.

Out in the driveway, a car was waiting for us, but it wasn't his usual hot-rod. It was a sleek, black limo sport utility vehicle with tinted windows and a smartly dressed driver, who opened a rear door and closed it behind us after we settled ourselves inside.

Alone with Lawton, I edged close to him and leaned over to whisper in his ear. "Can I confess something?"

"Anything."

"This reminds me of prom."

He laughed. "Yeah?"

"A little," I said. "Except we didn't have a limo." I eyed the setup in front of us. "Or a fully stocked bar." I grinned over at him. "Hey, is that champagne?"

"Oh yeah. It's a celebration." He put an arm around me, pulling me close. "My girl's birthday.

The way he said "my girl" sent a happy tingle from my ears straight down to my toes, stopping at a couple of key places along the way. "Your girl, huh?"

"Yeah." His gaze met mine, and I found myself lost in the moment, oblivious to everything but him, and the restrained intensity of his words as he added, "If I have anything to say about it."

Slowly, I nodded, forgetting that he hadn't exactly phrased it as a question. I felt my tongue dart out between my lips for the briefest instant before I caught myself. If my thoughts kept going

SABRINA STARK

on their current trajectory, we'd never make it out of the limo.

He leaned forward to pour us each a glass. "To you," he said, before giving my champagne glass a little clink with his own and downing the whole glass in one, long drink.

"Wow," I said. I wasn't much of a drinker, but the champagne was too fabulous to resist. It took me a little longer, but I drank until my own glass was empty and then grinned up at him. "So why the limo?" I asked.

He met my smile. "Aside from the fact it's a celebration?"

I nodded.

"How about this?" he said, leaning back against the leather seat. "I'm gonna skip answering just yet. At the end of the night, maybe you can tell me."

I narrowed my gaze in mock suspicion. "So there's gonna be a quiz? No one said anything about a quiz."

He leaned his head close to mine until our foreheads were touching. "Lemme give you one reason right now." His arms closed tight around me, and a moment later, our lips met softly at first and then not so softly.

I ran a hand behind his neck, feeling the thick strands of his hair sift over my fingertips as I savored the feel of his lips on mine.

When he pulled away, I was breathless and hungry for more.

"See?" he said.

"What?"

"Why it's better if I'm not driving."

"Actually," I said, "I didn't quite get that. Would you mind repeating it?"

So he did. Again and again.

What can I say? I'm a slow learner.

CHAPTER 45

Between long, lingering kisses and sips of champagne, I watched the landscape change around us from suburbia to highway and finally to an urban cityscape.

Soon, we were in the heart of downtown Detroit, passing ornate brick and stone architecture from the city's glory days. It was interspersed with signs of urban decay – a gas station with long-outdated prices, a boarded-up building that covered an entire city block, a burned-out car that hadn't been hauled away.

"It's not as bad as I expected," I said as we passed a bustling nightclub with a long line of stylishly dressed patrons waiting outside the main entrance.

"You don't ever come down here?" he asked.

"Not usually," I said. "At least, not so much anymore." I grew up in Hamtramck, a city almost completely surrounded by Detroit. In high school, I'd gone downtown every once in a while to hit Greektown or a museum, but mostly I stuck to the suburbs.

"Well, it's like anyplace else," Lawton said. "You got your nice parts and your not-so-nice parts."

I gave him a sideways glance. "Which part are you from?"

He was quiet for a moment as his gaze drifted past the tinted window, where an empty lot was littered with broken beer bottles. It was sandwiched between two massive office buildings, unlit and apparently unoccupied. "It wasn't the nice part," he said.

From the tone of his voice, it was pretty obvious that particular topic was closed, at least for tonight. It was probably for the best. Half-drunk with champagne and kisses, I'd never do any serious conversation justice.

I snuggled up close to him, feeling the hard muscles of his body shift subtly with every moment he made, whether to refill my champagne glass or to turn and look out the window.

Together, we watched the cityscape slide past us until we stopped in front of a gleaming, circular tower bathed in the blue and orange glow of sleek accent lighting and rows of well-lit windows.

Surrounding the tower were buildings of a similar, if slightly less, towering caliber.

"The Renaissance Center?" I said, although I knew exactly where we were. I'd been here before, although not very often. I sifted through my memories, recalling a Saturday afternoon shopping, and then another ill-fated afternoon at the movies with Josh. I'd lost my car keys and ended up having to beg my Mom to come get us.

She hadn't. All I can say is thank Heaven for Erika's parents.

Unlike that ill-fated afternoon, tonight I wasn't a pauper begging for a ride. Well, okay, I was still sort of a pauper. But I didn't feel like one tonight. I was with Lawton, and limo or not, I knew I didn't need to worry about how I'd make it back.

Somehow I knew that even if the limo went up in flames, or we were stranded somewhere off Eight Mile, everything would be okay, if for no other reason than I wasn't in any of this alone.

It was a good feeling.

That good feeling only got better on the seventy-second floor, where we dined and drank from a vantage point that was simply mind-blowing, with spectacular views that took my breath away nearly as much as the view of Lawton, sitting across from me, looking good enough to eat.

Based on not-so-subtle glances from the women at neighboring tables, I knew wasn't the only one who thought so. I tried not to notice when a table of three women, obviously out for a girl's night, ogled him with enough enthusiasm to make me want to march over there and slap them silly.

What was I saying? Slap them silly? That wasn't me. I wasn't the jealous type. Besides, I could see why they ogled him. Cripes, I wanted to ogle him.

Probably, I was ogling him.

I turned my shoulders away from the women, choosing to study the magnificent view outside rather than watch three bimbos drool over my date.

Okay, they weren't exactly bimbos. They looked like professional women. Still…

Stop thinking about them, I told myself. He's with you, not with them. I turned my gaze to Lawton, studying the dessert menu. If he noticed the women or their interest in him, he gave no indication.

As if feeling my eyes on him, he looked up. Our gazes held, and he smiled like there was no one else in the world but me.

Glancing out the window, I said, "Detroit sure does look a lot different from up here, doesn't it?"

He set aside the menu. "Got that right," he said in a tone that suggested he wasn't only talking about the view.

I studied him over the rim of my champagne class. He looked perfectly at ease in his expensive clothes and luxurious surroundings. From what I'd read, his life had changed an awful lot in a relatively short time. How long had it taken him to get used to the good life?

Maybe he still wasn't used to it.

Was he faking it? I faked it pretty good myself. Was I faking it now in my secondhand dress and cheap shoes? No, I decided. I wasn't. Tonight, for whatever reason, I didn't feel like an imposter. I felt like just a girl on a date with a beautiful guy in a beautiful place.

When one of the women got up and walked slowly past our table, her hips swaying as she gave Lawton a long, lingering look, I changed my mind. Turns out, I was the jealous type. Oh yeah, and she was a bimbo. Definitely.

But her effort was for nothing. Lawton's gaze rested firmly on me as he held my hand across the table.

The view below us was undeniably spectacular. It wasn't just of the Detroit cityscape, which looked a whole lot better from this vantage point, but also of the bridge to Canada, where the city lights of Windsor reflected before us on the Detroit River.

But honestly, the thing that really took my breath away was Lawton. I was falling for him. Falling for him hard. Sometimes, I thought he felt the same way, but then I'd remember all those girls. They had fought over him. And not just with words.

Had he made them feel special the way he made me feel special? It would be hard to resist something like that, especially packaged with his amazing looks and undeniable success.

When we left, hand-in-hand after Lawton paid the bill, I could barely remember what I'd ordered, or how it tasted.

But I did remember the feel of his hand in mine as we rode the glass elevator down, seeing the ground get closer and closer every second, and the look in his eyes when he told me he'd waited too long to show me off.

I'd laughed. "Show me off? For who?"

"For me." He lowered his voice. "Because I gotta tell you, the thought of anyone else looking at you –" He shook his head. "Not good."

I rolled my eyes. "Oh please, the way all those women looked at you in there, I don't think you're the one who's got to worry."

He grinned. "You worry?"

"No," I mumbled, looking down at my shoes. Now that I studied them in these surroundings, they really did look cheap. I looked up and met Lawton's gaze. "Well, not really."

"Trust me," he said, leaning in close. "You don't have anything to worry about. Besides, I didn't see any other women in there."

"Yeah, right."

"But I did see a lot of guys checking you out." His voice was quiet. "Lucky all they did was look."

"Oh please," I said. "No one was looking at me."

"You just keep right on thinking that," he said. "Come to think of it, it's probably a good thing."

"What do you mean?" I asked.

"I mean," he said, meeting my gaze, "that if you don't notice them looking, odds are, you won't be giving them any looks back." And then he kissed me, a long, lingering kiss that made me nearly as breathless as the downward motion of the elevator.

CHAPTER 46

As the night progressed, his decision to take a limo made more and more sense. We didn't have to stumble through some parking garage, looking for our car. We didn't have to worry about how much we drank, which was considerable, or which road to turn on as we navigated the city.

We went from dinner to a casino in Greektown, where he taught me how to play craps and blackjack, sometimes winning, sometimes losing, but always together, hand-in-hand, except when throwing the dice.

Around ten o'clock, we left Greektown and made our way to the same night club we'd passed on our way to dinner.

I'd already had way too much to drink, and my head was positively spinning.

When we pulled up, the line at the door was, if anything, even longer. People jostled each other in the chilly air as they stood under the long awning, waiting for someone inside to leave so they could get in.

I bit my lip, wishing I'd thought to bring a coat.

"Don't worry," he said, "we're not doing that."

"Doing what?" I said.

"Waiting in line."

I squinted up at him. "We're not?"

"Hell no," he said. "I got reservations."

I looked out at the crowd. "They take reservations?"

"Yeah. Watch."

We stepped out, and Lawton took my hand. Good thing, considering I might've been the teeniest bit wobbly on my feet at this point. He led us to the front of the line. "We got reservations," he told the guy at the door, a beefy guy wearing some sort of electronic headset.

"Hey," yelled a guy near the front of the line. "Buddy, haven't you heard? They don't take reservations."

Lawton didn't spare him a glance as the guy at the door looked at Lawton and then at me.

Then the guy smiled. "Come on in, Mister Rastor. Got your table all ready."

As we passed, Lawton handed him a folded bill, and not a small one either. The pattern continued as a woman in a tight red dress led us up a corded-off stairway to a VIP section, high above the dance floor. The sound pulsed through the place, making me move in time with the beat even as we settled into a comfortable booth, perfect for watching the action down below.

I leaned in close to whisper in his ear. "Mister Rastor? Well, aren't you civilized?"

He looked at me with hungry eyes. "Don't bet on it," he said.

When a tall redhead came to take our drink order, I glanced at Lawton. "I'm not sure I should have anything else to drink."

"Whatever you want, baby," he said. "You wanna order a Coke, go ahead. Or we can get out of here, head back to the house. Or wherever you want."

The music was hypnotic, with a steady beat that just begged to be danced to. "I don't want to leave," I told him. I turned to the waitress. "I'll have a daiquiri," I said. "Heavy on –" I bit my lip "– whatever isn't the alcohol part."

After she left, Lawton wrapped his arms around me and pulled me close. "Don't you serve drinks where you work?" he said.

"Sort of," I said. "But I don't make any of them. Mostly, I just relay whatever to the bartenders, then just drop it off."

He glanced down toward the dance floor. It was jam-packed with gyrating bodies. I saw arms raised, hips moving, hair flying. I hadn't done a lot of clubbing, even in college. Between working most weekends and my constant money shortage, it hadn't been a high priority.

But looking down at that crowd, I wanted to be part of it.

"You wanna dance?" he asked.

I nodded.

He took me by the hand and pulled me up from the booth. Hand-in-hand, we made our way to the dance floor and waded into it. He wrapped his arms around me, and we started gyrating to the steady beat.

It felt amazing. He felt amazing. Moving against him made me think of all the things we'd done in private, and all the things I'd like to do again. I threw back my head and gazed up at him as we moved in time to the music. Around us, people were watching. I didn't care.

We stayed out there for the next song, and the next after that. Then the music abruptly changed, to a slow, hypnotic song. I fell into his arms and floated into sweet bliss as he kissed me long and hard, his tongue snaking into my mouth, and mine into his.

The rest of the night was a blur of dancing and daiquiris. Of watching from above and wading through the crowd. Of feeling his lips on mine, and his strong arms shielding me from the crowd. Good thing, considering the place was packed, and I was getting more unsteady as the night wore on.

At midnight, he led me back to our table and gave me a small box wrapped in silver paper. In it was a stunning pair of diamond earrings. I hardly recall what I said. It seemed far too extravagant, but the look in his eyes told me I couldn't refuse. I was glad. Honestly, I wasn't sure I could have.

I put them on, right then and there, tucking the ones I'd been wearing into the box and handing it to Lawton for safekeeping. I don't know why I bothered. It's not like they were worth stealing, but I wasn't the type to waste anything, even if what I'd just gotten was so much nicer.

All in all, it was the best birthday ever. A night to remember, just like he'd promised.

Within the club, Lawton and I were inseparable. Even when going to the ladies room, he insisted on escorting me.

I remember smiling up at him. "Why?" I asked. "Because of the daiquiris? You worried I'll pass out under some table, and you won't find me 'til morning?"

"Nah, that's not it," he said as ne navigated me through the crowd. "On second thought," he said, as I stumbled a little over my own feet, "Yeah, I guess there's some truth to that. But mostly, I'm not gonna let you out of my sight. Not in this place."

"What's the matter?" I teased. "Don't trust me?"

"I trust you just fine, baby," he said. "It's those other guys I worry about."

I laughed. "There's no other guys."

"Yeah, I believe that," he said in a tone that suggested just the opposite.

At the hallway to the ladies room, I turned to him. 'I think I can handle it from here."

"You sure?" he said, giving me a wicked grin.

"Oh stop," I said, smiling up at him. "I'll be right back."

In the restroom, I did my business, then freshened up my lipstick. Why, I didn't know. If I were lucky, I'd be smearing it the second I ran into Lawton. His lips were a temptation I simply couldn't resist, much like the rest of him.

Stumbling maybe just a little, I made my way out of the ladies' room and looked to where he said he'd be waiting.

He wasn't there.

CHAPTER 47

I looked around, momentarily confused. Sure, I didn't really need an escort or anything. I was a big girl, perfectly capable of getting from point A to point B without a bodyguard or tour guide. But still, it seemed odd. Why would he be so insistent on coming with me, only to leave me wondering where he was?

When I didn't see him, I started wading unsteadily through the crowd toward the stairway leading to the VIP section. Walking, I peered upward, but didn't see Lawton at our table. Maybe he'd gone to the men's room?

I turned around, deciding I'd wait for him in the original spot. I was halfway there when I heard something that stopped me cold in my tracks. It was a male voice, hollering out from somewhere off to my left. "Hey! Dog girl!"

I whirled around, scanning the crowd.

"Over here!" the same voice called again.

Sure enough, there he was, one of player wannabes who'd been with Brittney and Amber that awful night at the restaurant. He was dressed the same as before. The only thing louder than his voice was his shirt, some black and gold sleeveless thing, no doubt designed to show off his overgrown muscles.

"All bling and no brains," I muttered, moving faster toward the hallway, determined to avoid him. I was nearly there when I felt a hard tug on my elbow. I whirled to see the player latched onto me like he had no plans of letting go any time soon.

His smile was a little off-kilter. "Aw c'mon, don't be like that." His gaze scanned me up and down. "Damn girl, I thought your work getup was hot, but you're double-smokin' now." He turned his cheek to the side. "C'mon, give me some sugar."

Ick.

Unsteadily, I shrugged off his arm. "I'm meeting someone," I said. "Go away."

"Now, that's just fuckin' rude," he said.

I glared at him. "Hey, you haven't seen rude. Where's your friend?"

"Why? You looking for a threesome?"

Double ick. "Seriously," I said. "Go away. Find your friend. Leave. Whatever. Just stay the hell away from me, alright?"

Over the guy's shoulder, I finally saw Lawton, wading through the crowd toward us. His jaw was tight and his expression dark. The player turned around to follow my gaze, and when he did, he visibly swallowed.

"Your loss," the guy muttered, and waded into the crowd, not exactly disappearing, but moving fast enough that he might as well have.

A moment later, Lawton was at my side. "You okay?" he asked.

I nodded. "Yeah, sure."

"Who was the guy?"

There were so many things I could've said. He's Brittney's second-choice squeeze. He's a pig. He's one of the worst customers I've ever had the displeasure of waiting on. But what I did say was. "He's no one. Just some guy who's had too much to drink."

Like I was in any position to talk.

Lawton's eyebrows furrowed. "So you don't know him?"

"Not really." Sure, I'd met him before, but honestly, I didn't even know his name. And hopefully, I never would. Besides, I didn't want to talk about him. I wanted to be with Lawton.

I wrapped my arms around him and said, "I looked for you earlier." I smiled. "You weren't trying to run off on me, were you?"

"Never, baby," he said, pressing his lips to my forehead.

"Then where'd you go?" I didn't want to be nosy or anything, but the whole thing did seem kind of odd.

"I ran into someone." He frowned. "No one you'd want to see."

I had a pretty good guess who that someone might be.

Brittney or Amber. Probably both.

From what I could figure, Lawton had somehow hustled them off to avoid a potentially awkward scene. It was thoughtful, really. Or at least that's what I told myself, in between wanting to give them a piece of my mind – or worse – for all the trouble they'd brought me over the past few weeks.

Lawton pulled me close and whispered in my ear. "How's my birthday girl?"

I liked being his girl. Somewhere in the foggy recesses of my brain, I realized that things were moving scarily fast. Somehow, in the span of just a couple weeks, I'd gone from being his friend or whatever, to his girl, or his baby.

I loved it. And it scared me half to death. This wasn't me. I'd never been one to get carried away. Too late for that, I thought.

"Wonderful," I said, pressing close to him, half because he looked so delicious, and half because, well, I wasn't exactly steady on my feet. "But you know, I still haven't shown you my birthday suit."

Five minutes later, we were heading out the door.

Inside the limo, I tumbled back onto the leather seat, laughing as one of my shoes slipped off and fell somewhere on the floor. Suddenly, I stopped laughing, a horrible thought occurring to me. "Oh my God," I said, turning to give him an intense look. "I'm not one of those girls." I gripped him by his jacket. "I'm not, am I?"

I might've been slurring, just a little.

Lawton was grinning at me. "What kind of girl?" he asked.

"You know," I said. "The sloppy drunk kind who laughs too loud and isn't half as cute as she thinks she is. I hate those girls." Brittney was one of those girls. As for me, I wasn't. Or, at least I wasn't usually.

Lawton studied my face, one eyebrow raised. "Well, you do appear to be drunk," he said, a grin flashing across his face as his gaze dipped lower. "But baby, you're anything but sloppy."

I glanced toward my shoe, lying on its side next to my little black beaded purse. "I'm kind of sloppy," I said, giggling just a little.

"Come here," he said, pulling me into his arms for a long, deep kiss. When we came up for air, he whispered in my ear. "If this is sloppy, I think I can suffer through it."

I gave him a mock shove to the chest. "Suffer through it? Just for that, I'm not picking up my shoe." I gave him a lurid smile. "Or," I said with the tiniest lick to my lips, "the rest of my clothes either." I gave a quick glance to the glass that separated us from the driver. "He can't see us, can he?"

Lawton shook his head.

"Hear us?" I said.

Again, he shook his head. "Not unless we press the intercom

button."

"Good," I said, reaching down to rub a hand over his thigh, and then higher. Through the fabric of his slacks, I felt his readiness. "Because I don't wanna wait."

"Yeah?" he said, his eyes half closed as he leaned his head back and spoke in a ragged voice. "Waiting. Yeah, it's hard."

I gave him a squeeze. "That's for sure."

He opened his eyes. "You know," he said, his gaze meeting mine. "You're not like anyone I've ever met. One minutes you're this, I dunno, upper-class neighbor girl, then it's like you're something else entirely. It's like you're two people, maybe three." He gave a little laugh. "But swear to God, I love 'em all."

I felt myself grow still. He'd used the "L" word.

CHAPTER 48

Was I falling for him? Definitely. Did this mean he felt the same?

It wasn't like he'd said, "I love you," but it was close enough to make me catch my breath. I didn't know what to say, so I pressed my lips against his and spoke the language that required no words.

Soon, the bodice of my dress was peeled down, and he was running a firm tongue across one nipple, then the other while I straddled him on the leather seat and freed his length from the constraints of his pants and then his briefs.

Technically, I never did show him my birthday suit. And I didn't get to see his either. But for some reason, that only made everything seem more decadent. There he was, in his designer clothes, shoes and all. And yet, I was touching him in the most private places. Stroking him, and watching his eyes close and his lips part as he said my name, or brought his lips to my skin in ways that had me sighing his name in return.

The cityscape shifted and changed, but I barely noticed it as his hands slipped underneath my dress. He reached under my panties to cup my ass as I nibbled his neck and ran one hand through his hair and stroked his swollen length with the other.

Shifting position, he reached between us. I felt his thumb rubbing lightly against that sensitive knob of desire that had been aching for his touch. I moaned into his neck, and felt him shudder just a little as he said, "Chloe, you're just so —"

He never finished the thought. Probably, it was my fault. I was stroking his length, squeezing and rubbing against him while his thumb continued its dance across my most sensitive spot.

Tinted windows, I decided, were the best invention ever. He looked amazing, and I had no intention of sharing him with any audience, not tonight, if not ever.

In my mind's eye, I could envision how we looked together. My little black dress was hiked high over my thighs, and my breasts were unconstrained by the dress or any other covering, except Lawton's mouth, or his fingers, which danced across one nipple, then the other. He was tugging, kneading, and pinching lightly before he replaced his fingers with his mouth, kissing one, then the other, running his tongue around in circles and sucking first gently, then harder.

My hips were moving in time with his motions now, my head thrown back, soft moans and whimpers escaping my lips as too many sensations competed for my attention. His hands, his lips, his tongue – it was all too much.

Slowly, and then all at once, a wave of almost unbearable pleasure washed over me. I don't know what kind of sounds I made, but I knew I wasn't quiet as I shuddered against him. I closed my eyes for only a moment, before I gave in to the nearly unbearable urge to have him inside me.

I didn't even bother to remove my panties. I moved the lacy fabric aside and positioned myself over him. He was massively hard, but I was slick with desire. As I lowered myself down onto him, he gave a low moan of pleasure that matched my own.

When our hips met, he said my name over and over as our hips rose and fell in time with the movement of the limo over the nearly deserted city streets. It was like nothing I'd ever experienced, and probably, I thought with a certain level of wistfulness, something I might not experience again.

As the pressure in my core grew, our motions grew more frantic. His hands were everywhere. On my back, running through my hair, on my still-exposed breasts, across my ass.

And then, I was riding the waves of pleasure yet again. I closed my eyes and leaned forward, grinding into him as he too began to shudder, his hips thrusting forward, and his grip around me tightening beyond all reason.

We rode the peak together, sighing into each other mouths as our lips met and moved in time with the slowing motions of our hips. We stayed like that long after our passion was spent. Somewhere, in the recesses of my brain, I realized I should've pulled out a condom. I'd actually brought a couple in my purse, so I had no excuse, unless you counted the fact that I simply hadn't wanted to.

And really, that was no excuse at all.

In spite of my lack of a social life, I'd been on the pill forever, so I wasn't worried about pregnancy. But the whole thing had been decidedly unsafe. I should've let it go. But feeling his strong arms around me, and watching through bleary eyes as the cityscape changed around us, I heard myself say, "I guess that wasn't exactly safe, was it?"

"What wasn't?" he said.

"You know what," I said, pulling back to put a little distance between us as I met his gaze. "I am on the pill though, so you don't need to worry about that. But the other thing –" I let the sentence trail off unfinished.

How to ask about the girls who he'd been with before? I felt a little shudder go through me, and this one wasn't from desire. Brittney. Ugh. She didn't strike me as the safe-sex type, and she'd been with him before me. "Never mind," I said, suddenly eager to forget the whole thing.

What's done is done, I told myself.

"Oh baby," he said, his eyes dark pools of intensity. "Don't worry about it. I'd never do anything to hurt you. Ever. I'm always safe."

I gave him a dubious look and summoned up a smile. "You sure about that?" I said, trying to keep my tone light. "We weren't exactly tonight."

"You're the first," he said. "You and only you."

"Really?" I said, feeling the tug of a genuine smile.

"Really. Like I said, there's been no one like you. Ever."

From the look in his eyes, I could almost believe it.

I'd like to say I slept in his arms that night, but it would be a lie. Somewhere between pulling ourselves together and arriving back at the Parkers', he mentioned that Bishop was back in town and staying at his place.

"But stay with me anyway," he said. "C'mon. Bring Chucky. We'll have a sleepover."

I laughed. "No way."

Lawton still hadn't confessed that he and Bishop were brothers, and the dynamic when Bishop was around was just too strange. I didn't want to stay in any house where some guy hated me, even if the owner of the house might feel exactly the opposite.

"Alright," Lawton said. "Then I'll stay at your place."

"Sorry," I said. "No guests, remember?"

He looked at me a long time, his face falling in and out of shadows in time with the passing street lights. I met his gaze, my own jaw set in a stubborn line I was all too familiar with. Probably, we were both hoping the same thing. That the other person would give in.

We didn't.

Later, I'd wonder if we were both thinking something else too. Just what, exactly, are you hiding?

In my case, it was simple. What I was hiding had very little to do with me. I wasn't some wealthy couple's daughter, a surgeon's love child, or even somebody's mistress. I was merely the house sitter, but that changed nothing about who I was.

In Lawton's case, I wasn't quite sure.

But as the limo pulled into the Parkers' driveway, I pushed all of those thoughts aside. As promised, Lawton had given me a birthday to remember, and no matter what happened tomorrow, I'd have a memory to last a lifetime.

When he walked me to the door and kissed me goodnight, I couldn't help but regret, at least a little, that I hadn't taken him up on his offer. Sleeping in his arms was a million times better than sleeping alone.

CHAPTER 49

At seven o'clock Saturday night, Erika showed up with enough bags and bundles to require three trips out to her car. I offered to help, but she flatly refused, telling me it was bad luck to help with my own party, even if it was just the two of us.

A few minutes later, we were settled in the kitchen, surrounded by takeout from my favorite Chinese place, a decorated chocolate cake, and a colorful pile of presents.

"You went way overboard," I told her, looking at everything she brought. Maybe she could afford it, but I couldn't help but wonder how I'd ever pay her back.

"Don't worry," she said, knowing me all too well. "I didn't spend a lot of money." She flashed me a grin. "Some of it's homemade."

I bit my lip as I eyed the cake.

She burst out laughing. "Not that, thank God. I want to treat you, not poison you, unless you want to spend your birthday in the emergency room."

"You're not that bad a cook," I laughed.

"Yeah, right." She reached near her chair and picked up a flat poster-sized package wrapped in colorful paper. "I made this though. And you know what? It's totally delicious."

I eyed the package with mock horror.

"Go on," she urged. "Open it. I'm dying to see what you think."

While she watched, I tore off the wrapping paper and felt my jaw drop when I saw what the wrapping paper had hidden. It was a movie poster, starring Lawton Rastor and – what the heck?

In the poster, Lawton was shirtless with beads of what I guessed were supposed to be sweat glistening on his bare chest, accenting his muscular torso and perfectly defined abs.

A woman's arms encircled him from behind, one arm clutched possessively around his taut waist and the hand of the other one working at the top button of his low-slung jeans.

Peeking out from behind him, I saw the face of a young woman who looked obscenely happy to be there.

That face was my own.

"Oh my God," I said, feeling the blood rush to my face. "How did you –" I stopped, speechless.

Erika burst out laughing. "You should see the look on your face," she said, almost choking on the words as she struggled to speak.

I couldn't help it. I started to laugh too. The thing was too ridiculous for words. "You know," I told her, "you are seriously twisted."

She put a dainty hand to her chest and assumed her best innocent face. "Me?"

"Yes, you," I said, pointing to the title of this so-called movie. "Riding the Rastor? What, like he's some kind of roller coaster?"

"Hey," she said, "if he is, buy me a ticket, seriously."

Instantly, a version of our nights together flooded my brain – Lawton kissing me in all those secret places, me tasting him in all his masculine glory, him carrying me up to his bedroom like I weighed almost nothing, him entering me as he cupped his hands –

"Oh hey," Erika said, plucking a napkin from the table. "You've got a little drool on your chin. Here, let me get that for you."

Instantly, my hand flew to my chin.

This sent Erika into another fit of laughter. "Did you actually believe me?" she said. "Girl, you must have it bad."

I did have it bad, but for some reason, I didn't feel like sharing the whole truth. Erika had always been more adventurous than I was, sexually speaking.

While I'd been focused on survival, she'd been focused on fun. But I couldn't resent her for it. She had a way of bringing something into my life that I sorely lacked, an escape from reality.

In a way, Lawton was doing the same thing, even if the respite was temporary. Erika, I hoped, would be around forever. Lawton, well, I knew he wouldn't.

But until the moment where we actually parted ways, I guess I wanted him all to myself. In an odd way, that included all the distinctly ungory details of our intimate time spent together.

"Wow, you're so serious all of a sudden," Erika said.

I looked up and gave her a smile. "Well, it certainly is thought-provoking," I said, raising my eyebrows suggestively. "Where'd you get these pictures?"

She shrugged. "The one of him was easy. It's from some poster from a few years back. The one of you was a lot harder. It made me realize I don't have hardly any shots of you."

There was a reason for this. I totally hated having my picture taken.

Erika pointed to the poster. "The arms aren't yours, but the face, that's from Erin's bachelorette party."

Oh yeah. Her sister's bachelorette party. I barely remembered it, thanks to cherry vodka shooters and nonstop goading by Erika. It served Erika right, though. From what I vaguely recalled, she was the one holding my hair, long after the male stripper had danced off into the sunset.

"Notice the text?" Erika asked, pointing to the so-called movie's promotional blurb. "Go on," she urged. "Read it out loud. I so want to see your face when you do."

"You are so bad," I told her as I held up the poster in front of me. I cleared my throat and started to read.

I'd gotten only a couple words in when she stopped me. "Oh c'mon," she said. "You can do better than that. Say it like you mean it."

Grinning in spite of myself, I started over. "What happens when a good girl goes bad? Very, very bad." I stopped, my face absolutely scorched from embarrassment. If Erika only knew. This was no movie. I was living it for real.

"Don't stop now," Erika said. "You haven't even reached the best part."

I looked down, scanning the text, laughing in spite of myself. "I can't read this," I said. "Seriously."

"God, you are such a lightweight." She snatched the poster out of my grasp. In an overdramatic, breathy voice, she finished where I'd left off. "Watch in all its naked glory as the innocent neighbor girl is spectacularly corrupted by the resident bad boy, Lawton 'Horse-Hung' Rastor, every girl's wet dream, every parent's worst nightmare."

When she finished, she looked up, awaiting my reaction.

"Wow." I didn't know what else to say.

Erika burst out laughing. "Oh. My. God. You should see yourself. Don't tell me you're actually speechless?"

"I'm definitely something," I said, wondering what she'd say when I told her that my date had been with Lawton. No doubt, she'd think it was hilarious.

"You know what you need?" Erika said. "To get laid." She slapped the table and gestured toward the poster. "And I know just the guy for the job."

I glanced at the poster. He looked good. No, better than good. Great. Spectacular. And I knew firsthand, he felt even better than he looked.

Memories from the other night flashed in my brain, snapshots that kept coming even as I tried to tuck them away for later. I saw his hands on my breasts, his lips on my neck, his pelvis grinding into mine as his sinewy muscles shifted and rippled in time with our movements.

"Wow," Erika said. "You must really like that poster." She grinned. "Just between you and me, I'm pretty sure I caught Debbie masturbating to it last Saturday."

"Oh stop it," I laughed. "She was not."

Debbie was Erika's roommate at college. I'd met her a couple of times, and honestly, she didn't strike me as the poster-masturbating type.

"Wanna bet?" Erika said. "I finished it up Saturday at the lab, and set it by the door so I wouldn't forget it when I packed everything up. But then when I get home Saturday night, the thing is propped up by her bed, and she's all funny about it, like she doesn't know how it got in there. But I can tell by the way she says it that she's gotten way too attached to it, if you know what I mean."

I knew exactly how Debbie felt. Somewhere in my phone, I still had that naked picture of Lawton. I meant to delete it. And yet, somehow, I hadn't. At first, it had been because I didn't know how. And then, every time I pulled it up, I just couldn't hit that delete button. But I needed to. Tomorrow, I told myself.

I slid the poster a sideways glance. It's not like I'd been planning to cuddle up with it or anything, but suddenly I wasn't so sure if touching it would be the best idea.

Erika put a hand over her mouth. "Oh crap. I guess I shouldn't have told you that. Don't worry, it's totally clean. I wiped it down just in case."

"Well, that's good."

She grimaced. "I'm making it worse, aren't I?"

I couldn't help it. I laughed. "Totally."

Soon, she was laughing too. She studied the poster with a critical eye. "Honestly, I can't blame her. Can you imagine getting a piece of that?"

"Oh, I can imagine, alright," I mumbled. Or, I could just replay the scenes from the other night.

"Speaking of which," she said, "I've got something else for you to see." She gave me a wicked grin. "I'm calling it tonight's entertainment, since I figured you'd nix my first idea."

"Which was?"

"Male strippers." She reached into her purse and pulled out a disk in a clear plastic case. Across the case, I saw the words "Rastor Sex Tape" handwritten in big black letters.

My mouth fell open. "That isn't –?"

"Oh, yes it is." She tossed the case onto the table and said, "Go on. Get your computer. I'll get the popcorn."

"Popcorn?" I glanced at the cupboards. "I don't think I have any."

"You do now," she said, reaching into her bag and pulling out a bag of microwave popcorn. "Go ahead, pop it up. Oh, but first, get your computer, will ya?"

I glanced at the disk. Sure, I'd heard about the infamous sex tape, and I knew it wouldn't be that hard to get, but did I really want to see this?

"What's wrong?" Erika asked.

"I don't know if I can watch that," I admitted.

"Oh c'mon. Why not?"

There were so many reasons I could've given. Sex tapes in general weren't exactly my thing, but that wasn't what made me hesitate. Lawton was a friend. More than friend, actually. It seemed like a gross violation of his privacy.

And then, there was the other thing. Seeing him with another girl, especially that intimately, I couldn't help it. It made me want to claw someone's eyes out – maybe my own if I were forced to watch this thing from start to finish.

"I dunno," I said. "I sort of know him."

She grinned. "Yeah, I know. I was with you that day, remember?"

"Well, actually," I said, "I've run into him a few times since then."

"No way!" she said. "You've been holding out on me? C'mon, you must know him pretty good if you're not wanting to see him –" she lowered her voice to a suggestive tone, "– in the flesh."

Oh, I wanted to see him in the flesh, alright. I just didn't want to see that flesh pressed up against the flesh of some other girl.

"Holy shit," she said. "Don't tell me he was your date."

"Uh, something like that."

"Oh. My. God," she said. "You slept with him. Didn't you?"

CHAPTER 50

Technically, Lawton and I didn't do a lot of sleeping. But looking at Erika's eager face, that particular fact didn't seem terribly relevant.

Looking at me, her eyes were bright, and her face eager. "You did," she said. "Didn't you?"

"What?" I stammered. "I never said that."

She was grinning. "But you did."

I stood. "Hey, you know what? I'm forgetting the popcorn."

She slapped her hand over mine. "Get up, and you're dead, sister."

"What?"

"You heard me. I want details." She leaned forward. "And I want them now."

I glanced at the disk, and then at the microwave, and then toward the front door.

"Don't even think about it," she said.

"Think about what?"

"Escape. There is none. Tell me now, before things get ugly."

At this, I had to laugh. "I wasn't plotting an escape," I said.

"Liar. Now c'mon." She held up a hand. "Wait! On second thought, I do need popcorn. You sit. I'll pop. You need to conserve your strength."

"For what?"

"For giving me every gory detail. And don't be cheap on me. I'll know if you're holding out."

I rolled my eyes. "If I tell you," I said, "do I still have to watch the tape?"

"Hell no!" she said. "Well, not unless you want to, um, for comparison purposes."

"Have you watched it?" I asked.

"Sort of."

"What do you mean 'sort of'?"

"Well, I walked in on Debbie watching it Sunday. So I caught the tail end." She held up a hand. "Don't worry. It's a new disk. She wouldn't let me have the old one."

In the end, I told Erika everything. She swore up and down that she'd never tell anyone, and I swore up and down that I'd share any new developments. To be honest, I wasn't exactly sincere, but I liked to think she was. In fact, I was counting on it.

And once I got started, I couldn't stop. I pulled out my phone and showed her the picture of him sleeping. I held my hand over the lower half, so she couldn't see all of him.

"But I've already seen him naked," she protested. "Remember? The tape?"

"Why do they still call them tapes?" I said.

"Huh?"

"Everything's digital now. But we still call 'em tapes."

"Who cares?" she said. "Show me the picture."

I gave her a look. "I'm not gonna show you a naked picture of my boyfriend. That's just creepy. Besides, I wouldn't like it if he did it to me."

"God, you're such a stickler." She sat up straighter. "Wait a minute. Did you just call him your boyfriend?"

"Um, well, honestly, I don't know what he is." I grinned. "But I do like him. More than like him, actually."

She looked down at the half-covered picture. "Wow," she said. "Just wow. So he really does look like that?"

I felt myself swallow. "Oh yeah."

"No wonder you don't want to share."

She was right. I didn't.

In the end, we popped in a romantic comedy and had the popcorn with that instead.

Sometime during the closing credits, I remembered the thing about Thanksgiving at my Dad's house. But when I invited Erika to join me, she shook her head. "Sorry, but I'm going skiing with my parents. You could come with us if you wanted."

"I wish," I said. But I couldn't do that to Josh, and besides, I had my responsibilities here.

She leered at me. "You know what you should do? Invite Lawton."

I rolled my eyes. "Yeah, right."

"I'm serious," she said. "Loretta would freak. It would be so worth it."

"Yeah, but I'm not sure she'd freak in a good way, or in a bad way."

"Either way, she wouldn't be giving you shit for a change."

I had to admit, Erika had a point. I wouldn't actually do it, but the thought was enough to make me smile. "I wonder if he'd wear a shirt," I said.

Erika grinned. "Let's hope not."

Way too soon, our little party came to an end, and I was helping Erika gather up her things.

"Let me walk you out," I told her as I turned to Chucky. "Stay," I said in my best mock commanding tone. In his basket, Chucky snuffled and rolled over. "Good dog," I said.

Erika laughed. "Uh-oh. You've got it bad."

"What?" I asked.

"The dog," she said. "It's like you're in love or something."

"Oh please." I wasn't. Not that I'd admit it, anyway.

"Hah! What'll you do when the owners come back?"

"I dunno. Visit?" Hey, it wasn't out of the realm of possibility. I could swing by at least once in a while, maybe take him for a quick walk or something. Turning away, I smiled to myself. Maybe I'd be visiting more than Chucky.

We finished gathering up her things, and my smile faded as I watched Erika shrug into her coat. "I wish I didn't work tonight."

"So play hooky," she said.

I rolled my eyes. "Yeah, right."

Sometime in the evening, the front light had gone out, probably a burned-out bulb. I made a note to replace it the next day.

When Erika's car backed down the long driveway, I stood at the curb, watching until her headlights disappeared onto the street, before I turned to go back inside.

I'd made it about halfway to the front door when I heard a sudden scuffling sound behind me. I whipped my head around, only to be tackled to the sidewalk by a big, shadowed figure in dark clothing.

My head slammed against the concrete, and an explosion of stars peppered my brain as I lay sprawled on my side, with whoever it was on top of me. Screaming, I tried to push away, using my arms, knees, and legs to try to get momentum, or do some damage to my attacker in the process.

Too soon, a gloved hand slammed over my mouth, reducing

my screams to a muffled string of profanity.

"Shut up," a male voice said, flipping me onto my back, "or I'll give you something to scream about."

CHAPTER 51

But I didn't shut up, and I didn't stop struggling, either. My eyes were wide, and my heart racing a mile a minute when I noticed another larger shadow off to the side. They both wore ski masks with only slim openings for the eyes and mouth.

The second shadow moved closer, crouching low as if hoping for a better look. "Damn," he said, "she is fine, isn't she?"

I was gasping against the hand, getting too little air and no chance to call for help. Raw panic consumed me, and I bucked up against him, jostling him just enough to give him a knee to the groin and a fist to his face.

"Fuck," he said. "That was close." His gloved hand ground harder against my face, mashing the back of my head into the concrete.

He leaned his head next to mine, and I felt the brush of the rough knit texture against my ear. "Try that again," he hissed, "and I won't be so nice." Something cool and flat pressed against my throat. A knife?

At that, I went completely still, gasping for air and trying to control my racing heart.

He lifted his hand toward the other shadow and said, "Get the car." Returning his attention to me, he said, "Time for a ride."

My mind was going a million miles a minute as my body froze in place. Was the thing at my throat really a knife, and if so, would he really use it? No matter what, I couldn't go anywhere with these two guys.

It would be suicide, or something almost as bad. Maybe now wasn't the time to make my move, but there was no way I'd be getting into any car of theirs.

For what seemed like an awful long time, we remained frozen in that position. I felt hot and cold all at the same time, with the frigid hard sidewalk pressing into my back, and the stifling mass pressing down on top of me.

I was afraid to move. And I was afraid to not move. His hand was still mashed down over my mouth, and I felt the vague coppery taste of blood in my mouth. In the quiet night, my desperate attempts to draw in air through my nose was a loud staccato, eclipsed only by the hammering of my heart.

Maybe when the other guy showed up with the car, I'd have the chance to escape. But it seemed to be taking a long time, even longer than the guy must've anticipated, because he started to fidget, a little at first, and then more as the minutes dragged on.

The only things that didn't move, though, were the knife at my throat and the hand on my mouth. Over and over, I debated biting that hand. And over and over, I rejected that idea as incredibly stupid. The gloves felt thick, and the knife wasn't wavering.

Had it cut my skin? I didn't think so. I felt pressure, but no real pain. And there was no blood. At least, I didn't think there was any blood. My exposed neck felt cold. And blood is warm, right?

The time ticked on as a car drove by, and then another.

Neither one stopped.

"What the fuck is taking so long?" the guy muttered, more to himself than to me.

My gaze was darting wildly around, from his slitted eyes to the darkened yard. Had they broken the light? Or maybe they hadn't needed to. It's not like I'd checked to make sure it still had a bulb. Shit, did it even matter? Whether by accident or design, the front yard was darker than I'd ever seen it.

From the street, we'd be practically invisible. In fact, we'd probably be invisible from ten feet away. A trickle of sweat dripped down the side of my face, making me long to wipe it away. But I couldn't wipe it away. I couldn't do anything. Not yet.

After who knows how long, headlights appeared at the end of the driveway. They grew brighter and brighter, until in my peripheral vision, I saw a dark sedan ease into the driveway and stop just a few feet from where we lay on the walkway.

My breathing was nearly out of control, and I felt like I was drowning in adrenalin and raw panic. No matter what, I couldn't let them take me into that vehicle.

CHAPTER 52

I realized I was trembling. The driver's side door opened, and the other guy got out, the ski mask still in place. He stood in the driveway looking over at us like he had all the time in the world.

The guy on top of me called out to him. "C'mon, move it, will ya?"

Holding something that looked like a tire iron, the guy held up a hand as if signaling for a brief delay. He then crouched down to inspect the front tire on the driver's side.

"Fuck the tire," the guy on top of me said. "C'mon! Jesus."

Ignoring his partner, the guy circled around to the passenger's side. He leaned over to inspect the other front tire. With a muttered curse, the guy above me sat up, his hand still pressed to my mouth, but the knife blissfully gone from my neck. I gasped for air as he craned his neck to see what the other guy was doing.

This was my chance. It might be my only one. Slowly, I made a fist with my right hand. I braced myself. Then, without warning, the guy flew off of me, almost like he'd been jerked on a string. Free from his mass, I bolted upright, gasping for air.

What I saw in front of me made me gasp for a different

reason. I didn't scream for help, because almost by divine intervention, it had already arrived. I saw Lawton, his face a study in cold fury, pounding the masked guy with his right fist while he held his neck with his left.

He hadn't even bothered to remove the guy's mask. The guy, whoever he was, was bucking wildly, clutching at his throat with both hands and twisting from side to side as if trying to worm away from the attack.

Almost too late, I noticed the second masked man striding toward us. The tire iron was nowhere in sight, but his destination was obvious. I jumped to my feet, hollering out, "Lawton! Behind you!"

Lawton whipped his head around to spot the guy behind him, but he did nothing to change position or defend himself from the coming attack. Instead, he turned back around toward the guy on the ground and delivered a vicious series of punches that had him flopping around like a rag doll.

Before I knew it, the second guy had a forearm around Lawton's neck. He yanked him backward, pulling him off the first guy, who, I vaguely realized, was no longer moving. Finally, Lawton acted. He broke free of the second guy's grasp, then barreled hard into him, sending them both rolling across the grass.

I looked wildly around and spotted the knife lying just inches from my feet. I scooped it up and charged, screaming all the pent-up rage and helplessness I'd felt just a few minutes earlier. With a final shriek, I leapt forward, knife raised, frantically looking for the best place to strike at the masked assailant.

His neck. His leg. Wherever. The guy was a big target. Maybe if I just started slashing, I'd hit something. When he bolted to his feet, dragging Lawton with him, I finally saw my chance.

With a guttural cry I struck out, aiming for the guy's forearm.

What I got was nothing because with lightning reflexes, a gloved hand closed around my wrist and squeezed hard. The knife fell to the grass with barely a noise.

"Let go of her!" Lawton yelled, his face flushed and his eyes blazing as he faced off against the second assailant.

"For fuck's sake," the guy muttered, releasing my wrist and taking a couple of steps backward, his hands raised.

Lawton rushed to my side. "You okay?" he asked, frantically searching my face and body for clues to my condition.

Nodding, I glanced toward the second assailant.

Lawton turned to the guy. "Take off the mask, will ya? Can't you see you're scaring her?

With a muttered curse, the guy pulled off the ski mask and tossed it to the ground. "I'd have taken it off sooner if she hadn't gone all Norman Bates on me." It was Bishop, Lawton's brother. His short hair was in a spiky disarray as he continued to eye me with undisguised annoyance.

"Norman Bates?" I glared at him. "As in psycho?"

He shrugged. "If the knife fits…"

My hands were shaking, and my head was swimming. There was too much to take in. The guy on the ground was still as death. Bishop was eyeing him with only mild interest. Next to me, Lawton was gripping my hand so tight, it felt like my bones might shatter.

I yanked my hand away, and whirled around to face Bishop. "Why'd you guys attack me? Is this your idea of a joke?"

Lawton turned to Bishop. "What?"

Bishop turned his gaze heavenward. "Oh, for fuck's sake."

I glared at him. "You already said that."

Bishop looked toward Lawton. "She thinks I'm the other guy."

"What other guy?" I demanded.

Shrugging, Bishop gave a quick glance at the car in the driveway. "The guy in the trunk. Let's just say we intercepted him."

I looked toward the car too. My voice shook. "He's not, uh – "

"Dead?" Bishop said. "No." He turned his attention to the guy on the lawn. "And we better hope that one's not dead, either."

Lawton's jaw tightened. "Speak for yourself. I don't give a shit if he's dead."

"Obviously," Bishop said. "You search him yet?"

Lawton shook his head and made a move toward the guy.

"Hang on," Bishop said. "I'll do it."

"Why you?" I asked.

"Because given half a chance, Romeo here –" Bishop flicked his chin toward Lawton, "– would probably finish him off. Then we'd have real trouble on our hands."

I took in my surroundings, starting with the strange car with a body, hopefully alive, in the trunk, to the ski mask on the lawn, to the unconscious guy lying a few feet away. If this wasn't real trouble, I didn't know what was. I started to shake. Not just my hands, but my whole body.

Lawton, very gently this time, took my hand. "Come here," he said. "It's gonna be alright." He put an arm around me and nestled me close.

I gave a shrill bark of laughter. "Alright? Seriously? This is so not alright."

Bishop was pulling the ski mask from the guy's face. I squinted into the darkness and was slowly able to make out some of his features. I sucked in a breath. I couldn't be one hundred percent sure, but I thought I knew him.

CHAPTER 53

Lawton turned to face me. "Wasn't this the guy from yesterday? At the club?"

His blood-spattered face looked a lot different than the last time I'd seen it. But it sure looked like Brittney's date, or friend, or whatever.

I nodded. "I think so."

I touched my throat. I could almost still feel the knife, but I felt no cut, no blood, no anything, except remnants of my own fear.

Somewhere in the back of my brain, I heard a muffled sound. It might've been a sob. Or it might've been a whimper.

Slowly, I became aware that the noise had come from me, and that Lawton's strong arms encircled me tighter now, wrapping me in a cocoon of warmth and security as I completely fell apart.

He murmured comforting sounds into my hair, but now that I'd started, I couldn't seem to stop. We stood like that for what seemed like a long time.

From someplace that seemed oddly far away, Lawton was saying something that seemed to require an answer.

With a final sniffle, I pulled back to look at him. "Sorry," I mumbled. "What'd you say?"

"I'm taking you inside."

I glanced toward the car. "But what about the other guy?"

I didn't need to look inside the trunk to have a pretty good idea who it was. I'd have bet almost anything it was the second guy who'd been with Brittney and Amber that night.

"He's not going anywhere," Lawton said.

"Neither is this one," Bishop said, walking past, carrying the other guy over his shoulder, fireman style.

"Oh my God," I stammered. "You sure he's not —"

"He'll be fine," Bishop said. He kept moving, heading toward the car.

I looked at the guy. He didn't look fine to me. His face was dripping trickles of blood that left a dark trail along the concrete.

"You sure?" I said.

"Trust me," Bishop said.

I glanced at Lawton.

He seemed to read the worry in my eyes. "If he says he's fine, he's fine."

In the driveway, Bishop popped the trunk and dumped the guy into it. I heard muffled thumping from somewhere inside. If nothing else, at least the other guy was okay. Sort of.

When Bishop returned, I said, "Shouldn't we be calling the police?"

Bishop and Lawton shared a long look. Neither one spoke until Lawton said in a low, quiet voice, "Is that what you want?"

It seemed an incredibly odd question. Of course, that's what I wanted. It's what any sane person would want.

And then something hit me. Whatever had happened here, no one but Lawton and Bishop knew about it. If the police were called, this would become a full-blown spectacle. It would be worse due to Lawton's involvement, because he was practically a household name.

This had tabloid fodder written all over it. And before then, there'd be police cars and flashing lights. Then there'd be interviews and lots of reasons for the neighbors to come outside and see what was going on.

The Parkers would surely hear about this, probably a lot sooner than later. This whole thing had nothing to do with them, other than the fact it had happened on their front lawn. I'd be fired for sure, and then, where would I go?

And then, there was the other thing. Somewhere deep inside, I knew who'd put those guys up to this. Brittney. She knew where I was staying, and she'd promised some sort of revenge. I could only guess that this was her idea of a sick, twisted joke.

I could practically see the headlines now, and none of them were good.

Next to us, Bishop leaned down to scoop up something from the grass. The knife. It had a short metal blade and a dark commando-style handle. His gaze narrowed as he ran a hand along its blade.

"What is it?" Lawton said.

Bishop shook his head. "It's fake."

On reflex, my hand returned to my throat. "What do you mean fake?"

"It's metal alright," Bishop said, "but I wouldn't call it a knife. Feels more like a movie prop." He turned to me. "Here. Hold out your hand."

"What the hell are you doing?" Lawton said.

"Humor me," Bishop said.

When I did, Bishop ran the blade along my palm. I felt the familiar sensation of metal against my skin, but no pain, no cut, no nothing. I felt my face grow warm. That explained why my

SABRINA STARK

neck had no marks, especially considering how hard the guy had pressed. How had I fallen for something so stupid?

"It's not even a knife," I murmured.

"Chloe," Lawton said. "What's going on?"

I shook my head. "I have no idea."

"So what do you want us to do?" Lawton said.

I glanced toward the car. "You sure they're okay?"

The two guys exchanged a glance.

"Yeah," Lawton said.

I looked at him a long time. "Don't lie to me."

"Alright," Lawton said, "yeah, they're banged up a little, but they'll be fine in a couple weeks. Maybe sooner."

"How can you be sure?" I said.

"Romeo fights for a living," Bishop said. "Remember?"

"Used to fight for a living," Lawton corrected.

"Yeah, whatever," Bishop said, sparing him a half glance before turning his gaze to me. "But it seems to me that you wouldn't be losing sleep over these guys. You worried about them?"

"No," I said. "Of course not. It's just that —" I shrugged. "I dunno. I don't want 'em dead or anything."

"About the police," Lawton said. "It's your decision. Yes or no?"

I bit my lip. I knew what I should do, but the whole thing was a no-win for everyone involved. And in a weird twist of fate, that included the guys who attacked me. I had no doubt who put them up to this. Maybe their ass-beating was the perfect end to this crappy story. Doubtful they'd try that again.

But did they make a habit of this sort of thing? If I didn't report them, and another girl was attacked, I'd never forgive myself.

"I don't want them doing this to anyone else," I said.

Bishop spoke up. "We'll encourage them not to."

"How?" I asked.

"Better if you don't know," Bishop said.

"You're not gonna hurt 'em?" I said.

"Baby," Lawton said, "want us to take care of it? Say the word, and you don't need to think about this ever again."

I felt myself nod. They weren't strangers, not exactly. If I needed to, I'd be able to find out who they were. Once I got a little perspective, I could always change my mind. Report them, threaten to report them, whatever. Later, when my head cleared, I'd know what to do. Now, I had no idea.

I'd also need to tell Lawton about the guys' connection to Brittney, but not in front of his brother. Bishop would get way too much satisfaction from the whole sordid tale, and I wasn't about to listen to his bullshit any more than I had to.

Lawton turned to Bishop. "You take care of them. I'll get her inside." With his arm around me, he turned to lead us toward the Parkers' front door. I followed his lead for a couple of paces, and then stopped as a horrible thought occurred to me.

I hadn't yet cleaned up from the birthday party. When I'd walked Erika to her car, I'd left everything out on the table. The cake, the poster, the sex tape. Oh my God. Lawton couldn't see any of this. And if he walked into that house tonight, there was no way he'd miss it.

CHAPTER 54

I stood silent on the sidewalk, eyeing the house with a dread that had nothing to do with the guys who attacked me.

"What's wrong?" Lawton asked.

"Nothing." I struggled for inspiration and found none. "It's just that you don't need to come in with me."

His eyebrows furrowed. He glanced toward the house. "At least let me check the place out, make sure everything's alright."

I shook my head. "No. Really, I'm sure it's fine."

"Baby," he said. "It's not fine. You're not fine. I can see it all over your face. Now tell me, what is it?"

"Nothing." I pointed toward Bishop, who was climbing into the driver's seat of the dark sedan. "You should go with him." I squinted at the car. "Where's he going, anyway?"

"I'm guessing he'll drive 'em home. Or maybe some public place. Hard to say."

"How would he know where they live?"

"Driver's license."

"Oh." How had I forgotten? The guy was a regular expert when it came to those. "So what's he gonna do?" I persisted.

"Drive them home and just leave?"

"Hard to say."

"You're at least gonna open the trunk before you leave 'em someplace. Right?"

Lawton glanced toward the trunk. "I dunno. Maybe." He returned his gaze to me. "Except it won't be me doing anything, because I'm staying here with you."

Again, I glanced toward the car. "You've done this before, haven't you?"

"Done what before?"

"I don't know." I couldn't put my finger on it, but they seemed way too good at dealing with whatever had happened tonight. "Stuff like this."

From the driveway, I heard a sudden burst of muffled thumps and angry voices.

"See?" Lawton said. "Second guy woke up. He's fine. Just like I said."

I'd seen the damage firsthand. "Fine" was definitely an exaggeration. I listened harder, picking up more thumping and even more yelling.

I bit my lip. "They're trying to get out."

"Maybe," Lawton said. "Either that, or they turned on each other." He gave a half shrug. "It happens."

I stared at him. "It happens? How would you know?"

From the driveway, Bishop rolled down the window and called out, "You comin' or what?"

"No," Lawton said.

"Yes, he is," I called back.

"No," Lawton said through clenched teeth. "I'm not."

Bishop looked at us, his eyes flat and his tone bored. "I'm leaving in five seconds. In or out. Your choice."

"Go ahead," Lawton said. "I'll see you at the house."

A moment later, Bishop was on his way. Together, Lawton and I watched as the car reversed out of the long driveway, then pulled out onto the street like the driver had all the time in the world.

When Lawton turned back to me, I blurted out, "You should've gone with him."

"Why?"

"Because I can't have guests over."

He gave me another strange look. "Baby, who's in the house?"

"No one."

"Uh-huh."

I gave him a pleading look. "Can't we just go to your place?"

His jaw tightened. "Sure. After I check things out here."

"You can't," I stammered. "I mean, I don't want you to."

"Chloe, be reasonable," he said. "A favor for me, alright?"

Miserably, I shook my head.

He stared at me a long moment, and then said, "Alright," in a quiet, clipped tone. "Have it your way."

"Great," I said. "Wait right here. I'll get Chucky."

Before he could respond, I dashed inside, locking the door behind me. Inside the house, I grabbed Chucky, along with his leash.

A few minutes later, we were driving to Lawton's place in my car. Lawton drove. I sat with Chucky on my lap. I tried to act normal, and from what I saw, so did he. But I couldn't deny that there was some sort of wall between us.

I hated that wall.

When I reminded Lawton that I had to work in a couple of hours, the wall seemed to loom larger, as if he didn't quite believe anything I was saying. But I told myself that couldn't be the case. He knew me, right?

Inside his house, Chucky dove straight for his favorite basket, a wicker thing with a checkered pillow. Lawton had bought it a couple weeks earlier, one of the things he'd used to lure us to stay. In an odd way, that seemed a long time ago.

Lawton and I wandered to what had become our favorite room, the one he'd brought me to that first time, the night of his interrupted birthday party. Silently, he pulled a throw-blanket out of a nearby chest and wrapped it around me.

Together, we sank back together on the sofa. I snuggled into him, and he wrapped his arms around me like he always did, but something was definitely off.

After a few minutes of awkward silence, I couldn't stand it anymore. I pulled away to look at him.

Slowly, Lawton turned his gaze on me, his body tense and his eyes troubled.

I felt a wave of guilt wash over me. Whatever he was feeling, I'd obviously caused it. Apparently, my evasiveness hadn't gone unnoticed. It was time to come clean, at least about some things. "I want to tell you something," I said.

"Yeah?"

I took a deep breath. "I did sort of know that guy."

"Yeah?" Somehow, he didn't look surprised.

"But not in the way you think," I continued, my words tumbling over each other as I rushed to explain. "He's a friend of Brittney's. They came in where I work. He and some friend. I'm guessing it was the same guy that came with him tonight. Anyway, they caused all kinds of trouble. With Brittney and Amber too." I looked away and mumbled. "They got me fired."

Lawton's expression darkened. "When was this?"

"I dunno. Maybe a couple weeks ago."

His gaze narrowed. "I don't get it. You still work there."

"Well, yeah. It's complicated." I looked down. "Anyway, I'm guessing that tonight, Brittney put those guys up to it."

"Why didn't you say something earlier?"

"It was just so ugly," I said, giving his question some thought. "And Brittney's, I dunno, a friend of yours, and I didn't want to come across as some kind of crazy, jealous chick, throwing around accusations I couldn't prove."

"So the other night at the club?" he asked. "What was that about?"

"Nothing," I said. "He just happened to be there, that's all."

"And you really don't know him?"

"No," I said. "Just from those couple of times. That's it."

"And you don't have any idea what he wanted tonight?"

"Well, Brittney did sort of threaten me, so —"

He jerked his head back. "She what?"

"It's a long story," I said. "She came into the diner maybe a week or so later. We didn't exactly hit it off, and —" I shrugged. "She said she'd pay me back or something, but I didn't really take her seriously. But if I had to guess, this was probably her idea of a joke."

I shrugged. "Or, it could've been the guys acting alone. But somehow, I don't think so. For one thing, Brittney knows where I live. They don't."

"I'm gonna kill her," Lawton said.

"You're not serious." I swallowed. "Are you?"

He turned to face me. "Is that what you think?"

"I don't know what to think. You and your friend, Bishop, you guys act kind of strange sometimes, like you might not always follow the letter of the law, if you know what I mean."

"He's not my friend." Lawton's voice was quiet. "He's my brother."

"Oh."

"But you already knew that, didn't you?"

"I thought, maybe," I stammered. "But uh, you never said so, so, uh –"

"Oh just forget it," he muttered, rubbing the back of his neck. "That's a different conversation."

"No, it's the same conversation," I said. "You hardly ever talk a lot about yourself. I'd really like to know."

He gave me a hard look. "Yeah, I know the feeling."

"What's that supposed to mean?"

"Look," he said, "I know you're not dumb, so stop acting like it."

I shrank back, his words hitting like a slap in the face. "I don't act dumb," I said.

"If you say so."

I didn't need this crap. My night had been awful enough already, and his veiled accusations weren't exactly helping. "You know what?" I stood. "I'm going home."

He gazed up at me, his expression stony. "Yeah? And where is that, exactly?"

I opened my mouth, and then clamped it shut again.

"Yeah," he muttered. "I thought so."

I shook my head, hearing my own voice soften as I said, "Maybe it's just time to accept it."

"Accept what?"

"That we just don't belong together."

CHAPTER 55

As soon as the words were out, I regretted them. It wasn't what I wanted. Not really. But I wasn't a fool. I knew this couldn't go anywhere long term.

I'd been acting like my Mom, neglecting my responsibilities for some pretty boy with obvious commitment issues. I thought I was in love. But I couldn't be. I didn't even know him. And he certainly didn't know me.

He closed his eyes and sucked in a breath. "Is that what you want?"

"I don't know." I ran a nervous hand through my hair. "I can't think right now." It was true. Too many other things had happened tonight. My emotions were running high. Apparently, so were his. This would be the worst possible time to decide anything.

His voice softened. "C'mon. Sit back down."

I looked at him, and then at the door. If I walked out now, I might never be back. The thought made my heart ache.

Slowly I sat, careful to leave some distance between us. When he was too near, I had a hard time thinking. At a time like this, distance was definitely a good thing.

Apparently, he felt differently. He closed that distance and wrapped his arms tight around me. "I'm sorry," he said, whispering into my hair. "You've had a shitty night, and I'm being an asshole. It's just that you've got me all tied up in knots, and I'm trying to go slow. But I can't. Not with you. Because I don't want to."

I felt myself relax into him. "Really?"

"Really."

I pulled away and met his gaze. "You know what scares me?"

"What?"

"It's that you're right," I said. "I know we're going too fast. But no matter what I do, I can't seem to make myself slow down. I guess I don't want to either."

"That's good," he said, running his hand along my face, "because there's something I want to say."

"Yeah?" said a male voice from the doorway. "Me too."

My gaze shot to the door, and there he was, Bishop, the irritation that kept on irritating.

"Will you stop doing that?" I said.

"Yeah. Sorry." He turned to Lawton, who was giving him a murderous glare. "But I'm serious. I need to talk to you."

"Later," Lawton said.

"No," Bishop said. "Now."

Lawton blew out an irritated breath. "Go ahead. Talk. But make it quick. "

Bishop's gaze flicked briefly to me before returning to Lawton. "Alone," he said.

"Well that's just special," I muttered.

If Bishop heard me, he gave no indication. "It can't wait," he told Lawton.

Lawton glanced from Bishop to me.

"Oh, just go," I said. "You know he won't leave until you do."

Lawton turned his gaze fully on me. "You sure?"

"She's sure," Bishop said. "Now, c'mon."

I turned to glare at him. "Thanks for saving me the trouble of answering for myself."

"Don't mention it," he said.

Lawton took my hand in his. "Don't go anywhere, okay?"

"I won't," I said.

Lawton stood, then leaned over me, his lips brushing mine right before he leaned in close and whispered. "We'll talk about everything when I get back. You're not getting out of it."

In spite of everything, I felt myself smile.

As Lawton adjusted the blanket around me, I glanced toward the door. Bishop was still there, a stony expression darkening his face as he stared at me with barely concealed loathing. I stared back, not bothering to hide how I felt about him either.

Family or not, I'd be glad when he went back to wherever he came from. The guy was nothing but trouble. Thankfully, Lawton had been too preoccupied with the blanket to notice our mutual loathing.

"Five minutes," Lawton promised.

I nodded, then watched as he left the room, and Bishop shut the door behind them. Like I'd eavesdrop or something. I felt the teeniest bit of discomfort at the realization that I'd done exactly that not too long ago. But that had been an accident. Besides, whatever Bishop was saying, I was pretty sure I didn't want to hear it. His opinion of me was obvious.

I huddled up under the blanket, waiting. I didn't have a watch, or even my phone to check the time, but I knew it was taking a lot longer than five minutes. The time dragged as I waited, growing more tense with every minute that passed.

It was at least an hour before Lawton returned. And when he

---

did, he seemed different somehow.

He returned to his spot on the sofa, and put his arm around me like before. But somehow, nothing felt the same. I studied his face in profile. His jaw was set, and his eyes unfocused as he stared across the room at nothing in particular.

And other than a perfunctory apology for it taking so long, he obviously had nothing to say.

And that's when I knew. Something tonight had gone terribly wrong.

CHAPTER 56

The possibilities were too numerous to consider. I felt myself pale. Had one of the guys died? Or maybe a neighbor had called the police? Or – oh God – what if his stupid brother had broken into the Parkers' house again. I could only imagine the things he'd say.

The minutes dragged, and the silence stretched out. Soon, I'd need to get ready for work. I had the briefest thought of calling in sick, but instantly shoved it aside. Thanks to the situation with Keith, every night I worked might be my last.

But I didn't want to leave without some clue to what had happened. After a long stretch of silence, followed by a string of one-word answers to my lame attempts at making conversation, I couldn't stand it anymore. I pulled away and said, "Alright, tell me."

"Tell you what?"

"What'd he say?"

"Who?"

"Now who's playing dumb?" I said. "Bishop. Who else?"

Lawton rubbed the back of his neck and muttered, "He didn't

say anything."

"Bull," I said. "You were gone forever. He must've said something."

Lawton shrugged.

"Something happened," I persisted. "What is it?"

"You really wanna know?" he asked.

From the look on his face, I wasn't so sure. Still, I felt myself nod.

"Forget it." He stared at the unlit fireplace, his expression stony. "You gotta work tonight, right?"

I nodded.

"Then you should probably just go."

I stared at him. "What?"

"Yeah." He dug into his pocket and pulled out my car keys. He held them out toward me. "Here."

I shook my head. "I don't understand."

"Yeah. Whatever." He stood as if ending a business meeting that had gone badly. "Besides, I've gotta go someplace too."

I got to my feet. "Where?"

"Downstairs." He looked toward the door. "There's something I've gotta check on."

"Fine," I said. "I'm coming with you."

"Suit yourself." He gave me a hard look. "Long as you take off your clothes."

I stared at him. "What?"

"You heard me."

"What the hell? I'm not getting undressed just to go downstairs."

"Alright. Then you're not coming downstairs." He made a scoffing sound. "What's the big deal anyway? It's not like I haven't seen it all before." His voice had a nasty edge I'd never heard before.

"What's the hell's wrong with you?" I asked.

"Nothing," he said. "But seriously, what's the big deal?"

"Do I really have to spell it out?"

He gave me a hard look. "Apparently."

"Well, for starters, it's weird. And you're acting funny. That's the big deal."

"If you say so."

I looked at what he was wearing. Jeans and a black T-shirt. It looked like plenty of clothes to me. "Are you getting undressed too?" I asked.

"You want me to?" He gave me a smile that didn't quite reach his eyes. "Just say the word, baby, because you know I'd do anything for you."

The words were right, but the tone was off.

I glanced at the door, and then back at him. His face was white, his fists were clenched, and the muscles in his neck were corded so tight they looked like knots about to come loose.

Still, his voice was eerily calm as he said, "It's your choice, Chloe."

It didn't sound like much of a choice to me. My gaze narrowed. "What's down there, anyway?"

"Looks like you'll never know."

"This doesn't make any sense," I said.

"Yeah," he said, "but when you see it, you'll understand."

"See what?"

"Look," he said, "We can go around like this all night. But it's not gonna change anything. The ball's in your court. You wanna go down there? That's the price."

I should've refused. I would've refused. But whatever was wrong with him, I needed to know. This wasn't him. This wasn't the guy I'd fallen for, the guy who woke me with kisses and played fetch with Chucky.

No, this guy was an asshole. I wanted my Lawton back, and so help me, I'd have done almost anything to get him. Where his brother had disappeared to, I had no idea. But his influence had obviously remained. I needed to get through to him, and if giving up a little dignity was the price, well, I guess he was worth it.

"All my clothes?" I asked, my voice very quiet.

He seemed to give it some thought. "No," he finally said. "Guess not. Just the outer ones should be good." He crossed his arms and waited.

"Fine. You win." Feeling incredibly awkward, I yanked off my T-shirt and threw it, hard, onto the floor. Then, I pushed off my tennis shoes and shimmied out of my jeans. In spite of my lost attire, the room suddenly felt incredibly hot as I stood in my black bra and panties. "There," I said, lifting my chin. "You happy?"

"Not particularly." He crossed the room and picked up my shirt. He ran it through his hands as if checking for something. Then, he did the same thing with my shoes and jeans.

"What are you looking for?" I demanded.

"Nothing."

"Drugs? Because I'm not on any, if that's what you're wondering."

Instead of answering, he turned and headed toward the door. "You still coming?" he asked.

I heard a note of challenge in his voice, and it grated on me in the worst way. Did he really think I was afraid to see whatever he had down there? If so, he had the wrong girl. "You bet I am," I said.

The basement door was located just off the kitchen. I followed him, barefoot, down the narrow, closed stairway. The light was dim, and I gripped the rail tighter than I probably needed to.

Vaguely, I wondered if I was the worst cliché, some stupid, half-naked girl walking cluelessly into dangers unknown, wielding an overly ripe banana or a pink powder puff to fend off some guy with a chainsaw.

I pushed those thoughts aside. This was Lawton. He wasn't a monster. He was – well, I didn't know what he was exactly. My boyfriend? I'd called him that earlier, but honestly, I wasn't feeling quite so sure at the moment.

As I neared the final step, portions of the basement came into view. I looked around. The place was gray and spotless with a painted floor that matched the painted concrete walls. I saw a few cardboard boxes, a weight bench, and some skis leaning against a far wall.

Near the center of the room, I spotted a big oak table surrounded by four huge oak chairs. Ahead of me, Lawton turned around at the foot of the stairway to face me as I took the final step. He motioned to the table. "Have a seat."

It was a lot cooler down here, and I felt my lack of clothing more keenly than I had just a couple minutes earlier. "Why?" I asked, rubbing my arms as I looked around. "What's down here, anyway?"

He walked over to pull out a chair. "Sit. You'll see in a minute."

With a sigh, I walked over and sat, resting my hands on my lap as I tried to figure out what exactly was down here. On the far side of the room, I spotted a sturdy-looking door with a deadbolt lock on it. Was he going to show me something from there? Because I sure as hell didn't see anything in the main area that warranted his strange behavior.

I was still looking around when almost before I knew it, my hands were yanked from my lap and pulled behind me.

From there, everything happened so fast I could barely

process it all, but the sensations were unmistakable – the feel of cold metal on my wrists, the sound of the cuffs clicking shut, and Lawton's voice, colder than the metal itself, as he said, "Alright. You wanted to see something? Well, you got your wish."

CHAPTER 57

"Lawton!" I shrieked, yanking against the cuffs. "This isn't funny."

"It's not meant to be," he said.

I turned my head as far as it could go. He stood immediately behind me, his arms crossed, and his face cast in shadows. He looked like a stranger, and I felt myself shiver. Still, with an effort, I kept my voice shockingly calm as I said, "Lawton, I'm serious. Let me go. Right now."

"No," he said. "I don't think so."

"Son-of-a-bitch!" I said. "I'm serious."

"So am I."

A moment later, I felt his hands on me, resting on my shoulders as he said, "Now listen up. I don't wanna hurt you. But I've gotta check for something."

I tensed. "What?"

"Electronics." Slowly, he ran a finger under my bra straps, and then over the bra itself. I felt a mortifying surge of heat wherever he touched, even when he went lower, skimming his hands over my panties, both the front side and the back.

"Well?" I said, when he was done. "You happy now?"

He didn't answer. Instead, he moved to the side of the table. With a guttural roar, he lifted it with both hands with one hard push, sending the heavy thing toppling over and crashing into the nearby wall. His face was a mask of unbridled rage.

I clamped my lips shut, too stunned to move, much less speak.

Then, as if the act of destruction had quenched whatever need had overcome him, he walked slowly to the opposite wall and leaned against it, facing me, his expression stony and his eyes devoid of any warmth.

I met his gaze head-on. No flinching. No looking away. My tone was snotty as I said, "Feel better?"

"No."

I gave him a nasty smile. "Good."

"Whatever."

I rattled the cuffs, and felt my temper surge along with my frustration. "Are you gonna tell me what the hell's going on?" I demanded.

He shrugged.

"I deserve to know."

At this, he made a strangled sound, half-laugh, half something else. Whatever that something else was, it was ugly and sad all at the same time. It scared me a lot more than the handcuffs.

"You talking about this?" he said, motioning to the basement, me, the chair, everything. "You know, it's a lot better than you deserve. So if I were you, I'd shut up while you're ahead."

"Shut up?" I said. "You asshole."

"Takes one to know one."

"What the hell's that supposed to mean?"

"Like you don't know."

I tried a few more times to get him to talk. I started out calm, well, okay not exactly calm, but a lot calmer than I might have been, given the situation. But it didn't take long before any civility evaporated into bouts of cursing and yanking against the cuffs. My wrists were raw, and in no time at all, so was my throat.

In the timespan of who-knows-how-long, I'd totally blown any resolution to squash my cursing habit. In fact, I'm pretty sure I invented some new words, mostly because I was wearing the old ones out by sheer frequency and volume alone.

And through it all, through my ranting, through my pleading, through my struggling, he just stood there, watching, his eyes dead and his mouth hard.

Meanwhile, another thought kept playing through my brain. It should've been the least of my worries, but every once in a while, it darted to the forefront in a way that had me even more pissed off than I would've been otherwise. I was supposed to work tonight.

What was I supposed to do? Call and tell them I was tied up? I heard a bitter laugh coming from my own throat. Yeah, that was about right.

"What's so funny?" Lawton said.

"Oh, so now you wanna talk?" I said, giving him the dirtiest look I could muster up. "Fuck off."

He bit his lip and looked toward the basement door. "You need some water?"

I stared at him. "Water? Seriously?"

He shrugged. He was still leaning against the opposite wall, arms crossed, eyes flat. He looked harder than the concrete behind him and just as cold.

"It's water or nothing," he said.

"You're an asshole, you know that?"

"I let you keep your panties, didn't I?"

In truth, water would be heavenly, but I wouldn't give the

bastard the satisfaction of asking for it, even if he did offer. I looked around the massive basement. I saw windows, or what I guessed were windows, high up near the ceiling. But they were all covered in black plywood.

I guess that's pretty standard if you're planning to lock someone up in your basement.

Except it didn't look like any of this was planned. Other than the actual handcuffs, I saw nothing that would have alarmed me if I weren't in my particular predicament.

"The guys who attacked me," I asked, "where are they now?"

"Trust me," he said, "It's better if you don't know."

"Trust you?" I rattled the handcuffs. "You're joking, right?"

"Believe what you want."

His calm demeanor grated on me. "How long are you going to stand there?" I asked.

"As long as you're here," he said.

My tone was brittle. "And how long will that be, exactly?"

He glanced at his wrist. "Another half hour should do it."

"Do what?"

"Again," he said, "better if you don't know."

My stomach dropped. What was he saying? I forced down the panic. "So you're saying you'll let me go in a half hour?"

At this, he glanced away. "Probably."

Shit.

CHAPTER 58

I felt myself start to shiver. The adrenalin was wearing off, leaving me too hollow to fight the creeping sense of despair, not to mention the cold, damp basement air that had been gnawing at me with more persistence as the minutes wore on.

At first, I'd been positively burning up with panic, then rage. But now, as my rage settled into a quiet loathing, I felt all the discomfort of my situation more keenly than ever.

I tried to pull my knees up to my chest, but with my hands secured behind me, I couldn't get in a decent position, and my feet kept slipping off the chair-seat. Finally, I gave up. I closed my eyes and leaned my head back, trembling from the cold, and probably more than a little exhaustion.

"You want a blanket?" he asked.

I didn't bother opening my eyes. "Fuck off," I said.

"I'll take that as a no."

"Whatever."

I must've dozed off, because I slowly became aware that I was no longer cold. Somehow, a blanket had been draped over my lap and tucked under my legs. Another one covered my shoulders.

Correction – my aching shoulders. The handcuffs were still there, and everything from my shoulders to my wrists hurt like hell.

Slowly, I opened my eyes. Lawton was still there, his eyebrows furrowed and his mouth tight. How long had I slept? I had no idea. It might've been minutes. It might've been hours. Honestly, I couldn't believe I'd slept at all, given the circumstances.

And then Lawton spoke, his voice soft and eerily calm. "Why'd you do it?" he asked.

"Do what?" I mumbled, still sleep-addled, or maybe just exhausted.

He reached into his pocket and pulled out an unfamiliar cell phone. He fumbled with it for a few seconds, then held it with the screen facing me. The screen came to life in the form of a video, shaky, but clear enough.

It was Brittney's friend, the guy who attacked me. His face was a mass of blood and bruises. I heard Bishop's voice, off-screen. "Go ahead," he said. "Say it again, just like you told me."

The guy took a ragged breath. "It was Chloe," he said. "She paid us a couple hundred bucks to you know, pretend to kidnap her, maybe rough her up a little bit."

"Why?" Bishop's voice asked.

"I don't remember," the guy mumbled.

"Want me to make you remember?" Bishop said.

"No, no," the guy stammered. Then, he looked straight at the camera. "She said Lawton had some kind of hero complex or something. Figured if he rescued her, you know, he'd fall for her, maybe get him to propose or I dunno, move in with him."

"And about the other thing?" Bishop said.

"Yeah. Well, she was planning some sex tape thing. Lots of money. She said we'd get a cut if we did a good job making him, you know, come to her rescue and shit."

Instantly, I was wide awake. "He's lying!"

"Sure he is," Lawton said, in a tone that suggested otherwise.

"I don't even know him," I yelled, anger coursing through me, and not just at Lawton. My shit list seemed a mile long.

"Except you do," Lawton said. "You admitted as much."

"No," I said through clenched teeth. "Just because I know him, it doesn't mean I know him."

"That's not what he says."

"You're gonna take his word over mine?" I said. "You are such an asshole."

"Yeah. So you keep saying." He gave me a hard look. "But tell me something? You ever hear of this movie, called uh –" He looked away. "Riding the Rastor?"

I felt myself pale. So Bishop had gone into my house? I should've known. "I don't fuckin' believe him," I muttered.

"Who?" Lawton said, his voice barely interested.

"Bishop. He went in my house, right?"

"No," Lawton said, his voice very quiet. "He didn't. I did."

"What?!"

"Yeah." He made a scoffing sound. "Bishop came in, showed me this." He held up the phone, now silent. "I said 'no way, the guy's lying. That's not Chloe. I know her. That guy, he's full of shit. It's some story. I don't know where he got it, but it's not true.' But then –"

"Then you broke into my house?"

"Except," Lawton said, "it's not really your house, is it?"

"I'm living there now," I said. "Isn't that good enough?"

"You know what?" he said. "I don't really care. Not anymore."

In spite of everything, his words sliced through me. I hated him. And I loved him. And regardless of which emotion was in charge, the guy was a total dick, and I wouldn't give him the satisfaction of breaking up with me, assuming we'd ever been in a relationship in the first place.

"Yeah. That makes two of us," I said.

"So tell me," he said. "Is Chloe even your real name?"

"What the hell?" I said. "Of course it's my real name."

"Look," he said with a nasty smile, "you think you're the first girl to try to pull this kind of shit on me?"

"I wasn't pulling anything," I said. "Now, are you gonna let me go, or what?"

"Not yet."

"Why not? What are you waiting for? What are you planning to do? Kill me for whatever you think I've done?" I glared at him. "Which, by the way, I haven't."

"No," he said. "Believe what you want, but I'm not gonna hurt you."

"Except you already have."

"Sorry."

"You don't sound sorry."

He shrugged.

"Then what exactly are you waiting for?" I said.

"Well, here's the thing," he said. "Yeah, I was in that house of yours, or whoever's, and I saw all that shit you had laid out, but I got to wondering 'what else was there."

"What do you mean, what else?"

"I mean," he said, "videos, pictures, you know, the kind of crap that's gonna turn some waitress into a fuckin' star."

I lifted my chin. "There's nothing wrong with being a waitress."

"Except you obviously don't think that way. Otherwise, you wouldn't need this, would you?"

He reached into his other pocket and pulled out a different cell phone. Except this particular phone, I recognized. I closed my eyes. I knew exactly what he was going to show me, and I didn't want to see it.

"Open your eyes," he said.

Slowly, I did. And there it was, the naked picture of Lawton asleep. Taking it had been an accident, but if I were being honest, the fact I hadn't yet deleted it wasn't exactly accidental. I should've deleted it. I certainly meant to delete it. Just somehow, I couldn't bring myself to get rid of it.

Still, I hadn't showed it to anyone, and never would. Okay, I'd showed it to Erika, but not the X-rated parts. Still, the realization made me feel more than a little ashamed.

My voice was quiet. "I took it by accident," I said. "It's a new phone. Did you even see all the other pictures on there?"

If he'd bothered to check at all, I knew what he'd find. Pictures of my dashboard, my shoes, the ceiling, just about anything but what I wanted to capture for posterity. It was official. I hated that phone. If I ever got any money, I'd throw the damn thing out the window.

He held out the picture. "So this was an accident, huh? Pretty good composition for something you didn't mean to take."

"Yeah? Well, scroll through them," I said. "Show me one other picture that looks like I took it on purpose. Just one."

"I already did," he said.

"Do it again."

With his gaze still half on me, he scrolled through the images. His eyebrows furrowed. "This doesn't prove anything."

"Well, I guess that's where we're different," I said. "because I didn't think I'd have to prove anything to you."

"Yeah?" he said. "And what about that movie poster? You got big plans for it? Nice of you to think of a name before you got a product. Or, have you got one of those too? If you do, and if it's in the house, Bishop'll find it. I guarantee you that."

So that explained the delay? Suddenly, it all made sense, including why it was taking so long. There wasn't anything to find, but if I knew his brother, he'd keep on looking.

"There's nothing to find," I said.

"Didn't seem that way to me," Lawton said.

"That poster?" I said. "It was my birthday present. My best friend, Erika, she's a graphic design major. It was a joke." My voice rose. "Just a stupid joke! What the fuck is wrong with you?"

"Yeah," a voice said from the doorway. "What the fuck is wrong with you?"

"Oh great," I muttered, turning my gaze toward the sound of the voice. And there he was. Lawton's dick of a brother. I turned to glare at him. "Come to join the fun? Well, come on," I said, in voice that bordered on hysteria, "the more the merrier."

There was only one problem. He didn't look very merry. And neither did Lawton.

CHAPTER 59

Bishop still hadn't moved. He was staring at Lawton. "Just what the hell are you doing?" Bishop said.

"What does it look like?" Lawton said. "I'm talking to Chloe."

"Is that what you call this?" Bishop said.

"It's the only place that's secure," Lawton said. "No wireless. No nothing. Shit, you've only been drilling that into me for months." He gave me a cold look. "I already checked for recording stuff."

Bishop turned his gaze on me. "I suppose that explains the blankets. What? You made her take off her clothes?"

"No," Lawton said. "She did that herself."

I made a scoffing sound.

"You did," Lawton said.

"Only because you lied to me."

"I did not," he said. "I told you there was something you had to see. I showed it to you, didn't I?"

"The video? Oh yeah. That was real priceless. And by the way, the guy's totally lying."

"He is not," Lawton said, turning to Bishop. "Go on. Tell

her."

Bishop looked down. He shook his head. And when he looked up, his gaze rested on Lawton with the kind of disapproval only a big brother can manage. "You know you're acting crazy, don't you?"

"You're one to talk," Lawton said.

"And she's right," Bishop said. "The guy was lying."

Lawton's face froze. "What?"

"And you were supposed to stall her, not drag her down here and tie her up."

"Actually," Lawton said, "I used handcuffs."

"So," Bishop said, "you couldn't think of a better way to stall her than this?"

Lawton swallowed. He looked away. "It's just, I dunno." His voice broke. "I couldn't believe she played me like that."

"I wasn't playing you," I said.

"Yeah," Bishop said, "you know your pal, Brittney?" The way he said "pal," his opinion of her was obvious.

"Yeah?" Lawton said.

"Well," Bishop continued, "turns out, she orchestrated the whole thing, even gave him that fake story in case he got caught."

Lawton stared at him. "And you know this, how?"

"Lemme put it this way," Bishop said, "the guy's friend was a little more forthcoming, especially with the right encouragement."

"Yeah?" Lawton said. "And how do you know he wasn't lying the second time?"

"This time," Bishop said, "I got it from the horse's mouth. And by horse, I mean Brittney herself."

"That bitch!" I said. "I knew it!"

Lawton and Bishop turned to look at me, almost as if I'd been momentarily forgotten. "Well, she is," I muttered.

Lawton's face had gone a shade paler in the last couple of

minutes. He looked at me as if he had no words to convey whatever he was feeling. "Chloe, I —"

"Forget it," I said. "Now are you gonna let me go or not?"

"No," he said.

"What?" I snapped. "You're kidding, right?"

"I mean," he continued. "Yeah, I'll let you go. I'm so sorry about this. But I don't wanna let you go, not like this, I mean in the other way." His eyes were haunted. "I am so fucking sorry."

"Oh please," I said. "You're a total psycho. I should've known better. Now, seriously." I spoke very slowly, as if he were too stupid to understand even the most basic of instructions. "Let. Me. Go."

Glancing away, he reached into his pocket and pulled out a key. "I wasn't really gonna hold you here, you know."

"Whatever."

"Wait," Bishop said.

I turned to glare at him. "Wait? Seriously?"

"Before you leave, there's something we need to discuss."

But Lawton was already behind me. I heard the sound of a key working against the cuffs, and a moment later, my hands were blissfully free. Gingerly, I changed position, wrapping my sore arms around my equally sore body and tugging the blanket around my shoulders just a little tighter.

I pushed away from the chair, standing, a little wobbly, but more or less okay. I turned to Bishop. "And what, exactly, do we need to discuss?" My voice was a cold, strange sound in the dim basement.

"Are you gonna call the police?" he asked.

"Well, you two seem to have some sort of problem with the police," I said. "I wonder why that is."

"Call 'em," Lawton said. "Whatever happens, I deserve it. I mean it. Whatever you want." He reached out for me. "I'm so sorry."

"Stop saying that!" I pushed his hands away. "Don't. Touch. Me." I glared at him. "Ever."

As if oblivious to the drama with me and Lawton, Bishop said, "You never answered my question."

"Yeah?" I said. "That's because I don't know the answer."

He nodded. "Fair enough. But I want to remind you of something. That little party, or whatever it was in the house, along with that picture of him you took. Well, it doesn't make you look exactly like an innocent young thing."

I glared at him. "What are you saying?"

"Just that if you start something, you'd better think it through. And I'm not just saying it for Lawton's sake."

"Liar."

"Think what you want," he said. "But I'm telling you, and Lawton can tell you too, things can get ugly real quick in a situation like this."

Lawton turned to glare at him. "You threatening her?"

"Oh, this is special," I said in the snottiest tone I could muster. "So now you're coming to my defense? Gee, thanks. Where were you when some psycho handcuffed me in his basement? Oh yeah, sorry, I forgot, that guy was you. Asshole."

Bishop made a sound that sounded suspiciously like a laugh.

I turned to glare at him. "It's not funny!"

"You're right," he said. "Look, I'm not threatening you. Lawton's right. You want to report him, you have every right. If you were my sister —"

"You'd have me report it?" I said.

"Fuck no," he said. "I'd beat Lawton's ass until he was sorrier than any law enforcement could make him."

"Do it now," Lawton said. He turned to me. "Baby, would it make you feel better if he beat the crap out of me?"

"Definitely," I said.

CHAPTER 60

Lawton held up his hands. He turned to Bishop. "Come on. Do it. Beat the shit out of me. I won't even hit you back."

"Oh, for fuck's sake," Bishop muttered.

"I mean it," Lawton said.

"But as it is," Bishop continued as if Lawton hadn't spoken at all, "he's my brother. And I hope –" At this, he turned to give Lawton a long, meaningful look "– that once you hear why he acted like such an ass, you'll get why he lost it so bad."

"Lost it?" I said, rubbing my sore wrists. "Is that what you're calling it?"

"Oh baby," Lawton said, kneeling in front of me to reach for my hands, "You've gotta believe me. I don't know what happened."

"Yeah, well I do." I yanked my hands away. "Now, will one of you dickheads get my clothes so I can get out of here?"

While Bishop went to retrieve my clothes, Lawton kept apologizing. But honestly, at this point, I was barely listening.

Aside from the trouble with him, I'd probably just lost my waitressing job for good. If I were smart, I'd demand money out

339

him, at least enough to cover what I'd lost tonight. If I were
n smarter, I'd demand enough to cover my expenses for the
t month, until I found another job. Any job.

But I guess I wasn't smart. Or maybe I was just too proud.
t like Grandma. Too bad I wasn't more like my Mom. She'd
reeze him but good.

When Bishop returned with my clothes, and then melted away
wherever, I made Lawton turn his back while I got dressed.
'd gotten his last look of me, if I had anything to say about it.

I should've known better. The guy was a psycho. But then
gain, I guess I knew that going in, hadn't I? What exactly had I
xpected?

I was crouched down, lacing up my tennis shoes, when he said
something that made me falter.

"Chloe, please," he said, his voice ragged, and his eyes
glistening. "Don't go. Not like this. I love you. You know I do.
Stay, please?"

"And what if I don't? What are you gonna do? Handcuff me
again?"

"You've gotta understand – "

"No," I cut him off. "I don't have to understand anything.
You didn't need to keep me here. If you wanted to know
anything, about any of that stuff, or whatever, all you had to do
was ask."

He swallowed. "Baby," he said, "I did ask. You never
answered. I'm sorry, but –" He pushed a hand through his hair.
"Look, I know I fucked up. Majorly fucked up. But I guess it just
all made me kind of crazy. I mean, I'd fallen so hard for you, and
when I thought you were just using me like –" He shook his head
and looked away.

"Like what?" I said.

"Like who," he corrected.

"Okay, then who? Brittney?"

"No," he said. "Someone else."

"Who?" I demanded.

"Brandy Blue." He made a sound of disgust. "Well, that's the name she goes by now anyway. You know, I hate that name. Sounds like a damn porn star. But I guess that's what she is, huh?" He looked away. "And me too. Thanks to her."

I knew I shouldn't encourage him. But I couldn't help it. In spite of everything, I wanted to know. "What do you mean?"

"Anyway, she was this cocktail waitress, and –"

"There's nothing wrong with being a waitress," I said.

"Yeah, I know, honest," he said. "But Brandy, you know, she had her sights set on something else. Wanted to be a star. Not that I knew that when I hooked up with her." He shook his head. "Best fucking actress I ever met."

"What are you talking about?"

"The world I travel in, well, it's not exactly filled with the nicest people."

"So what?" I said. "You're not nice. What do you care?"

"You're right," he said. "I'm not nice."

I glanced around the basement. "Obviously."

"But I guess if I'm being honest," he continued, "the thing with Brandy, I took it out on you. I am so fucking sorry. I should've known better."

"Yeah," I said. "You should've."

"You wanna hear the rest of it?" he said. "Let's go upstairs. I'll make it up to you. I promise."

I stared at him long and hard. I wasn't that girl, the one who'd take this kind of abuse and say it's okay because something bad happened to him in his past. I had always been smart. Well, except for when it came to him.

It was time to reclaim whatever brains I had left and get out while I still had the willpower. "You can't make it up to me," I said. "I don't even know you."

"That's not true," he said.

I rubbed my sore wrists. "Is Chucky still upstairs?"

Lawton nodded.

"Good," I said, "because we're leaving."

"You won't listen to the rest?" he said. "C'mon, baby. Please."

"I'm not your baby," I said. "Not anymore."

I turned away and walked toward the stairway. I heard him follow, but I refused to look back. Upstairs, I found Chucky nestled in his basket, blissfully asleep. It seemed a shame to wake him, but I did anyway.

Lawton followed after me, his voice ragged and his tone pleading as he tried to convince me to stay. When I had all my stuff, including the supply of toiletries I'd started keeping in his master bathroom, I held out my hand. "Keys."

With an anguished expression, he reached into his jeans pocket and held them out. "Won't you at least let me drive you home?"

"No," I said. "And the gate had better be open."

His voice was quiet. "It will be."

"Good."

He held out a hand, but didn't quite touch me. "But only because I hope you'll be coming back through it."

"Yeah, well, keep hoping that," I said.

And a few minutes later, as I pulled out of his gate and onto the quiet street, I finally let the tears fall as I considered everything I'd lost tonight. And through it all, his final words kept echoing in my brain. "I'm not going to force you, but I'm not giving up, either. You wait. I'll win you back. And then, baby, I'm never gonna let you go."

I hadn't responded. Instead, I'd just walked out the door, away from him and toward who knows what. Sitting in the Parkers' driveway, I rubbed my wet sleeve against my nose one final time, picked up Chucky, and got out of the car.

For all his pretty words, he'd forget me in a week, if not sooner.

And I was glad.

Or, at least that's what I told myself. And I'd need to keep telling myself that if I didn't want to lose my mind entirely. Because I knew one thing for sure. Lawton was my drug. And he'd proven himself impossible to resist.

Hopefully, he wouldn't tempt me. Because for all of my own lofty words, I wasn't truly sure I could say no.

To anything.

THE END

Now Available

Rebelonging

The Exciting Conclusion to the Belonging Series

ABOUT THE AUTHOR

Sabrina Stark writes edgy romances featuring plucky girls and the bad boys who capture their hearts.

She's worked as a fortune-teller, barista, game-show contestant, and media writer in the aerospace industry. She has a journalism degree from Central Michigan University and is married with one son and two kittens. She currently makes her home in Northern Alabama.

ON THE WEB

Learn About New Releases & Exclusive Offers
www.SabrinaStark.com

Follow Sabrina Stark on Twitter at
http://twitter.com/StarkWrites

8580967R00205

Printed in Great Britain
by Amazon.co.uk, Ltd.,
Marston Gate.